Book Two Of

River Rule Trilogy

Broken Rule

By

Ameeta Davis

Published by Ameeta Davis. Contact ameetadavis@ameetadavis.com
First published in UK in 2020.

ISBN: (print) 978-1-9998928-4-5
ISBN : (eBook) 978-1-9998928-3-8

Author's website is www.ameetadavis.com

This book is dedicated to my mother Mrs Sumitra Choudhry.

Other Books by Ameeta Davis

Book One of River Rule Trilogy

River Rule

N
W
E
S
Dev's House
BLESSED
TERRITORY
Major's
House

St Anthony's
School
Sid's House
(Modern Ruin)
FORCED BLESSED
TERRITORY
RIVER RULE
PLACE
Robber's
Cave
Army
Cantonement
Temple
MONSOON
RIVER

Chapter 1

The Morning After the Night Before

Muddy water droplets splattered on her bloodstained face, hands, knees... everywhere... and all over her foetal-positioned naked body.

Between the patter of the nonstop rain, loud reverberations like the ones her mum's Tibetan bowls made, slinked in with the rain through the air pockets in the muddy walls.

Thoughts of her Irish mother turned Buddhist swamped her. It was her fault. All her fault. If she weren't dead, she would soon die here.

Here was where the persistent rain permeated the unusually thick mud walls and floor to fall on and be absorbed by her naked body.

Tickled, she shifted on the ground. Fragments of material lay scattered on the ground underneath her. She grabbed at a larger piece hoping it was something she could cover her cold wet body with.

Her eyes were useless in the dark, but she knew what the fragment was.

Horror filled her as her fingertips snagged on the familiar, stitched school emblem Johnnie Walker – Gopan – wore on his borrowed shirt. She let rip a guttural scream as she flung it as far away as she could.

SHUT UP, UNA! CRAP! That bastard... Wolf can't have told the truth! I know he can't have! Fucking liar! He's lying... For your own sake, Una, zip your mouth, no thoughts now before they find you.

***

Avi sat on the one hundred and eighth step of the temple, shocked. She really was here… did that mean…? Wide-eyed he watched the rain spear through the green haze of the surrounding jungle and hit the swelling belly of the torrid river as it broke its banks. Its level already above the twelfth step of the temple.

Sick to his core, Avi pondered the idea of jumping into the river and allowing it to sweep him to the Forbidden Blessed territory to avenge his cousin's death and rescue Una. Even if she were here, he couldn't believe she did it.

The memory of the mutilated body whose scent he had hungrily picked up on and then discovered made him want to gag. It took much to stem the vomit that Wolf triggered when he hinted it could be Una. He had held on until he called the other Blesseds and his great grand uncle recognised the mutilated body of his grandson, Gopan. Somehow knowing the victim made it worse. Avi shook his head, Una was difficult, wayward, and stubborn, but a man-eater? No way. The image of blood oozing from her mouth nearly had him retching again. This was no time to show weakness.

Avi straightened himself and wiped his mouth just in case he had actually thrown up. His mouth was clear. *"Wolf lied..."*

"He didn't, didn't you just hear her and thought talk with her?" the Sharman interjected.

Avi had forgotten to block his thoughts from his nana, the Sharman. "How do you know? None of us saw the killing." Avi snorted.

"I know."

The Sharman grimly continued to ring the ancient bell as he looked on as Avi glared at him. Exasperated, Avi puffed out some air. "If you know that then you know what she has become…" Avi's voice tapered off. "To kill another so savagely can only mean she has become one of the wolves… another bitch in Wolf's pack?"

The Sharman didn't answer. He hadn't shared the knowledge of the killer with anyone. Instead he was rallying his brethren to hunt for the man-eater animal and Forced Blessed. His arms were aching, there was no reason to continue ringing the bell, most of the Blessed were here. What would they think of him if they knew he was only ringing so the Wolf had fair warning of their imminent hunt. He never thought it possible that he would give his Forced arch enemy a heads up.

Each strike of the silver clapper in the bell reverberated one hundred and eight times, calling out to Blesseds further afield. The morning was in its infancy, but most were already assembled on the steps above the river's water level. Hunger and revenge etched deeply on their faces and stance. The Blesseds had cut short their hunt last night in respect of their loss.

The Sharman knew that several of them believed he or Avi had instigated the heinous killing. He also knew it was likely to be his brother and sons who were spreading the damning accusations. It wasn't that long ago when his brother had talked about Avi's unsuitability to succeed him and hinted that Gopan would be a better candidate. Despite the danger to himself and his grandson he had to hide knowledge of Una's presence and Blessed form even if it meant the Blesseds turning on them later.

The Sharman was sure Wolf understood Una's superficial value. But he also knew Wolf did not really know her true value. Still, the Sharman was confident Wolf would keep Una's Blessed form under wraps. Eyeing the magnolia trees dotted around the temple, he knew it wouldn't be long before the Blesseds found out Una's truth. The Sharman looked below at his brethren and sighed. Wolf had recruited from the Blessed youth. He and the rest of the elders had never believed it possible even when Burfani had not reappeared in any form, ethereal or otherwise, after Rosetta died.

Wolf's easy victory over Rosetta; her inability to help her heir complete the Blessed journey, rattled the youth. They loudly jeered at Burfani legends and quietly defected to the Forced Blesseds. Anger flared once again, and the Sharman jerked his hand off the bell. He'd given ample warning; he'd stalled long enough. He hoped the hunger on the assembled Blesseds lead to Wolf's fitful death. In truth, he was the real killer but as always Wolf never got his paws dirty.

Despite their obvious hunger the Sharman didn't think they would eat Una or Wolf if they discovered the truth about what happened yesterday, but the mutilation would be far worse than Gopan's. Even the Forced Blesseds held to that rule even if they dishonoured the sacred rule of giving all animals, humans and Blesseds, a clean death. Rosetta was a clear example of that. The Sharman might not expect his kin to eat Una, but he did expect them to tear her flesh from her limbs and shred her into thin strips and scatter her to the four winds. For Una's sake he hoped Wolf had found a good place to hide her. Perhaps the best outcome despite all his earlier unfruitful ministrations to bring Una to the Blesseds was that she had drowned in the river as he thought she had when he witnessed her falling out of the army truck.

It was at this point Una's raging screams permeated through the ground and not just in Avi's head. All the Blessed heads eerily turned in the direction of the last unidentifiable scream.

The men with the spears were ready to hop the rocks in the torrid river when Avi darted ahead of them. He still had some of the snow leopard characteristics. He unclutched his left hand and then used his spear in the right to catch something in the river, and then held up what he caught. A large exclamation followed by a hush was heard over the rain, river, and stamping feet. Avi boldly held up the magnolia blossom. He counted in his head and waited. He got to five and then one of the tribesmen standing on the rocks exclaimed out loudly. "Can it really be true? The magnolia only appears out of season when Burfani appears."

Smiling, Avi rushed all the way up the steps, parting the tribesmen in two waves before he disappeared into the shadows of the temple and brought out a box covered in a black shawl.

"I thought it was an ordinary cat, but could this thing stop Wolf?" Avi turned to face his nana.

Cries of joy filled the air.

"Burfani is back! We are saved!" chorused all around.

"The Sharman was right, she always comes when demons arrive," shouted out one elder.

Avi knew he had stalled the hunt for the killer – Una. In jubilance he raised the cub by its paws over his head. The tribesmen were now crowded around him. Above the hushed but excited voices, Avi sought out his nana. The Sharman, in his human form, looked very pale.

"Where did you find that snow leopard cub?" the Sharman asked through thought talk.

Unnerved by the austere tone, Avi answered, *"I thought I heard screams and had an eerie sense that Una was close, but when I got closer to where the screams were coming from, near the bridge, I found the cub stranded on a rock between the fast-flowing currents of the river. I'm sure it is the same cub that Una foolishly called Cat! I didn't realise he was Burfani. I suppose I was just pleased that I had mistook the cub's distress calls to be human screams. This will keep Una safe for now, won't it?"*

Avi was confused when he heard the Sharman's last stark, but clear, thought. *"Now we are truly doomed."*

Chapter 2

An Olive Branch

The ringing was incessant. It was noisy, urgent, and oh-so loud.

Could it be the bell in the temple where Avi was?

Did that mean Avi could help her escape Wolf's underground mud chamber?

She wanted him to save her.

She was so scared. Scared of the monster in the mud cell.

Then she remembered the night before and what she did.

Seriously… save her? More like she wanted him to kill her.

How often, and how many months ago, had he warned her to leave and she stubbornly stayed on in Khamosh Valley lulled by the temporary security of her boarding school and age.

For heaven's sake, I'm still seventeen.

She shouldn't have turned for another year according to the River Rule. A rule Wolf had ignored and broke. In the habit of rule breaking herself, she already had something in common with him. She was caged in this mud prison for the very precise reason that she broke Wolf's rules. She'd escaped only after a few hours of being captured by him but was then recaptured because she had no knowledge of the land or how to even survive in the terrain. There were no kind words of introduction when he cornered her. He was ready to feed her to the wolves, his wolves, unless she murdered Gopan first. Unlike heroines in books and movies she did just that. Granted, survival was a deep-seated desire. But that wasn't why she did it. She did it for Dad.

Una fisted her angry tears away.

Did monsters or wild animals feel remorse?

Would Avi understand why she killed Gopan?

She had to connect with him and explain herself.

She had to connect if only to plead with him to stop the ringing.

With the single purpose of connecting to Avi in mind she relaxed her body, breathed in, and then slowly let it out. She tried her hardest to find and connect with traces of his thoughts. Nothing. She was blocked out.

She tried to access his feelings like he had in the past.

Feelings? *Uh-oh! Had he accessed more than her thoughts this time?*

Was that why he was blocking her?

Her hope to connect depleted. She was alone. She felt a deep loss. She had somehow expected him to be with her in thought like he had when they first met. In fact, he had gone further than her thoughts. He had used her body to see, hear and feel when she was hiding from the tribesmen, when they came to bargain for her in exchange for the land her grandfather's house stood on. Petrified, she had called out in her thoughts and he had answered. It felt like a lifetime ago, yet only eight months had passed since she left Manchester and arrived in the Himalayas. It was eight months ago that her father brought her here. She thought her father had abandoned her. Gopal never said what happened to her father when he kidnapped him although he hinted at something dark. That's why she killed him. She killed him with one clean bite. Horror invaded her senses as she remembered seeing his body flop instantly. One moment he was alive the next he was a lifeless doll. She had taken his life instantly. Una stilled. It was a clean bite! A bite at his throat…

She had been duped.

The Gopal's shredded shirt had nothing to do with her… Una couldn't think anymore.

The bell ringing had hastened to a feverish pitch. A pitch like the horn blown before a frenzied fox hunt in the British countryside. Was Avi leading a hunt? A hunt to find her. Was that why he had blocked her? Una's disbelief turned to anger and then to cold terror as she waited to be set upon.

***

It was unthinkable that she had fallen asleep, but she had. The bell, wherever it was, appeared silent. She was glad that her anxiety had fled too and, in its place, a yawning hunger for sustenance filled her mind and body once again. Her skin was warm under her coat of fur and her claws had broken through her paws.

Claws she hoped would help her escape her prison. Una scrambled up and in vain clawed at the mud walls but couldn't find purchase. She roared in frustration and realised that, despite her wide mouth, her roar was pitiful and no more than a growl, not much worse than a hissing meow. Caged, she walked forwards and backwards in frustration. There wasn't even enough room to pace. "Fuck you, Wolf!"

As if she had uttered "OPEN SESAME" or "ABRACADABRA" the manhole opened, and a wooden pole was shoved through unceremoniously. She scarpered towards the mud walls to avoid it. Unnecessarily, as it never touched the ground but remained suspended a foot above her head. Initially terrified of what was going to drop down she stayed close to the mud wall.

She thought she'd spent hours staring at the pole, but it was quite possible that it was just a few minutes – snow leopards didn't own watches. In the end she'd had enough, and her curiosity got the better of her. The worst that could happen to her was death. If they wanted her dead, she would have been for a few hours already. With that thought she rose to take on the pole. She circled underneath it. She had to have a better chance of shimmying up the pole with her claws and limbs than with her hands. Her stomach growled. *Enough thinking,* she thought, and lunged forward and grabbed at the pole, which bounced a bit. She managed to hang on.

"Thank God for claws!" Una muttered as she lifted herself out of the manhole and onto firm ground.

"Hunger does that to you."

"Does what?" Una half answered Wolf.

"Makes you give in and throw caution to the wind. You could have been ambushed again." Wolf chuckled in amusement.

"I didn't smell more than one dirty dog." Una surveyed the area surrounding the manhole carefully. His pack were missing. "Looks like I was right."

"I underestimate you."

"Where are your hommies?" asked Una as she stared into Wolf's bright yellow night-vision eyes, which were quite close to where she stood.

"Hommies?"

"Your gang, your posse."

"I know what you meant; I'm questioning why you thought I would need them."

"I outran you yesterday." Una began to project the memory of her outrunning the Wolf's cohort, finding her way up the cliff and resting on a branch overhanging the valley below.

"If you watch the memory to the end you will remember why you stayed. But for our new friendship's sake I'll remind you that memory casting drains you."

Una hurriedly stopped. She didn't have enough strength after the chase she led the others on the night before. Only a day in and she understood she needed all her energy to find food. She also didn't want to be reminded of the truth: that she didn't know how to survive the jungle.

"Exactly!" Wolf moved forward. Una had forgotten that he could read her thoughts easily and she needed to shield them. "So, I know you will cooperate and not run, in fact…" Wolf stopped and looked intently at Una. Being stared down by a wolf's keen eyes unnerved her and the shackles on her back began to rise.

"If the Blessed find out that you're the one who killed one of the precious Sharman's family and, according to fresh rumours, the expected next leader, then…"

"What would they do?"

Wolf watched Una's snow leopard wary eyes as he forced her to walk backwards by pushing his nozzle forward, almost touching hers.

"They intend to tear you from limb to limb, fur from skin, skin from muscle and muscle from bone, like Gopan was by you."

"You liar! I killed him cleanly..." Una mewed in shock as her hind leg backed over the open manhole and hung over it momentarily. Mewing sharply, she hastily moved forward onto solid ground. "You bastards must have fucking done that..." Una paused from her cussing and gave Wolf a meaningful look. "How do they know it was me?"

"They don't know it was you or what you are, but they are looking for a man-eater. To protect my... What did you call it, posse? I will give you to them if you trouble me." Una pushed her leopard shoulders back. Wolf's eyes grew cold and hard. "You need my protection and instead of wasting time and wondering if you can run away or trust me, you should understand my usefulness. You need to feed and if you are seen on the boundaries then you might be hunted before the night is over."

Una held her frame tight to overcome its determination to tremble, and spoke with little emotion, "I should be able to outrun them and retrace..."

"You won't get far; they will be in their animal forms and will spear you from some dark place or another. Do you want to chance that?"

Una stood silent.

Wolf became impatient and moved towards the cliff.

There was a heavy silence until Una heard a stomach – her own – rumble.

She darted forward and stopped just ahead of him. Bemused, Wolf threw back his head and howled. Una turned around. Just in time to catch the gleaming light in his eyes, keen and commanding. Una stalled and let him pass.

As she waited to follow him into the dark wilderness, Una's mind flashbacked to her first night in Khamosh Valley when she looked for the taxi driver in the dark and found gleaming eyes watching her from behind her grandad's gates. That night seemed so long ago.

Chapter 3

Up the Rabbit Hole

Two months later

Chattering teeth filled her head. Cold air elbowed her exposed ribs and like all mornings the invisible washing machine in her body, set on spin, rattled her awake. Her usual morning wake-up call. Yet, stupidly, eyes still closed, she placed her knuckles on her cheeks to check how cold she was and yelped. Vigorously rubbing her knuckles to melt the ice shards off her fingers drew blood. Warmth finally. Blood used to gross her out but not anymore. Now she found it quite nourishing.

Fully awake, despair flooded in like it had the previous mornings. Not because she was half animal but because she was still half human. The impenetrable manhole metal cover allowed no light, yet she knew it was morning. Each dawn her warm living blanket seeped into her skin leaving her naked and exposed to the chill of the icebox she lived in. Each morning she resented her human form.

The nights were so much kinder. Since her first night, Wolf lowered the pole and accompanied her on her hunts. The nocturnal fresh air and expansive terrain was something she desperately waited for and cherished. Her snow leopard body brought freedom while her human body kept her cramped, cold and in captivity. It was a limited freedom, no doubt.

Two long months had passed. Notching a tally with her hardened and sharpened nails enabled her to keep tabs on days if not hours.

Today, however, was an exception.

The familiar grunt of metal came at an unfamiliar hour. Her first sunshine ray after a long time shimmered before it was momentarily blocked by a flying shadow. A paper package landed on her upturned squinting face before it slipped down her cheek, flying past her naked body, and dropped close to her feet. With stiff fingers she grabbed and tore at the paper. Tears of disbelief ran down her face and chin as she glanced at the clothes. Combat clothes she'd seen Wolf's gang wearing when they arrived at the same time as the tribesmen at Grandad's nearly a year ago.

Had she passed some sort of quarantine?

Was she finally accepted as one of them?

Had she just been through an initiation period and did these clothes mean it was over?

Truthfully, two months down the line, she no longer cared. She grabbed the clothes: shirt, jacket, and multi-pocketed trousers. The shirt and jacket were a godsend, but the trousers were too difficult to put on in the semi dark. Scrabbling on the floor her toes found something soft. They felt like gloves but were too long – they were socks. Without much thought, Una put her hands through them and roughly massaged her long legs to get some blood circulation in them before she put them on her feet. She lay the trousers ready. She got one leg into a trouser leg when the manhole lid completely shifted, flooding the manhole with light.

Una's head shot up in alarm and then ducked with temporary blindness.

Whoever opened the manhole had the sun behind them.

"Take your time getting dressed, Una, I'll look away." It was a girl's voice; one she'd heard before. A vision of marigold wedding garlands came to mind.

Disorientated and in slight disbelief at hearing a familiar voice again, she hesitantly said, "A bit late now, Grace, to care now that you have seen all of me."

A "Yes, suppose" from Grace was followed by an awkward silence.

With shaking hands, Una belted up her trousers. "Is there anyone up there with you?"

The shadowed head appeared again. "Yes, so don't try anything silly. We have weapons and will not hesitate to shoot."

Una put both hands up above her head to signal she was ready to play along with them.

A rope ladder unravelled itself and ended at Una's hips.

"Run out of ladder…" Una quipped under breath.

"Just get up here. I can change my mind and shut the manhole again."

No chance of that. Una hastily grabbed the rope and swung her leg up. It was tough work climbing up. She no longer remembered how to use her limbs properly. She'd lost practice. She was all over the place, her limbs flaying to begin with until she got the hang of it. Her hair caused even more trouble; it kept getting entangled with the rope ladder rungs as she trod on them. "Ouch…!" Her hair had grown past her waist and was far thicker than she remembered.

Finally, at the top, she stayed on all fours. She wasn't sure if she had the strength yet for standing on two legs. She had mostly slept during the day especially when the ground warmed up. From where she was crouched, she surveyed the land and thought her hunting ground looked so different in the daylight.

Hunting ground... really, Una! As far as I can tell, you've not caught much more than chipmunks.

Una couldn't see Wolf. She did, however, notice a pair of boots at the edge of the opening. Una swiftly dragged them to herself… the terrain was too stony without her padded feet.

"I'd check for scorpions first, if I were you," Grace uttered.

Una shifted her hair from her bent head. Grace looked pretty serious. Una banged the boots together while turning them upside down. She could follow instructions well when they suited her.

Looking up from tying her second shoe, Una paused. It was

startling to see so many eyes trained on her. When had they arrived? She could swear that Wolf's minions had not been there a minute ago. In the lonely hours Una had wondered about the shades of their uniform, which she'd seen when Wolf first appeared at her grandfather's house, when the tribesmen had pushed through his property. She'd worked out they didn't need the camouflage of green and khaki shades in a jungle when they had the ability to become the jungle in their individual animal forms. However, here against the face of the rocks they blended in with their sky blues and greys.

She looked carefully at the rock faces; they were littered with ropes and climbing grooves.

"You can stop gawking now, boys. There's nothing here to see," Grace shouted at the minions and then spat in annoyance to Una, "Hurry up!"

"Now don't be jealous, little sis, Blessed changes emphasise your features." Wolf abseiled down a rock. Una was shocked, although she could hear his voice and had scoured the rock surface, she hadn't spotted him.

"Pleez, bhaiya, Una was pretty before. If she hadn't been, you might have saved our friend Meeru…"

The mention of Meeru's name dropped the temperature a few notches and galvanised Una to finish the task of tying her boot laces.

Grace held out her hand, despite the earlier exchange between herself and her brother. Her words lacked hostility but were tinted with envy as she sighed. "He's right about the blessed change in your hair – it's just something indescribable."

"A nuisance would be a better word, I'm sure. It got in my way when I was climbing." Una grabbed a fistful of her hair. "If it makes you feel better you can cut my hair off."

Grace jerked Una's hand down.

"What…" Una blurted.

"You can't! Seriously you can't mess with your hair! It'll impact your snow leopard body; it could be an important part of your body…"

"How do you know?"

"Several of the initial Forced Blesseds did that and when they morphed after making alterations, important parts of their animal body, like whiskers for sensing movement, were stunted. They had to wait for their human hair to grow again. You must learn which part of your body morphs into the other. I would say based on the position of your hair, and length, it must be part of your tail…"

That would seriously affect my balance and... my climbing.

"Hmm, maybe we should cut it to stop you from running away again."

Una caught Wolf's glance.

Gosh, where would I run to? He doesn't realise how desperate I was to get out of the manhole, and I have no wish to be there again.

He broke their deadlock stare with a wink and then directed his gaze at his sister. "I'll leave her to you, sis." He pushed a folded newspaper clipping into her uniform's breast pocket and left.

Grace waited for him to disappear before she signed for Una to follow the path he took.

Una nodded. Grace had to steady Una a few times while she found her legs as they walked down the trail between the rugged rocks.

Paying attention to where she placed her booted feet, Una asked, "Grace, why today?"

"What do you mean?"

"Something must have changed for you to let me out of the manhole during the day."

"Yes… You."

"But I changed on the first day, into a snow leopard, so why now and not then?"

"You morphed at night but in the day your human self… how do I explain it?"

"Try."

"Fine, wait." Grace paused and sat on the rock she had been standing on. Slowly she unfolded the newspaper clipping from her pocket and placed it on the rock beside her. Una was glad of the break from walking on her pins and sat down, trapping her hair beneath her bottom.

"Ouch!"

She had to stand up again. Feeling sorry for Una, Grace passed her the clipping and stood up too.

Wide-eyed, Una read the local newspaper headline dated two months ago.

"Seventeen-year-old girl goes missing in Khamosh Valley. It is believed the girl called Una Dev was abducted on her way to her friend's house in the army cantonment area." Underneath the headlines were her passport photograph and a school photograph from an inter-house competition. Una read on: "Her grandparents, her local guardians, are frantically looking for her. Vivek Dev, her father who lives in Manchester, UK, has paid for an investigation and is working with local authorities." There was a photograph of a man with her father's name in the caption. The only problem was it wasn't her father!

"Who is the man? Why would they say he is my dad?"

"You will have to ask your grandfather that. Anyhow, that's not important here."

Una looked at her incredulously. "If that's not important then explain why you have let me out in broad daylight when the authorities and my grandparents are supposedly looking for me. How…"

"Work it out for yourself." Grace pulled out a polaroid camera from her backpack and took a picture of Una.

Una was too shocked to close her widened mouth to finish the sentence.

Grace waved the photograph in the air and then handed it to Una.

Una stumbled. She didn't recognise herself in the photograph. Even after the summer growth spurts, she had evidently continued to grow taller. Her new, lean muscled body was a product of her nightly explorations. Her hair was shockingly long, and so much of it. The way it fell changed her face completely even without the bleached thick brush strokes. She slept most days after the night exertions so hadn't found it a nuisance but on the contrary, she had thought it a soft pillow. Her green eyes were more emerald and glasslike. They reminded her of Cat, the scrappy cub, which she thought was a kitten and was reluctant to name. Una let out a snort. So much for not getting attached… Cat had gone beyond attachment, to changing her into what she was now.

Now, if she even stood next to a full-sized cardboard cut-out of her prior self, she would find it hard to say she was the same person. People could mistake her for being related perhaps but would not believe she was the same person. Shock and confusion iced over her body, fixing her to the spot. She couldn't speak or think. Grace felt a pang of compassion. She motioned for Una to sit. Una couldn't move. Grace took pity and with just one touch of her index finger pushed Una down.

This time Una didn't notice or care about her hair when she sank down on the same rock.

Grace examined her finger in disbelief of the ease with which she was able to push Una down. "I think I've made my point."

Grace had. Una's heart pumped warm blood through her previously frozen arteries. Rage of injustice came after despair. If she were seen working around the area no one would recognise her and make a report. Her own grandparents would deny that she was their grandchild because no one could change as much as she had. Besides, they were already lying with the fake photograph of her father, so would they really want her back even if they did recognise her. The photograph suggested her father was still missing… if he were still missing then there was no more money coming in… so why would they want her?

Una stared at her hands. Wolf didn't have to hide her because she literally had nowhere to go. Over the weeks, she had moved a long way from her normal life but now she couldn't even return to the mundane existence at her grandfather's house. Una looked up at Grace. She didn't want the pity Grace was radiating. She was not helpless.

"Aren't you?"

"Get out of my head, Wolf!" Una screamed.

"Then get your butt down here."

"Fine." Una scrunched her fists and dusted herself down.

Grace didn't need instructions to move.

Una could see they were making their way down to the dreaded river again and she stopped. Horror stricken she stared at Grace's head and this time she stopped her by the arm.

"I can't go down. I've stayed, haven't I? I've been initiated..." She was ranting and failing to drag Grace's body backwards and impede her descent down the slope.

Grace prised Una's fingers off her combat jacket.

"Don't worry, Una, it's not about you this time, it's another firstborn."

"We all have to be present. The Blesseds come to make sure we only take firstborns."

"You are a third born, so how is it you are Forced Blessed?"

"I'm not."

Una stood back in shock and disgust. Why was Grace here if not a Forced Blessed? Surely, she didn't approve of the barbaric practice.

"Don't you dare show revulsion. Save it for your own relatives."

"They're not as repulsive as Wolf or even you."

"You're right about that. They are far worse... My brother was forced into this situation by your grandfather and Major. They knowingly ruined our lives by selling us forbidden Blessed land on which to build our house. All we have done is make sure your grandfather's firstborn suffers the same fate."

"Wait, didn't you say it was the initiation of a firstborn? But that can't be true. There aren't any more. Not only that, you've got both firstborns from both households."

"You will see for yourself that you are wrong."

Chapter 4

Scouting for Una

Half an hour earlier.

Avi sped up the rock surface bordering the Forced Blessed territory. Every now and again he stopped to listen. He was so sure that he'd heard her thoughts earlier… something about a manhole… but after picking up those thoughts he couldn't pick up any more of them.

"I know I didn't imagine her," he growled, out of breath as he followed the cliff line. He was exhausted from scouting for her the last two months and now when he finally heard something, he'd lost her again.

Avi's brooding came to a swift halt when broken cliff fragments clattered onto his head from above followed by the tickling of his snout by the end of a nylon rope that suddenly dropped down. Nylon rope… the type you used for climbing. Avi backed his body a few steps. If he ever had a doubt, he didn't now. He was not near; he was in Forced Blessed territory. Avi was glad of the protection his thick fur afforded him when more shingle fell from above. Avi stayed very still. He wasn't ready for a skirmish with one of Wolf's minions on their own territory. He could smell them, but they were moving away from him. Fifteen minutes passed. There was no more movement from above. If he wanted to know where Una was, he had to go further into enemy territory and for the very first time he wished he were in his human form. It would be easier to shimmy up the rope far more quietly than his bear persona would manage up the rough terrain.

Tough… time was pressing on.

Inwardly grimacing as he caused more shingle to shower down, Avi bounded upwards and ultimately made his way to the top. Whoever had been there had left a little while ago. He was alone on a wide ledge with a perfect bird's-eye view of the entire Forced Blessed territory, and his best chance of finding Una. Unfortunately, the jungle canopy was thicker on the Forced Blessed side. That and his eyesight made the task of spotting her difficult. Still, even though his eyesight was weaker in his sloth bear guise, his ears picked up on something heavy like metal being dragged along the ground just below him. The metallic glint was enough enticement and vindication for him to leap down the slope into Forced Blessed territory. Halfway down he caught Una's thoughts again.

Gosh, where would I run to? He doesn't realise how desperate I was to get out of the manhole, and I have no wish to be there again.

"Una?" She didn't answer and he could no longer hear her thoughts. His own thoughts, however, came gushing. *Una had been trapped in a manhole? For two whole months? All the time he had been looking for her.*

Avi crashed through the trees. He made a sudden stop less than a few centimetres from the heel of a boot. With great care he tiptoed backwards. Phew! That was close. Too close! Peeking above him, he saw many mountain camouflaged Forced Blesseds abseiling.

All the Forced Blesseds were cutting short their training and making their way for the River Rule initiation.

You idiot!

Avi was never self-complimentary, even in thought.

Una's release and the initiation were on the same day. That could only mean... That nana was mistaken. Una hadn't been initiated yet. He was right, Wolf had lied about Una killing Gopan. Bastard!

Today's initiation of a firstborn made complete sense. It had to be Una crossing over.

Two months ago, the local newspaper Kulkil brought on the way back from school, said she was missing. Kulkil only showed it to him out of loyalty. He had rightly guessed how Avi felt about Una on Meeru's wedding day. When he acted as a gofer between the two of them. On that day Meeru chose to die instead of being wed. Wolf had tricked and abandoned her, but she still chose suicide over marrying another. Wolf had killed his mother and then indirectly his aunt and now the bastard had imprisoned his Una in a manhole for two whole months. Avi didn't care that he was outnumbered, he would finish Wolf now. Or so he thought.

"Get back here, Avi!!!" Avi had forgotten to block the Sharman out. He had no choice but to turn back. If he didn't the Sharman would come to his aid and put himself at risk.

Avi made a hurried retreat to the Blessed territory. Only seconds before more Forced Blesseds had begun to make their way down the cliffs.

Still angry, Avi couldn't help making a dig at the Sharman through thought talk. *"You should have known that Una wasn't involved. If she had been, we wouldn't be having an initiation right now."*

"Not necessarily."

Not necessarily? Avi mulled over everything he'd learnt over the last nine months… and was sure that only firstborns could cross over. His paternal uncles had children. Yes, but all of them were safe, under ten years of age. Plus, by the time they were of age he was going to make sure that they didn't suffer the same destiny.

"Nana, it has to be her. There are still the same number of houses: Dada's, Dev's, and Sid's. There aren't any new families in Khamosh Valley."

"Finally, you are here."

Avi was not surprised to find the Sharman in his frail looking human form on an uphill climb away from the temple, between a thicket of trees not too far from the Forced Blessed territory. He was caught bear-pawed coming out of the Forced Blessed territory. Territory forbidden to the Blesseds. Needless to say, the Sharman wasn't radiating pleasure at seeing him.

"Avatar?"

Avatar… his name conjured an image of something he wasn't. He hated when he was called it at school and even more so now.

"Avatar answer me. Why were you in their territory? You knew they would be out in force. You must have known you could be caught easily? On top of that you knew all Blesseds have to be present at the riverbed right now for a firstborn River Blessing…"

"That's a nice euphuism for a barbaric sacrifice," jeered Avi.

"Barbaric? Not at all. Your arrival to our world would have been in the same way and neither your life nor your mother's would have been at risk."

Avi stood still. Frustrated, the Sharman finished his words, walked back to where Avi was and grabbed hold of Avi's closest sloth ear. Despite his deceptively frail form, he easily dragged Avi towards the temple. Avi swung his head left to right and right to left to shake the Sharman's hand off his ear, to no avail.

Avi protested loudly, "You forget I was there when you and the other Blesseds tried to grab Una, and what happened when me and my friends used to hang out in the dry riverbed initially, until we realised the perils. That wasn't even about initiation. Why do you think my uncles kept rope in the cowshed…?"

"We won't talk about all this again. We keep going in circles. We really haven't got time. Today you must keep your thoughts to yourself and you must not intervene."

Avi mocked, "In that case, why don't I just stay here? There's no need for you to take me there."

"You are an insolent brat; no other tribesmen, Blessed or not, would dare to challenge me." With that he pushed Avi down the slopes. Avi rolled himself all the way to the now dry, post monsoon riverbed. Thud!

Avi brought his ungainly body up to stand and roared whilst shaking off the twigs and debris he collected on the way. It didn't bother him that the Sharman was covered in it now.

The Sharman held his breath while he dusted himself down. "Again, you are wasting time. I've explained to you before that all Blesseds must be there. All Blesseds must be accounted for, so no mistakes are made in the conversions. We do not duplicate animals unless there is a lack of numbers in the animal kingdom."

"One doesn't want to be here and the other shouldn't be here," the Sharman shouted. "Kulkil, why are you here? Go back!"

They both heard footsteps.

"I've brought Burfani!" Kulkil eagerly rushed over to them, holding the snow leopard cub.

Avi noticed his nana bristle and avert his eyes from the bundle in Kulkil's arms.

"He can't come," the Sharman spoke curtly.

Kulkil's face dropped. "But why? He's not that ill, besides, he is our leader…"

"Avatar, did you know that the snow leopard is ill?" Kulkil's eyes popped out as did Avi's. They both noticed that the Sharman hadn't addressed Burfani with respect.

"The snow leopard… surely it's blasphemy not to use the correct title."

The Sharman realised his slip and whispered, "The Forced Blessed are near we don't want them to know Burfani is here, silly boy."

"But then why did you say snow leopard, surely his presence is meant to be a secret too."

"Kulkil, you are trying my patience! Take him back quickly, I think I can hear the Forced Blesseds coming now!"

"And you, Avatar, follow him and change back into your human self."

Avi protested, he didn't want to be a human again. If he was forced to live in the jungle, then he preferred his animal guise. He didn't want one of his relatives on either side of the path to stumble across him. Only a few Blesseds knew of his final Blessed form.

The Sharman softened. He understood Avi's reluctance, he himself preferred his monkey state. Still, it couldn't be helped.

"I've already told you our numbers are counted, and we must

be careful that some are not missed because we are in our animal guise. Especially as the native jungle animals like to stand with us. His tone now was far gentler.

"Look, the infidels are already making their way down rapidly."

From afar, for a little while, both grandson and Sharman watched the Forced Blesseds making their way down the cliff rocks before making their way to the four boulder posts on the riverbed.

"They must have been training when you were in their territory."

"Yes…"

"You fool!"

"Who's a fool? We need to know what they are up to."

The Sharman grunted.

"We can't sit back when only a few of us have undergone army combat training. They are preparing for combat and not in their animal forms. There's no way we can defend ourselves from the Forced Blesseds in their human form. I've already told you about the weapons they had when they curbed Ma's flight. Our tribesmen's' spears and brute force is just not enough to overcome an attack. Our Blessed forms will be useless against their weapons."

"Stop for now, Avi…" Avi halted mid-rant. He placed his hands on his grandson's shoulders and pushed him in the direction of the temple. "I've got to go, and you have to change, so get on with it."

Avi waited for his grandfather to disappear behind some bushes before he quickly retraced his steps to the Forced Blessed boundary. If all the Forced Blesseds were coming this way, then Una would be too. Therefore, it was still possible to save her from becoming a Forced Blessed.

He realised how unrealistic his attempt to save her was when he was forced to duck down in the bushes as the Forbidden Blesseds, led by Wolf, passed him by. There were too many of them.

Avi counted them as the line of combat boots jogged past him in unison. He didn't move. Instead he consoled himself with the thought: *If she's here and is at the end of the line I might still be able to grab her.* Of course, he knew that wasn't likely and admitted he was still there because he wanted to see her after all this time.

Standing behind the bushes on his hind legs was not very comfortable but he didn't miss her.

The line came to an end.

Unless Una had turned into a boy she wasn't in the group. Disappointed, Avi turned away and made his way to the temple to get changed, thinking aloud, "Well, that just proves that she wasn't yet initiated and might be on the other side of the initiation curtain on the riverbed."

Unlucky for him he missed the rear end of the Forbidden Blessed cohort when Una came trundling down the path.

Although Avi's transformations were much quicker they were not instant yet. He caught himself in the reflection of the water pitcher, morphing. He looked like a monster, half human, and half animal.

To be on even ground with the Forced Blesseds psychologically, Avi decided to not wear his usual dark jeans and T-shirt and thrust his arms through his army uniform which he wore while still training with them. His hand wavered over his army cap wondering if it was too much but then he swiped it off the hook. He hesitated when he caught his reflection in the water again. It was like meeting someone from a distant past. He kicked the water pitcher and his form disappeared. Fixing his cap on his head he left the temple and made his way down the numerous steps.

Wolf and his cohort had not seen him in human form since they chased him on the day, he lost his mother, Rosetta, the leader. Avi wondered if Wolf and the others would recognise him. Would Una?

Chapter 5

Coming of Age Party

Una was revolted by the bubbles of excitement that surfaced when she thought of seeing Avi again. This wasn't some high school prom.

She'd lost her humanity, was now a murderer and yet her utmost emotion was of joy about meeting Avi again!

Didn't Wolf say that Gopan was Avi's relative?

Yes, he did.

Then shouldn't she be terrified of seeing him?

God, she was gross!

Una was so ashamed of herself and didn't recognise herself. Had she really become blasé about other's suffering?

Had she been in the manhole too long?

Una shook in repulsion. She couldn't believe she was almost rushing, with lots of near falls, to go and witness… not partake in… a barbaric coming of age initiation. Her bloody heart twisted sharply, wringing out her temporary amnesia.

Memories of unbearable pain in her sockets when her arms were pulled backwards by stronger, more savage ones through an invisible wall flooded in, drawing her breath in. Unconsciously she rubbed her arms. Avi had saved her that day ten months ago.

For the first time ever, Una appreciated what Wolf had saved her from. After all, falling off a bridge was kinder and much gentler than what she envisioned happening soon.

Una's mind wandered off herself and back to the possible identity of the new victim. Had another family moved into the valley? Did she know the victim? It wasn't Avi, she was sure of that. She'd heard him thought talk and was sure he was already in the jungle on the side of the Blesseds. The side that was desperate to avenge Gopan. Gopan was part of the Sharman's family; Avi's cousin. How had Gopan felt when his cousin had thought him only as her grandfather's help? Now that he knew who Gopan was it quite likely meant that Avi wanted her dead too. Clammy fear crept up; fear not of death but of losing their relationship which she hadn't even understood completely and truthfully, and still didn't. Forget the new Blesseds' destiny, she wondered about hers and Avi's.

"A few more steps and we will be in the open. Watch out, even at this early hour the morning sunlight is quite bright after living under the jungle canopy and in the shadows of the mountain cliffs."

Grace finished her warning just as they came upon the edge of the dry riverbed where one of the four boulders was firmly embedded in the subsoil of the riverbed. This time Una wanted to run into the jungle rather unlike her first evening as a Forced Blessed when she tried to trick and escape from Wolf. If only dream casting could predict the future. That way she would know what the outcome was when she was spotted by the Blesseds today. Her arrival on the Forced Blessed side for all to see would surely cause a fuss. Would they link her arrival to Gopan's death? What if Avi has told them already? Would he be the one to exact their revenge…? Her imagination was running wild. Dizzy with her pain and a growing pain clamping her lungs she stumbled forward on the river pebbles.

"Fainting already? You aren't allowed. You are our very special poisoned weapon. We need to rub you in their faces."

Una looked up at Grace whose face was contorted in sadistic glee.

"It's a shame Wolf said you can't stand in the front line and shock the others. I for one would love to see the Sharman's face when he spots you in the line-up. Anyhow, let's get you up." Una flinched from Grace's helping hand.

"Did you hear me? Get up! We need to get you where you are less conspicuous." Grace was losing her patience. Una wasn't quick enough it seemed. Agitated, Grace tugged at Una's arm and grabbed her around the waist as she manoeuvred them both to the boulder posted quadrant where the Forced Blesseds were lined up in two rows. Once she was positioned not a murmur or scrape of a boot or foot on the noisy shingle could be heard. Una fell into place and stance. As the minutes passed, there was a growing air of anticipation that grew until the Sharman and Blesseds, from nowhere just likes ghosts, emerged from the foliage without a sound and flanked the opposite side of the quadrant.

Strangely though as soon as they lined up the quiet air came to an end. Something spooked the Blesseds and their lines were soon in disarray. Una was confused by all the whispering and agitation. She was hidden from view, so it wasn't her. Could it just be that the Forced Blesseds were present?

"Aren't the Forced Blesseds meant to be here?" she whispered to Grace.

"We are, it's mandatory," Grace answered, matter of fact. There was too much emphasis on "We". Considering she wasn't really Forced Blessed Una let it go.

"So why the unrest?" quizzed Una, giving Grace a side glance.

"They're wondering how the numbers are increasing."

"They've increased? How?"

"Well, it's not by births, that's obvious. There's only me," Grace whispered in amusement.

Una didn't like the sound of that. Had she been recruited for this very purpose?

Before she could ask Grace grinned and whispered, "Although, I can see merit in Meeru's idea of offering you and her darling nephew, Avi, to procreate for the Forced Blessed team." Una flung her fist at Grace, only to connect with Wolf's arm as he walked through the lines. "Una, pull your cap down and, Grace, come here, I've changed the plan."

Dread filled Una yet she still couldn't resist peaking between the sea of heads. Her search for Avi after hearing his name was interrupted by Grace digging something hard into her back to make her move. It was a pistol.

Una cooperated. She concentrated ahead. It looked like she was making her way to the bushes that edged the stony path she once walked on happily as an ordinary girl. Was she was going to be taken to the cowshed again? Was this her initiation? A deep fear overtook her.

Had Wolf double-crossed her?

Even worse than that she thought of another outcome.

Was she being handed over as their great grandson's murderer?

Chapter 6

Unrest at the Quadrant

Avi didn't have to lift his cap or walk closer to the quadrant to know what had upset the Blesseds. His sense of smell was enough. A by-product of sniffing out ants, he guessed. It wasn't that he smelt many more than the fifteen Forced Blesseds he'd counted when he shared Una's and Rosetta's visions, and the additional numbers of defected Blesseds. It was that the extra numbers smelt different to firstborn Blesseds. They smelt like… Avi screwed up his nose. They smelt like humans who had spoiled – gone off.

Could it be that they were the reverse of the Blesseds who were a heightened mixture of human and animal, and instead were an inferior mix? Less than both human and animal?

Avi moved in closer.

Even without their weapons the Forced Blesseds were formidable. Their stone-cold stares pierced through the Blesseds and beyond, creating enough tension.

"Have mercy, Hanuman!"

Avi's attention was brought to his own side, and to his nana's, who unlike the rest of the Blesseds was not staring at the Forced Blesseds but at him.

"Avi, I warn you, don't let anyone suspect that you have known of Una being here for some time."

Avi said nothing in reply.

Agitated, the Sharman continued, *"Stay hidden behind the others."* Then with greater emphasis, said, *"Please don't cause trouble today."*

Furious with the Sharman's need to warn him he almost walked back and then stopped. He had to be there for her initiation. Not because of the rules but because there was a slim chance of rescuing Una or at least making sure she was initiated in the least painful way possible.

There was no doubt in his head that they were gathered for her initiation. No new families had joined the area, so it had to be her. It was strange to him that he preferred her to be initiated here with some pain rather than already be one of them and out of his reach. Of course, he understood that the Wolf would hinder his attempts to save her from him.

"What are your plans for Una?" When no answer followed Avi continued in thought talk, *"Let me help you."*

The Sharman spoke after a short interval.

"What can you or I do now?" There was sadness in the Sharman's voice. Avi heard defeat and then the plea that followed. *"Stay quiet and behind the lines, you and I will soon find out what is happening with her."*

Avi retreated behind the ranks as Wolf strode over to the Sharman who was already standing perpendicular to both lines.

The Blesseds gasped in unison. Wolf had broken a significant tradition just by standing next to the Sharman. Even Avi could see Wolf had cast doubt on the Sharman's authority.

The timing was odd to all the Blesseds, including Avi.

"Nana, what do you think this means?"

Again, the Sharman said nothing.

The Blesseds began to protest. Almost as if Wolf had heard Avi thought talk, Wolf walked in front of the Blesseds' line-up and openly sneered at them. Avi couldn't help feeling that he would have done the same when he compared both line-ups. Both were in their human form. However, the enemy line-up looked like steel, sleek and sharp in their sky-blue uniform while his kith and kin elders in their tribal garb and the young in jeans, with animals peppering the lines with their presence, looked like rabble.

"Nana, if the initiate has a choice, then I'm afraid the Forced Blesseds

look more commanding than us."

The Sharman didn't even flinch at the dig. Avi became flustered. *"It must be time to summon Kulkil to bring Burfani?"*

The Sharman did not answer. Avi couldn't believe his nana didn't see this as an opportunity to reveal their trump card. Avi pleaded, "Nana, can't you see that this would be a good time to show the Forced Blesseds our true strength?" If nothing else at least our defected Blesseds would return.

Avi finally got a reaction from the Sharman.

"IT SEEMS YOU HAVE NO RESPECT FOR THE BLESSEDS, AND ME IN PARTICULAR." The tiniest of pauses was taken. *"DO YOU WANT TO JOIN THE FORCED BLESSEDS JUST SO YOU CAN WEAR A FANCY UNIFORM OR DO YOU SUFFER FROM THE SAME DELUSION OF WOLF'S THAT YOU CAN HEAD THE BLESSEDS BETTER?"*

The onslaught of the raging thought speech rattled Avi and puffed out his strength.

"IT DOESN'T MATTER WHAT WE LOOK LIKE, SHE WILL HAVE NO CHOICE BUT TO BE ON THE FORCED BLESSEDS' SIDE. THIS IS JUST A SHOW FOR US BLESSEDS, TO MAKE US BELIEVE THEY HAVE BROUGHT HER OVER LEGITIMATELY."

Avi shook his head, exhausted but not defeated.

"How can you be so sure that she's already a Forced Blessed?"

"Because it is true!" The Sharman paused and then in a gentler tone asked, "Avi, are you terrified that she might be a wolf and that's why you can't accept the possibility? Beta honai ko koi nahi taal sakta – What will be will be."

"*Aap galat ho, dekhna* – You've got this all wrong. You will see," Avi murmured.

The Sharman was tired of the conversation. It was getting them nowhere and they just didn't have the time for it. "*Let's not battle each other right now. For Una's sake and ours just be quiet.*"

That got Avi's attention.

The Sharman turned in Avi's direction. *"Let Wolf follow through with the deceit. In this instance it's useful. It will remove any suspicions of having something to do with Gopan's death if they believe she has arrived today."*

"You still think..." Avi stopped and instead kicked at the river pebbles in frustration.

Chapter 7

A Hyena is Born

"You look really strange in uniform." Avi wasn't the only disobedient one. Kulkil had crept up unnoticed behind him. Avi's mood lightened. Kulkil was like having a loveable Labrador especially when they jostled. Avi couldn't resist and stepped back on Kulkil's toes. "It's not your time… it will happen soon enough to you. Go back before the Sharman notices you."

Kulkil stared ahead defiantly. "Everyone knows that Una is coming through even though it's not her eighteenth, so why can't I? That Dev is really sneaky, claiming his granddaughter is missing and putting it in the newspaper so no one will suspect him of handing her over as promised to the Blesseds."

Avi knew Kulkil was wrong but it did make him wonder if Dev had made a deal with Sid instead of the Sharman. What was the truth behind Una's arrival in the jungle?

Kulkil pulled on Avi's cap. "I can feel that scowl from back here. Cheer up, man! It's all good. Those long, long legs in short dungarees are coming soon."

Avi swore. Inappropriately timed images of Una in her dungarees and then in the white Kaftan in the summer swamped him. His unbridled mind conjured her vanilla scent… then a motorbike piston backfired and brought him back to his senses.

A motorcycle was heading straight for them from across the path and through the quadrant of the river. The roaring of its engine sounded further away despite its proximity due to the buffered white gelatine-like wall membrane that kept the Blessed world protected from the Others.

"Avi, I'm here."

Avi began to move forward but Kulkil grabbed him from behind. *Damn! She was either going to drive through willingly or undergo the awful ritual and be dragged through it.* Unlike last time he would be the one pulling her through the membrane to danger rather than pulling her away from it.

"This is what you saved me from before... I didn't know..."

"Did I really save you?" asked Avi. Then without thinking, shouted, "Una, drive away…"

Kulkil smothered Avi's mouth with his arm from behind him. Avi didn't realise he had switched from thought talk to voice. Luckily, his outcry was smothered by the stamping noise of the tribes' feet. With bulging eyes and nearly free, Avi watched as a hand made a surface print on the thick fog. It seemed to be looking for a way through.

Was Una really willing to come over and hoping to tear through the membrane by riding through on a motorcycle?

The stomping came to a sudden standstill. Unlike last time no one moved forward to pull her through. Instead they all held their breath and waited. A dark, male hand ripped through the opaque wall.

"It's not Una!" a tribesman shouted.

Avi witnessed the Sharman's face blanch in disbelief.

Wolf chortled. "*Kyo kaisa laga meri chaal, tum nai socha bhi na tha* – How do you like my move? Bet you didn't predict this twist."

The Sharman was too shocked to answer.

Avi frantically tried to see through the membrane.

"Una, where are you...?"

"I'm here, Avi."

"Where?"

"In the Forced Blessed line-up."

She'd only been a few metres from him all this time? Avi's heart sank. A few metres away in distance but in that moment, he felt the metres ran into an unsurmountable distance thus parting them and putting a wall between them for eternity.

He was such a fool. He scrutinised the hand and was taken aback.

As was Una. It was especially difficult for her to forget the dark, short, and stubby hand with a large ruby on its pinkie finger. Both Avi and Una shared the same reaction: of queasiness and incredulity.

"Let the initiation begin." Wolf usurped the Sharman's position and announced the beginning of the River Rule initiation.

"*Ruk Ja Nalayak!* Stop, Wolf! You've gone too far!" The Sharman pulled Wolf back. "Only the Sharman, and that's me, can initiate the River Rule."

"*THEEK HAI!* OKAY! I'll graciously give way… this time." Wolf's facial expression contradicted his words.

The Sharman took a deep breath in and let it out, then began chanting in Sanskrit.

On the last Om two animals stepped forward from both camps and stood in front of the opaque wall, ready for the initiation process. A mongoose stayed at the Sharman's heels. The fidgety wolf pup from the Forced Blesseds' camp bare its teeth. Wolf knelt and picked him up and pretended to listen, and then laughed. "I agree, the ring is vulgar, a bit like the initiate." He pretended to listen to the pup again. "You want to help by removing the ring, of course, let me assist you." He held the wolf by its scruff, stepped back and rocketed the pup at the initiate's hand.

The air was filled with terrifying yells of anguish as the gaudy ring, still on a finger, fell. The excited pup pounced on the severed finger and grabbed it in its mouth.

At the same time the ethereal wall was obliterated as the initiate's motorbike jolted out of control from underneath its leathered driver and threw him amongst the assembled.

"Gag!" both Una and Avi thought shouted.

Gagan was writhing on the ground, having urinated in his leathers, clutching his hand, posing far too much temptation for the wolf cub, who dropped the severed finger promptly and jumped into the air to attack him. Before it landed on Gagan's neck it froze for a moment, mid-air, emitted a strangled yelp and then fell on Gagan. It was dead.

Everyone expectantly turned to Wolf, who was immobilised on the spot and then turned to look at what he was staring at. Avi held Wolf's gaze as he walked through the Blessed lines, plucked his knife from the pup's body, and then dropped it at Wolf's feet. Avi enjoyed the shocked recognition on Wolf's face. It was the knife Meeru had kept from her wheel of fortune days. In short it was Wolf's knife.

"Avi, you shouldn't have done that." The Sharman's curt remark shocked and hurt Avi.

"Are you serious?" Avi swung to face the Sharman's thunderous face. Avi couldn't tell if he was furious with him or with Wolf. Most likely both. "Would you rather Gag was blinded and maimed? He's not even a FIRSTBORN. HOW COULD YOU NOT INTERFERE?"

"No one interferes, not even me!" answered the Sharman, barely keeping his temper in check.

Wrong answer. It fired Avi even more. "I had a right to stop him from taking my half-brother and stop him from being maimed. He doesn't belong here. Send him back. Don't you see that you have to?"

Gagan stilled and suddenly went from crying to half crying and laughing in pain.

Gagan shook his head.

"Oh, but I am a firstborn."

Avi looked incredulously at Gagan and then at the Sharman. The Sharman shrugged his shoulders not knowing what Gagan meant. Avi kneeled where Gagan lay sprawled on the riverbed. "Don't be stupid, why would you lie about that. Just save yourself and tell them the truth." Gagan shook his head.

Frustrated, Avi tried again. "Seriously, how can you be so stupid – I know we both have different mothers but we…"

Gagan interrupted. "We have different fathers too."

Avi stumbled backwards onto his forearms. "How can that be?"

Gagan looked at Wolf with pleading eyes.

Wolf grunted. "You mean how could his ma trick your papa? She did and very well, and it seems they are possibly still duped. When she returned with Gagan from her parents to find you missing she asked your dada where you were. That's when he explained that a deal had been made with the Sharman that all firstborns of the residents were to be sacrificed for the land they bought from the tribe. That day, his ma took him out of school and went back to stay with her parents and told your dada some cock and bull story about Gagan needing time to overcome your destiny. When your precious dada sent for this prick to help with Meeru's wedding, she refused to send him back. Luckily, the devious sod was bored and thought it would be more fun at the wedding and sneaked back to Khamosh Valley. And that's when I made a bargain with Gagan. Isn't that right, Gagan?"

Gagan whined. "A bargain, this ain't no bargain. You never said anything about being mauled... Oh my God, where is my finger?"

Wolf smiled but there was a dangerous glint in his eyes. "You will soon learn, if you haven't today, that no one dares to bargain with me." He shrugged his shoulders in a deceptive carefree manner. "I had to put you in your place."

He eyeballed Gagan. "Did you think you could be the same rank as me?" Content that Gagan wouldn't dare reply, Wolf continued, "No one gets to choose to be a wolf, the honour is bestowed on the lucky ones."

"But you promised..."

Avi read the disappointment and cold anger in Wolf's clamped up expression. *God, Gag, you stupid idiot, he had no intention of letting you live.*

"Well read, Avi. Will you tell him, or shall I?" Avi gave nothing away. Wolf scoffed then bent down to hover over Gagan. "I promised to allow you to transform into the animal of your choice, but

I didn't intend for you to survive your initiation."

Wolf rose and booted Gagan in his ribs. Gagan babbled louder.

"However, fair is fair. Since you have survived the attack, we will let you live for now and even join us. Though your mauling means you are a damaged wolf and that puts you at the bottom rank, below the dumb animals, and also probably means you will eventually die if you can't fend for yourself."

Gagan was not listening, he was rolling in agony. Wolf's attention was on Avi while he seemingly addressed Gagan. "Gagan, for now be thankful that Avi saved…" Wolf was forced to stop before he could say "you". Avi had broken his gaze with Wolf to look over at Gagan. Wolf followed his gaze. Gagan was howling in agony as his body contorted every which way as he began to morph. At the end of the process most turned away. Gagan was a terrible sight, of mottled coat. His right foreleg was shorter than the others, putting his body off balance. The significance of a missing digit causing unbalance to a Blessed transformation was brought home to Una. Her hand went to her hair subconsciously.

Wolf circled Avi as Avi got up and shook himself down.

"I must thank you."

"What for?" asked Avi.

"Without realising it you've made your so-called brother hate you more. Hatred is as good as gold here."

Avi huffed.

"He's never going to forget that he is marked and inferior, especially as it was his wish to outrank you. He will grow to hate you daily when he realises that if you hadn't interfered, death would have been better than being an incapacitated mutt in a jungle. His hatred of you suddenly makes him a useful weapon against you and the Sharman, thus increasing his usefulness a hundredfold."

Avi sidestepped several times to halt Wolf. Frustrated, he shouted with his arms spread open wide, "Who says you get to choose to have Gagan. He's from my household and that's why he will be with the Blesseds."

Wolf inched forward so both their faces were centimetres apart.

"I'll say you have guts going up against me. Looks like I have the wrong brother." Avi pushed Wolf back. Wolf chuckled. "That's a shame… but then again, I can see you are a handful for your nana, the Sharman, and the Blesseds. While I'm sure Gagan can guarantee me his loyalty." Wolf then addressed the Sharman who was silent all this time. "Tell him he is mistaken."

In a flat tone the Sharman agreed, "Avi, you were born Blessed from a Blessed lineage, from your mother's side, but Gagan has no such lineage so he can choose where he goes."

Without being asked the sad creature that was now Gagan limped towards the Forced Blesseds. The neglected mongoose took the opportunity to greedily feast on Gagan's finger and the other animals present fought over the remains of the wolf pup. All of the Blesseds and Forced Blesseds then dispersed except for two individuals.

***

Avi could not discern her features as she had her cap tipped downwards to cover her eyes. But since when did he need to see her to know who she was. Before she could walk over and engage with him, he loudly thought spoke, *"Don't!"* She stopped.

"Avi, please!" she thought pleaded.

Avi hastily raised his arm.

After giving her tough advice about not talking to him he turned his back on her and disappeared into the jungle. She tried to follow him, but his army greens camouflaged him well.

Hiding in the branches, Avi made up his mind. He didn't want anything to do with any of his previous life. The sight of her sank his conflicted heart, rousing disturbing emotions as well as disgust and rising fear of what could come next, and from whom. Whether that be Gagan or Una. God knows what deal she'd made. She must have made a deal because she didn't use the opportunity to break away or ask for help. She obviously had been set free. Was Wolf plotting a trap of sorts if he engaged with her? Well that was not going to happen, at least not today. Avi wasn't sure if he could follow his own rule of staying away from her, his past. But for today he knew, once he removed his uniform, he would change back to his animal guise and no one would be able to find him.

Avi wondered if the rest of the dysfunctional family he left behind knew that Gagan was missing. Would they guess correctly and then wonder why the jungle chose him to be Blessed? The irony was Major, his dada, had unwittingly prized the cuckoo over his own flesh and blood.

Chapter 8

Connections and Reunions

Twenty minutes earlier.

The unnecessary circular march led by Grace through the bushes that bought her back to the back row of the Forced Blesseds' line-up made no sense to Una. She knew it was circular before she saw the edge of the riverbed again because her Forced Blessed self-had somehow picked up on the individual heartbeats. It was a cat's equivalent of thermal vision, she supposed. With shivering, unsteady human legs she first stumbled her way, bending low between bushes, towards the cowshed and imminent death by the Blesseds. The heartbeats had dimmed behind her and then as she moved forward, she began to hear the same number louder and louder thus making her realise that she had circumnavigated the river.

What was Wolf playing at?

Was this the sadistic bastard's choice of punishment for misbehaving in the line or a reminder that he could control her movement?

Whatever, it revealed an ability to hear heartbeats, which she could probably use when she finally escaped. Una sighed. She had been plotting her escape since she arrived in Khamosh Valley, for almost a year. She was tired of it.

Meanwhile, it was easy for both Una and Grace to slip back unnoticed into the line-up as a revving motorbike somewhere near the cowshed end of the quadrant held everyone's attention. Una glanced ahead to where everyone was focusing. A red spot was shimmering on the previously whitish gelatine wall.

A gaudy ruby caught the sun and sparkled audaciously as it poked through the rip, stilling the collective heartbeats of all bound by the thread of consciousness – Blesseds or Forced Blesseds. Thus, making a complete mockery of the stance of a separate identity, by the Forced Blesseds, in Una's mind.

Wait! Una thought. *The stubby finger was familiar... it was Gag's. He'd wriggled a ruby finger at her when he stopped her on Major's driveway during Meeru's ill-fated wedding preparations. How did Gag, Avi's younger brother, become the sacrificial goat? Did Grace walk her back to avoid the newcomer. Had Wolf alerted her?* None of it made sense to Una.

The stillness from the collective was eerie but the coiled energy in all, ready to spring on the suspecting being, was unnerving. Between heads she saw something move with such speed that its physical body reduced to haze like the blades of a fan at top speed. A piercing squeal followed. It was Gagan for sure. Long teeth cut through the ringed finger's flesh which then remained in a bloody wolf pup's mouth. Una's stomach lurched. Barely had she stood straight when a knife ricocheted in the air and fell, this time producing an ear-piercing yelp from the greedy guzzler.

Una pressed forward between shoulders expecting to see Wolf claiming the knife. Instead, a lone, tall regular army uniformed male figure parted the feather and beaked headdresses ranks to reach the centre of the river quadrant. His solitary Blesseds peaked cap threw shadows on his face making it difficult to recognise him. Although he came from the Blesseds camp, he looked out of place amongst the tribesmen in their traditional dress. Their feather haloed faces showed equal measures of wariness and shock, akin to those on the Forced Blesseds' faces in her line. Una thought it out of place for the Blesseds to give one of their own such a look. Such a look she had seen given to another individual by Major's family. First sadness and then pain filled Una. This was not another individual, it was him. It was Avi and he was not accepted here either.

The pup's howls fizzled out.

Tension brewed. Una observed hands in the front line and on either side of her clasp their knives. Her own hand involuntarily touched the area where the pouch would be on her body if she had one. She shuddered. Once again it was brought home to her that she was imprisoned by collective thought. Just a few hours in daylight and she was already acting mechanically despite not a single order being issued. The Blesseds' eyes recognised the threat and they too swiftly took a stance to throw their spears; they were far enough to wield them at their enemies.

First Wolf spoke and then… Avi.

His voice had changed, it was deeper and curt, but it was him. He was laying claim to the despicable human on the ground. She should have cared about what was said between the trio, but she was oblivious to everything but Avi.

For so many months she had heard this boy… now man, in her head but it was the first time she'd glimpsed him in the flesh. He looked dangerous and his measured stance against Wolf showed he was impervious to the atmosphere he was a catalyst for. The Blesseds had parted a little too easily whilst squeezing together to give him the widest berth as if he were a leper walking amongst them. Their distrust and despise was greater than that of the Forced Blesseds. The Forced Blesseds' energy, in contrast, did not belittle his action. Avi was out of place and an outcast even on this side of the path.

She caught the gist of the exchange between Wolf and Avi but was distracted by Avi's thoughts. Even when she sensed he was near in the summer she was unable to talk to him because of the impenetrable shield surrounding his thoughts. Sharing his thoughts now were more intimate than an embrace. Her rapture however gave way when the turmoil raging through Avi pushed at her heart.

Such a big lie, a lie that relegated my mother to a beast.

And then an emotion akin to laughter bubbled through his thoughts.

So, they were all duped... their misguided love wasted... my father and grandfather thought they had an heir and a spare and now they have nothing.

His light-heartedness changed again to loathing.

I was the mongrel spare.

Una comforted him. *"Not to everyone. Meeru loved you and she knew who you were."*

Una trembled at his shock. He had momentarily forgotten that she could hear and feel what he did. He turned in her direction, she couldn't explain why she did it, but she hid behind the person in front of her, blocking herself from view.

She saw his profile shrug and then a more overpowering sensation took over the collective.

Gagan was morphing.

She couldn't help herself from thinking: *he's ugly as an animal too. His ugliness matches his screwed-up mind.*

Avi might have blocked himself from being eavesdropped on but he was listening.

"How do you know what he is like?"

"I met him when I kneed him in front of his gang at Meeru's wedding..."

She knew he could see the images of her encounter with Gagan. She tried to stop before she saw the elaborate wedding string lights turning off in Major's house, when Meeru chose to hang herself using them.

A pause and a change in his emotions overcame him. Meeru had been dear to him. Less aunt, more, older sister.

There was silence and then she heard him thought talk to her.

"Watch out for Gag. He was revengeful before but now you are in sight and together in the Forced Blessed jungle."

Una's disgust and misgivings grew as she watched a bedraggled wolf with unsymmetrical legs limp towards the Forced Blesseds' line. His head tilted up and down as he staggered up and down the Forced Blesseds' line-up until the first line disappeared behind Wolf. When he found what he was looking for, despite his reduced circumstances, he gave her a wry smile and said, “Found your papa yet?”

Una hadn’t expected that. Her gaze never left the abomination on all fours as it caught up with the rest of the Forced Blesseds.

Grace pushed her sideways. “Come on, if it’s any comfort he will be stuck in the manhole instead of you, until he is ready and his family stop looking for him… Oh shit! That will be soon! The idiot has left a trail with the stupid motorbike. Oh no! Wolf!” She ran off to find her brother.

Chapter 9

Living in a Bubble

The animals gorging on the wolf pup fought and sparred and soon the unfortunate thing had disappeared entirely. Even the spilt blood and stains on the pebbles had been licked clean. The only person left on the river besides herself was the tall uniformed figure. Una knew it would be up to her to take the first steps. She lifted her foot to move forward.

"Don't!" Avi's word stalled her.

"Avi, please!" she thought pleaded.

Avi hastily raised his arm and hand and looked around them.

"Stop! Right now!" She stopped, it felt like her life depended on it. *"How is it that you don't even know how to shield yourself?"*

His tone was a mixture of incredulous concern and anger.

Una didn't say anything.

"Don't you dare ever try and thought talk to anyone because you will leave them unshielded and vulnerable." Una saw him shrug both shoulders before he let them drop. It seemed he really wanted to shake her. *"Don't you know how to shield your thoughts by now? It's been two months."*

Una was hurt.

"I do... but it's difficult to be clear-headed all the time and you need confidence..."

"Confidence? Who says? It's nothing to do with confidence."

"Then what's it to do with?" Una angrily replied.

"Seriously. You don't know?" Avi turned his back to her and then

turned to her again. *"Of course, he hasn't told you."* Una noted his incredulous tone once more. How it must suit him. Avi's expression showed some sympathy towards Una. *"This is my last encounter with you, so you don't need to worry about me. I don't care if you've chosen Wolf but for God's sake don't let him fuck with your brain too much."*

"I haven't..."

Avi pointed to her feet and then up her body to her chin and then to her head. Una looked down at her uniform. Her open mouth slammed shut.

"For not lying to me I'll show you an easy way of stopping others in your head and here I mean Wolf. It might be easier for you to first close your eyes. Once you get used to this you won't have to even do that."

Una did as she was told.

"Stopping people from reading your thoughts is not difficult. All you have to do is imagine you are in a big bubble. If you want to allow someone in, you create a bubble around the image of both of you in your mind. Now look hard at the image you have created."

Una did. She could see a thin bubble around them.

She stepped closer to Avi's image.

"Stop!"

"Why?"

Avi's image stepped back against the bubble. Then a worried expression came over his face.

"What did you see?"

She had seen herself! Through his eyes!

Una was flustered and without thinking, lied.

"Nothing, just your image. What else was I meant to see?"

It seemed like Avi didn't want the truth any more than she wanted to tell it. Plus, she wasn't even sure if she had used his eyes to see herself because now all she could see was Avi's image. Una corrected herself, she had to stop lying to herself at least.

First disappointment then repulsion featured on Avi's image.

"Nana was right after all about the Forced Blesseds."

Una's real body and her image flinched.

Avi indifferently carried on. *"Now pay attention, if I don't want you in, all I have to do is redraw the bubble."*

And just like that he removed her. Una was standing outside Avi's opaque bubble in her mind and she could no longer see his thoughts. She opened her eyes.

Avi held her gaze and then turned his back on her and disappeared between the bushes, disappearing from her sight completely.

"Please, wait, I just want to…!" she hurried forward to where she thought she had seen him leave, "…thank you."

There was no one, just dark patches amongst the autumn fall and evergreen bushes, pinecones and… his uniform.

Chapter 10

Lost and Found

Una picked Avi's uniform up and held it to her nostrils. Her animal pheromones had already forgotten the bloody scenes from before. His chemical signature was all over them. She held them tightly to her chest.

"Give me the clothes!"

Something poked her back, a knife, no, it felt more like a…

A couple of self-defence moves brought her assailant down and she snapped his weapon – a stick – in two. She recognised the teenager's voice from the mango tree incident when the Sharman had spoken to her about joining the Blesseds in the summer. If she'd known she would be captured by Wolf, she might have done so. The teenager was a boy no more. He'd obviously had a growth spurt or two.

"Una!" Her assailant was more shocked to see her than she was to see him. Kulkil sat up. "How… you can't be here without initiation…" He then jumped up. "Wait, you look different."

Una waited for the realisation and then it came. His face turned the shade of dishwater grey. "It can't be… you are already initiated… No… it can't be." He looked around him and with urgency shouted, "I must tell Avi!"

Una interjected, "He knows, and he ran."

"He ran? Why…" Then he looked at her outfit. "Oh…"

Una suddenly no longer felt happy about her new, clean set of clothes.

"How could you? You knew he was Blessed. Why did you choose their side?"

"I didn't, I was forced but it doesn't look like Avi has chosen the Blesseds either."

"He hasn't, he can't choose. He was born Blessed."

She knew that she was there when his mother, Burfani, revealed her snow leopard self. For the first time she remembered that Avi had to be a snow leopard… like her. That had to mean something. *Isn't that what Grace implied Meeru wanted. She had to meet Avi before she was forced to return to the Forced Blesseds' camp.*

Una held the clothes high. "If you want Avi's clothes then you can tell me where he is?"

Kulkil wasn't tall enough to reach her extended arm yet. Kulkil protested, "Avi won't see you and you will never find him unless he wants to be found…" Kulkil gave up. "I guess you can keep the clothes."

Una could hear other heartbeats coming towards her. It was time to stop messing around with Kulkil. She hurriedly offered the clothes back to the youth. "You never gave me your name."

"Kulkil."

"Cool Kill?"

"Kull said like bull, kil, like… kill."

"Kulkil…"

"Una, why didn't you return?" Wolf sprung from nowhere.

"I was lost. Kulkil was…"

"Has disappeared." Wolf smirked. "I have that effect."

Una just ignored him.

"Good thing I came back then, or you might have run off with the boy. Although he's a little young for you."

Una passed the steps leading to the temple and saw a langur sitting on the topmost step watching her with interest. She swore he was the same one from the traffic jam that got rid of all the rhesus monkeys when she first arrived. Who was she kidding, how would she know?

Kulkil was now with the langur, at the top, folding Avi's uniform.

Una couldn't help herself thinking, *Kulkil, you obviously care for him, he'll run away from you too, just...* and then she stopped. Kulkil was distracted. With a tug he removed something out of Avi's outer combat pocket. It was a silver chain… no, it was a locket.

Una put her hand to her neck… her locket was missing. She must have lost it when she transformed into a snow leopard and fell from the bridge.

Kulkil was staring at her as he held the locket high, and then carefully put it back in Avi's uniform pocket. She knew it was hers. She raised her hand up as if to ask for it back but then let her hand fall. Wolf was watching her carefully.

Walking up the path, Una patted her breast pocket above the combat jacket and felt her heart race. She wondered if it was significant that Avi carried her locket just above his heart?

Chapter 11

A New Family

Why didn't Kulkil give her the locket back? She could tell he knew it belonged to her. If anything, by his taking it out in her view, it suggested he wanted her to know. *Know what? Know that Avi cared?*

Yet he walked away. But then she too was walking away… for now. Both had been tested. Both were barely surviving. She was exhausted from the roller coaster of emotions. For now, she was content to just concentrate on where Wolf was taking her.

"Glad you are focusing on what is essential to survive." Una stopped in her tracks. Thought blocks were hard to maintain when she was tired. Una gave him a sidelong glance and bristled at the half smile on his lips as he signalled to something ahead. The bastard was taking her to the manhole… Worse still, Gagan was already standing there. The creep's eyes, even in his motley wolf state, lecherously roamed slowly over her. The hair on her body prickled in disgust. She couldn't ignore it but was too tired to sound intelligent. "You make me gag, you fucking hyena! You're just a GAGGING HYENA," she sneered. Wolf laughed – "Wrong continent for a hyena but not a bad name. Of course, we will have to remove the swearing."

"Hyena! Hyena!" the cheers began. All the Forced Blesseds were there. A smug smile broke out on Una's face despite her usual loathing of name calling. It was plain that Gagan didn't know what a hyena was, but he knew she had insulted him and sneered back.

"You better look out for yourself because I'm still a male wolf and nothing outranks one, bitch!" Una yawned extravagantly and then stopped mid-yawn. She caught Wolf grinning back at her. It made him look… human. Handsomely human and carefree.

They all looked carefree. Yet they were the same Forced Blesseds who had intimidated the elders of the Blesseds, showed no empathy to Gagan when he had been maimed and had even been ready to fight with their knives when Avi killed the wolf pup.

"How can the same line be on the brink of a knife fight and then be chanting like immature schoolboys half an hour later?" Una addressed Wolf.

"Because they are just high school boys after all, but don't forget you called him names first." Wolf chuckled.

Wolf's laughter somehow took some of the weight off the frightful morning.

"Snap out of it, Una." Grace clicked her fingers and signalled for her to follow her. "Don't go falling for him, he is one hundred per cent wolf. He charms men and women alike but he's quite fickle. Remember what happened to my best friend, Meeru."

"Meeru and Wolf were a couple?" Her hunch about him having some feelings for Meeru was right.

"She thought he had forgiven her when he asked her to do one last thing on her wedding day before he took her back."

"And what was that?" Una got the impression that Grace saw Una as Meeru's competition and quite clearly didn't like it.

"Did you receive a kitten…"

"A cub. Wolf said it was the Blesseds that gave it through Meeru."

"My brother said that?" Grace was flabbergasted.

"Yes, but why are you so surprised?"

Grace ignored Una's question. "We are finally here."

Una protested, "What did Wolf ask Meeru to do?"

Again, Grace ignored her. Una gave up, her earlier fatigue and dread replaced the light respite from earlier. Una blindly followed Grace but wondered why they were sneaking through a garden hedge instead of remaining in the jungle, now behind them.

"Grace, where are we?" Una asked as she followed her through a man-size opening in the hedge, camouflaged by another hedge growing in front of it and creating a corridor.

"St Anthony's school?"

Avi's school. "Why are we here, besides simple trespassing we can't even pass off as boys?" Looking down at herself it was more than evident she was a girl; her favourite Jimi Hendrix T-shirt would never fit her now and her mass of hair…

"Don't worry about that. Papa donated a dormitory building on his land to the school. It was only completed a year ago."

"That may be, but it doesn't change the fact that we are still in a boys' school."

Grace was hurrying and didn't want to engage in unnecessary chat. "Look, Papa has set it up so that no one is going to ask questions."

Una was not convinced. "What authority does he have?"

Grace stopped, her hands on her hips. "He's the housemaster. Just before the construction of the dormitory, the usual long serving housemaster sadly had a nervous breakdown. He said a wolf was stalking him – can you imagine that?" Grace couldn't resist winking at Una.

Una stood with her mouth open. Doing a bad job of acting innocent, Grace continued, "Luckily Papa was available to fill in the gap. As housemaster, Papa of course gets living quarters which are joined close to the dormitory and he is allowed to have his family living with him. And of course, I am family too." A niece…

"Daughter…"

"I don't look anything like any of you…"

"Oh, your genes are a throwback to my great-grandfather – an English railways' station manager. Of course, unlike us you have more of the Anglo than the Indian in your Anglo-Indian gene. Which is not a lie, is it, Una?"

Yeah, she was of mixed heritage, an Irish mum, and an Indian dad but Grace and Wolf's parents were the Raj time Anglo Indians.

Surely people could see that she was first generation Anglo Indian. Una shook her head in disbelief.

"Do you remember those photographs Papa took of us at Meeru's wedding? Well, he framed them and as far as other staff or his students are concerned, you are his daughter who is London returned. Sorry, I mean Manchester returned. We will tell them the truth, that you went to a co-ed grammar school and just finished. Stretford Grammar, wasn't it? They are excited because this school was modelled on Manchester Grammar school. Lucky you are a girl and couldn't have gone to Manchester Grammar School otherwise you would have piqued the interest of the staff and seniors in this school."

Una was stumped. "How do you know which school I went to. I've never mentioned it, especially as they threatened to..."

"Expel you for truancy and exploration of shady places like the dock's empty warehouses?"

"How would you know that?"

Grace just smirked.

Una was on edge. She could tell that something elaborate had been planned by Wolf and Sid, which was much bigger than balancing the jungle or winning points against the Sharman. Something dangerous and evil. Worse still, somehow, she was integral to it. Her father bringing her to India no longer felt like a coincidence. Was it all planned... here... by them?

Grace's voice changed. She had picked up on Una's trepidation. "It's not as if you are going to do lessons at school. Una, cheer up. We are just going to live here with Papa, until we finish."

"Finish?" Una's ears pricked up. "Finish what?" she asked suspiciously.

"Our martial arts training. You are also going to be slogging in the library, mugging up on the valley's history and tribal myths and laws." Before Una could ask anything more, Grace cut her short, "Anyhow, we will talk more later. We are at our destination."

Una looked ahead of her. The building was breathtaking with its beautiful veranda and many columns. How could something so beautiful be built for sinister purposes.

"We'd better get in before all the boys return."

Una pushed past her. Grace screwed her nose and stepped back. "Seriously, Una, you really need to have a shower."

Una sniffed her armpit. She didn't need to be told twice.

Grace waited on the other side of the shower door and was rewarded with, "Aggh! Fuck, aggh! Grace, you could have told me there was no hot water." Grace smiled. She'd purposefully omitted to tell Una about the lack of hot water despite the hot and cold dial. Hot water meant loitering and that didn't happen in this block.

Una stepped out of the shower, her body a shade pinker, and wrapped herself in the only towel which was rough as hell. Luckily, the night clothes were clean boys' kurta pyjamas. They looked comfortable enough.

Grace had left. Una was too tired to care. She collapsed on a bed in a sea of beds and crashed.

Chapter 12

Sleeping with the Boys

"Perhaps she's Goldilocks…" uttered a male voice.

"Nope, she didn't break a chair or eat our porridge… not that we eat our slimy porridge either," another answered.

"She's Sleeping Beauty then," said a third.

"Nah! She's Snow White," answered the second male.

"Oh, you are so damn right! She's got black hair and a white face!" exclaimed the first male.

The third male agreed. "Yeah, I can see what you mean."

"Role play is not usually this much fun," chuckled the second male.

"Guys, whichever sleeping fairy-tale character she is playing, who gives a fudge. Let's decide on who out of us gets to kiss her first?" shouted a fourth.

A clamour of footsteps approached Una's bed.

Una awoke disorientated; to many eyes peering over her with puckered mouths. She jumped up and smacked her head against an unsuspecting boy's chin. The dormitory rang with laughter. It took a few minutes for Una to adjust to the scene. She was clean, in a pair of loose pyjamas. It all looked innocent like it had in her boarding school until her nose picked up the smell of testosterone. She was not in her school but in the brother school, St Anthony's. Instead of girls the dormitory was full of boys, dressed in emergency services uniforms and outfits. There was something awkward about them. They appeared more like people dressed in guises at a fancy-dress party… a dull fancy-dress party at that. But surreal, nonetheless. Una peered at the boys; she recognised a handful of faces but was puzzled by them. They looked innocent yet her mind wanted her to reject their innocence. And then she remembered where she had seen them. To make sure, one by one she locked gazes with the older dorm-mates and realised they had all been in the Forced Blesseds' line-up.

"Rude much?"

Una turned to face the speaker who was wearing a police official's beret. It was the Forced Blessed who was Wolf's right-hand man… she recognised him from the morning… although his tattoo was missing. That was it! All their faces were wiped clean of their tattoos. Even after spotting the difference, something else about the right-hand man niggled at her. He looked a little older than her but not by much. Although he had called her out for staring at them, he himself ardently held her gaze in earnest as if he were urging her to remember him. She mouthed: *I saw you in the morning.* He made a gesture with his hand and mouthed back: *think further back.* It seemed important to him that she placed where she first met him. She couldn't remember an earlier account and shrugged in defeat. His shoulders dropped in disappointment. Still he beamed at her and ventured a hand forward. "Raul. You must be Ms Rao."

"Ms Rao?" She hesitated. "My name is…"

Raul interrupted hastily, "Ms Rao, we aren't permitted to use staff first names unless you study here, and you don't." He quelled her protest.

"Please sit comfortably and as a favour you can judge the auditions."

Sit comfortably… when was the last time she had sat comfortably. She was grateful to be away from the Blesseds and Wolf. "Auditions?"

"Yes, our juniors are auditioning to join our house which specialises in martial arts. The current house boys, including myself, will be graduating from school in the summer.

"What does martial arts skills have to do with acting?"

"You will see by living in this block."

Una made herself comfortable. "Do all houses have auditions?"

"No, this a new house and the boys are recruited from other houses based on their athletic training, martial arts, shooting and discipline. Of course, everyone is desperate to belong to the house because it has the best dormitories and its own dining mess and gym," explained Raul with pride.

Martial arts, shooting and athletics... discipline. Did they need to be disciplined like the Forced Blesseds' line-up? Had the new Forced Blesseds been initiated in this dormitory... Una scuttled backwards on the bed. "Has this audition got something to do with this morning?"

Raul hesitated. *She had to be right.*

"Do the boys know what happened in the morning?"

"Raul, what does she mean? What happened in the morning?" one of the juniors asked whilst sitting next to her on the bed. Raul's face took on an ugly scowl. Una became quiet.

"Nothing much happened, boys." Then catching her eye, he added in a tone, "Martial arts and shooting are important to our house and school. So, some of us who have represented India in world athletics and the Olympics gave Ms Rao a demonstration with real targets in the jungle."

"Ms Rao, why have you chosen to train and live here?" another of the juniors asked.

"So, she can be our eye candy of course!" Una swooped towards her bed companion and held his head in a vice grip.

"I surrender!"

Una didn't give.

"Ms Rao, let him go, he was teasing."

Una loosened her grip and the boy escaped.

"Ms Rao is going to train alongside us just like Ms Meeru did. Remember the school allows outside candidates to train."

Several "Oh's" were muttered in the group. Raul must have thought that was the end of the subject, but Una wanted to know more.

"Does Wolf train here too?"

"Who?" The junior boys looked at each other and at their seniors in confusion.

"Wolf… you mean Wolfgang?" answered Raul. He warned Una once again. "Take care, Ms Rao, we don't use first names, just surnames."

Raul then addressed the boys, "Boys, his name is Mr Hamilton to you." He then turned back to Una. "We call your father's friend's son and your childhood friend Mr Hamilton here." To mask Una's confused expression, Raul added, "Ah! Sorry, Ms Rao, perhaps you didn't know that while you were away, Mr Hamilton, your friend, has become our main archery and martial arts teacher."

Not sure of what she would say next Raul reached out for Una's forearm and pulled her up and discreetly gestured for her to follow him out of the dormitory. "Tell you what, Ms Rao, why don't I show you the gym?"

She followed him out of the dormitory. Once alone in the corridor he came to a sudden stop.

"You can't ask questions about Wolf or about the Forced Blesseds in the school. Is that clear?"

Una ignored him. "But didn't Wolf attend the school? Come on, they must know of his connection with Sid?"

Raul sighed loudly and angrily slammed the wall behind Una. "Fine! Just this once and then that's it."

Una nodded.

"They know that Sid's son, Warwick, attended but has passed away. He is remembered as a model student and that's why the school accepted Mr Rao's donation of his land."

"Don't tell me they can't recognise Wolf."

"Wolfgang looks much older and is barely recognisable. There are only a couple of teachers from his time and they don't cross paths with Wolf. Wolf only comes here to this building and the library and they don't frequent those parts."

Una wanted to ask more but a few boys had opened the door

and were making kissing sounds and were fake kissing their hands. Una laughed.

She winked at the boys and lightly brushed Raul's cheek with her lips.

Raul almost jumped out of his skin. "Look, Ms Rao... that was..."

"Too much... too soon?" Una asked coquettishly.

"What? Stop it... you've given them fodder to rag me indefinitely which is not great if I am to lead them."

"Oh sorry, did I offend you?" Una pretended to care.

Raul had a sense of humour after all and replied, "I didn't really mind..."

"Of course, you didn't," Grace angrily interrupted. She *really* wasn't happy.

Forget Raul, Una almost jumped.

Were Raul and Grace an item?

Una looked at her quizzically and mouthed: *sorry.*

Realising she had everyone's attention, Grace's expression brightened. She gently touched Una's shoulders and tucked her hand in hers. "Don't worry about what Raul thinks. His street cred has increased a whole lot."

"Especially as the pretty Ms Rao kissed me."

Both girls turned around and thumped him to the ground.

Grace walked arm in arm with Una back to their private quarters. As soon as they got through the door, Grace let go of her arm. Clearly, she was still upset. *Great! Grace now thought she was hitting on her boyfriend as well as her brother! Way to go, Una!* Una wanted to hit herself. Grace in the meantime brusquely stopped Una in the entrance to one of the bedrooms.

"We share this one, and your stuff is in this cupboard."

Una opened the cupboard wondering what possible stuff of hers could be there. Her jaw fell. In the shelves and on hangers were all the clothes that had gone missing from her bedroom cupboard in her grandfather's house on the day of her escape. Gopan was truly a snake. He must have packed and delivered her belongings, as well as her, to Wolf. Wolf had said Gopan was in cahoots with the Blesseds, but she had already worked out on the first day that Wolf had lied. Una draped her Jimi Hendrix T-shirt against her and wondered how her torso, like her legs, had grown longer too. A tear rolled down her face. She'd lost her life and now the possibility of wearing her tatty T-shirt. Somehow it tipped her over the edge.

Grace's anger dissipated in sympathy and she sighed. "Wolf was annoyed with the clothes arriving here. He told me to get rid of them before you got here. But we were sort of friends and I thought they might comfort you." *Friends! How was that even possible. Grace had been plotting with her brother to bring Una here. Friends indeed.*

Not realising her own duality Grace carried on talking. "Wolf was right, you will need to have new ones. Anyhow, in the main you will be expected to wear your Forced Blessed uniform when you aren't in your animal skin."

Una gave in. It didn't really matter how she got here. She wasn't going anywhere anytime soon. Gratified that Grace was no longer upset with her she cheered up and moved away from the cupboard and sat on the soft, made-up bed. Still fatigued she saw the bed as a sanctuary from the disturbing existence she now had. Her body complied with her wish and let out the widest and loudest yawn.

"It's nap time for you, Una. You will soon learn this is your natural time to sleep."

"Don't the junior boys find that strange?" Una's head was already on the pillow at the head of the bed.

"The junior boys have morning lessons to get through and the rest of us keep a low profile till late afternoon when we join the boys for your favourite activity, I imagine – wall climbing." Grace removed her indoor shoes before she lay on her own bed.

Una half wanted to explore more of the school and thought that once Grace went to sleep, she would sneak out. However, for the first time in her human form on the jungle side of the path, not shivering in sub-zero icy temperatures, her body relaxed, and she fell asleep straight away.

Chapter 13

Avi After the Initiation

Gagan's appearance and disloyalty to Avi did not upset him as much as it should have. Weirdly it was almost a relief. He no longer had to feel guilty about not liking his own brother. However, the deceit of forcing him to live as a tainted twin, when really, he was the only son, dug at his innards. The pain lessened when he gave himself a talking to. No matter what, Avi was always going to be abandoned because of his Blessed DNA. Gagan or not, Avi knew Dadi. His grandmother would've married his father to someone else to make sure he had more male heirs and might still do that. He'd just been reared and tolerated as a pawn on Major's chessboard.

While Gagan's appearance shocked and hurt him momentarily, Una's held him hostage. Deep-seated shame and guilt washed over him. Unbeknown to anyone, including the Sharman, he'd known that Una had fallen into the river in the jungle. Yet he had not managed to rescue her or find her all this time.

Whilst he didn't witness her entrance into the jungle himself, his body knew the very moment she fell into the jungle.

Their peculiar connection, that was greater than the average Blessed connection, sent him into free fall two months ago while he was morphing from a human to a bear. His nearly bear body had gone into flight or fight mode. His eyes had painfully dilated, and for no reason at all he began hyperventilating. His vision messed up and all he could see were the rocks of the river with the rest of the surrounding foliage out of focus, even though he was based in the forest end of the jungle acres away from the spot. Her desperate whimpering and something like a last prayer hurried him to morph back into a human.

Like before, through extreme emotions their bodies had connected again, and she was in pain. He hadn't thought she had morphed but now he wondered. On that day he'd ran as fast as he could to the river. When Avi finally arrived at the river, he swam across to where he thought she might have been. There was no sign of her. He bobbed along until he saw something glitter in one of the tree branches overhanging the river. Avi swam forward and yanked it off the branch. It was Una's locket. All he could think was that she had fallen through the tree into the water. Anxious, he dived deep into the belly of the river. The current was strong. Still with his head under he saw something above the surface stranded on a boulder in the fast-moving river. He thought it was a cat, but he now knew it was Burfani.

Avi had hoped he had been wrong about Una's arrival on that day but now he couldn't deny what he already knew. His heart twisted as he remembered her standing in a Forced Blessed uniform.

With the recent memory of her came questions like: *Why didn't she flee to the Blesseds' side to be with him? Had she been closely guarded, or could it be possible that she had killed Gopan? After all she had been hiding in the back line.* Then it came to him.

What if she had tried to change camps but he ran off?

Chapter 14

The Stockholm Effect

Humming? Why did she hear humming? Was some chirpy idiot sharing the shower with her? Nope there was no one else in her shower cubicle.

Then that could only mean that she was the chirpy idiot. Una stopped the vigorous rubbing to compensate for the icy water, only to freeze on the spot as the arctic water from the showerhead sluiced over her head.

Bugger! Was she suffering from some kind of Stockholm Syndrome?

Did she really believe that she was as happy as a lark and that the freakin' Forced Blesseds were her friends? All because she was no longer stuffed in a friggin' hole in the ground trapped under a fucking manhole cover?

Una slapped her face hard.

She'd forgotten her hands were really strong and gave herself a cracking good wake-up call.

Una stared at her reflection as she trailed her fingers over the stinging red marks she'd left on her left cheek. *Good! Perhaps now she won't forget that she's a prisoner.*

Somehow, she had to outwit the Forced Blesseds and leave. Una sighed. But how?

Outrunning them hadn't helped her when she didn't know where to go, and how to survive. Moreover, it really hurt to admit, she was humming because it was a relief to live in familiar quarters with younger people. She'd loved the camaraderie of her boarding school and these dorms were no different. Due to their close relationship and sharing a founder, both boarding schools shared similar routines and social grouping. In any case the group, or cohort, which Wolf liked to call them, had accepted Una surprisingly easily.

The other recruit though was unlucky.

Gagan was instantly disliked by all of them. For some reason them not liking him was her fault. Despite their dislike it cut Una that the twerp had been allowed to leave the manhole permanently after just a couple of days. She liked to think it was because he could only manage to get out of the manhole in human form.

Grace put pay to that explanation when they both were getting changed in their room. It seemed that Gagan had volunteered to come across and therefore was allowed early release from the manhole.

Still, it amused her to see how "racked off" the senior Forced Blessed members were with Gagan because of him bringing his motorbike. It meant extra work for them as they had to write posts to his friends on Facebook with him posing with his motorbike on some phantom motorbike expedition with a group of new friends.

What was the point of that when no one in the valley had access to the internet?

How was it that his family were getting the information? Una could just imagine one of the Forced Blesseds masquerading as his friend and bringing "fresh news" to the family. The series of photographs meant they hadn't found out about Gag's truth yet.

In any case the boys from the dormitory were very inventive with their dress-up box and donned leathers and all sorts to pose with him and his bike against "borrowed internet backgrounds". Raul was enjoying posting crass remarks he believed Gagan would make or sometimes really dweeb ones that made Gagan a laughingstock on the internet with the blessing of Wolf.

Una soon learnt that Wolf was in command of them all, all of the time.

Sid, his father, was just a figurehead who they barely saw. Una expected to be treated like a prisoner like in the Vietnam and World War II movies she'd watched, sat between her mum and dad on the sofa. But no, Wolf was reasonable, and she was treated just as any other new recruit in the cohort.

Una knew deep down why she had been humming earlier. Wolf wasn't a tyrant, he made it very easy for all to follow him. Una was surprised that none of the boys had willingly chosen to be Forced Blesseds but soon understood that, like her, they had decided to make the best of it. The more she spent time with the Forced Blesseds, the more she realised they didn't do anything without a purpose. She caught herself agreeing with them. Surely it was better than feeling completely hopeless?

OMG! She was definitely suffering from Stockholm Syndrome.

Appalled, she turned the shower on full force until her body prickled all over and her temperature plummeted even lower.

Una chided herself, *I mustn't accept my captivity. Remember, I'm only here for Dad.*

Her body prickled with heat this time.

She pulled her wet hair away from her face and stared in the mirror. *When had she stopped looking for Dad?*

Una racked her brain.

Unbelievably, she had completely forgotten that she had willingly agreed to join the Forced Blesseds so she could infiltrate the camp and find him.

Sickened by herself, Una turned off the shower and, Bambi-like, slipped on the bathroom tiles as she stepped out of the shower cubicle.

Tears flowing, Una remembered how, in the first few days, at every opportunity she had painstakingly combed the dormitory block she was in. Opening all the doors unlocked and locked to see if her father was hidden anywhere. She even sneaked around Sid's house. After every attempt to find her father, her regret for killing Gopan diminished until she felt nothing but grief and guilt that her dad was dead. If only she had read his letter when he left, she could have picked him up from the airport and saved them both.

The fact that the Forced Blesseds did not eat humans gave her hope that he was still captive but since she hadn't found him, she wondered if he really was alive. Una aggressively towelled herself dry. She had to stop the downward spiral of her thoughts. Until proven wrong she had to believe he was alive somewhere. With haste she threw on her camouflage combats and boots and with wet hair rushed through the building and ran all the way to the base of the cliff – her refuge.

Una's love for heights was shared by very few of the Forced Blesseds, and like most days she found herself all alone as she went about tightening the ropes and climbing holds on the cliff edge for the younger boys' morning training session. Remembering her thoughts from earlier, Una shook her head. Again, she had slipped into contentment, forgetting that she had been abducted. She couldn't believe it. Wolf had made sure she fit in easily by allowing and occupying her with the things she loved. *Was this how he had brainwashed her and the other initiates before her? Had he allowed then to fashion a life of their choosing to keep them happy?*

SCUMBAG!

Wolf was a geek amongst many things. He'd only worked out what made her and the others content and found the path of least resistance. She was so glad that she kept herself protected in thought bubbles from Wolf. Although so he didn't become suspicious, she still hummed songs to keep him out. Saying that, she had forgotten to create the bubble in her room and shower this morning and only remembered as she left the building. There was a good chance he had heard all the earlier stuff. She didn't care. In fact, she wanted him to hear what she thought of him at this very moment. She removed the bubble from around her but then vented her anger using her voice instead.

"YOU FRIGGIN' SCUMBAG!!" shrieked Una. Her fine words carried over the cliffs. She still didn't care until she realised her folly as a knife came swirling at her. Her catlike instinct moved her body before her brain engaged and her arm shot out to catch it.

"Pretty impressive..." said Wolf coming up the hill, rubbing the wolf-patterned shaved hair above his right ear.

"I don't think scumbag is a word anyone uses here, but then your old flame who you have aptly titled, does. He is well read like me and was the librarian at school."

"Excuse me, what's Avi got to do with anything?" exclaimed Una, dragging her attention from Wolf's fingers, which were still stroking his head. How did Avi come up in conversation and how did Wolf know where she was? The second question was easy to answer. Wolf always knew where she was. Una tightly gripped the handle of the knife. She had witnessed enough clipped ears in the dorm, and nicks in the dormitory walls and practise walls, to know how Wolf caught the other's attention.

Una recovered her composure. "You can have this back... scumbag!" Una aimed and threw the knife at Wolf who grabbed it easily just before it somersaulted between his eyebrows.

He pretended to be deeply hurt. "Scumbag? Moi?" Una shrugged her shoulders. "Seriously? You're calling ME," Wolf pointed at his chest, "a scumbag?" He loved teasing and bantering with Una. *All part of the act of seducing her mind*, thought Una. She was late to stifle her betraying smile. Wolf noticed and chuckled.

"I thought the British Una had been replaced by a more docile and obliging one. Still, I'm sorry to disappoint you. The knife, my dear, is a Blessed one. It looks like someone in the Blesseds camp has worked out who has killed Gopan or has made a pretty good guess."

"No! Really?" asked Una, with deep green saucer-like eyes. Just for a moment she believed him but the smirk at the end of his words gave him away. Una was picking up on his tells. *Another sign that she had become comfortable around him.* Angry and frustrated with herself, she tugged at his arm and examined the hilt of the knife in his grasp. She was right. He was lying. It definitely belonged to him; it had his wolf icon imprinted on it as bold as day.

"Got you!" The genuine smile and laughter were back for a moment before Wolf became his serious and true cold self again.

"Be worried, Una. Next time it could be them. They are actively looking for Gopan's killer but before they do, we need you to become Burfani."

A shiver coursed through Una's body. *Her become Burfani?* How? Rosetta was already Burfani.

But then, where was she?

Una had not picked up on another female snow leopard scent in all the time she had been in the jungle, which, come to think of it, was strange. Nor did she see her in the line-up of Gag's initiation. Wolf, unable to read her thoughts due to her shielding, mistook her quizzical worried glance across the jungle for something else.

"Can you see them too?"

See who?

"Let me show you what I mean."

He stepped one foot into the overgrowth. "One, two…"

A shower of darts rained from the sky.

Wolf laughed and ducked back to where Una stood. "The Sharman's pesky monkeys guard the boundary with their blow pipes. We are lucky it was them. Sometimes it can be an onslaught of parrots beaks."

"Wolf touched the faintest of scars on his left hand. "They really can injure and maim."

The colour drained from Una's face. On the day, the tribesmen came to her grandfather's place a colony of green parrots had landed on his roof. By quickly shutting the roof door on them she had narrowly escaped their menacing beaks. Her memory turned into reality when a green cloak of wings and beaks circled and speared down overhead. Wolf grabbed Una's hand and ran.

"Surely it's better to run in our animal form? Well, at least for you it is," Una asked Wolf. She hadn't mastered turning into her snow leopard self yet.

"Don't even try. They mustn't know what you are, or even suspect that you are a predator of any kind." Wolf glanced at her over his shoulder. *"Think what would happen to your father if you were dead?"* Her hand turned clammy. She tried to free it, but Wolf was having nothing

to do with that. He tucked it under his arm and continued to run.

Una nervously looked over her shoulder as they approached the school campus. The parrots were squawking and circling the boundary between both camps.

"Don't worry they can't cross over." Wolf smiled, his face breaking into his boyish smile again.

"Then why did you grab my hand and make me run…" And in thought she asked, *"How do you know I'm looking for my father?"*

Wolf didn't speak until he forced her to come to a standstill in front of an unfamiliar school building. He chose to ignore the question she voiced and answered the other instead.

"I heard you thought talk when you were in your room, just as I did a moment ago." Una knew because she realised it after she had showered and left the building.

"Did you really not think we would notice you sneaking around the dormitory block, and in my home? Since the first day you've taken rash risks like running away and trespassing. I'm sure you can see that I can't afford for you to do something stupid like accidentally die."

Una couldn't deny that she wasn't rash and a risk-taker.

"I was on your trail, so you didn't do something stupid like investigate on the Blessed side of the border. Admit it, you've exhausted all the other places." Wolf paused and waited for Una to respond.

Una was thinking. If he needed her so badly and she wanted to leave, he had to have a bargaining chip and that chip had to still be alive… she hoped.

"You have my father."

"Yes," Wolf replied without hesitation.

"And he's still alive?"

"Yes, but he won't be if you are killed by the Blesseds before I overcome them and take over the jungle."

Una hesitated. Wolf was openly showing his cards. If she tried anything or didn't side with the Forced Blesseds wholeheartedly, she knew her dad would die. Gopan's death and Gagan's initiation showed Wolf to be ruthless.

He truthfully had no heart and although she already knew the answer she had to ask.

"If I promise to stay in the boundaries will you let me see my father."

"No, absolutely not."

"Please, just the once."

"Una, the discussion is over."

Una gave in.

Wolf cleared his throat. "For now, you must join the other trainees in the library and for the next few months, swot as much as you can about the Blesseds, the history of the tribes and Khamosh Valley jungle. Learn everything you can about Burfani. The Blesseds will not go against Burfani and so I will be able to defeat them easily. Once, and only once, I have control of Khamosh Valley will you be able to see or hear from your father. My cohort is superior to the Blesseds in a fight so don't think I can't control Khamosh Valley without you. Work with me and keep your father alive, don't, and you will see his body disappear like that of the wolf pup."

"Who can forget it?"

"I hoped you wouldn't. I never do anything by halves. That show was as much for you as it was for Gagan and the Sharman."

Bile rose to Una's mouth.

"Are we all clear?"

Wolf didn't need an answer, he knew she had no choice, but it still made him smile when she compliantly replied in the quietest of voices so that he nearly missed it. "Yes."

Chapter 15

The Library

Una studied the building ahead of her. Like the dormitory and training ground, she had expected the library to be hosted in a modern hi-tech building. Therefore, she was surprised to find herself staring at a mock Tudor brick building with an antiquated Indian twist to it. It was complete with wooden staircases protruding from it. It even sported an English styled balustrade balcony similar to one's aristocratic homes had back in England. Una found the building comforting, perhaps because it reminded her of "home", which she was most unlikely to ever see again.

The rest of the cohort were already assembled in the jasmine covered portico. She could imagine a Victorian viceroy pulling up. There was even a stone bench on the inside wall for guests to take in the jasmine perfume as they waited until they were cleared for entry.

As Una stepped onto the enclosed veranda her mind's turmoil caused by Wolf's words and mock escape from the monkeys and parrots was replaced by the onslaught of her sensory organs. Familiar smells and ghostly visions sped through her mind telling her that this was her place, her sanctuary and most importantly it belonged to her. It was impossible, the familiarity suggested she would have frequented the library often, even before she was born. She was confounded. She hadn't yet set foot inside.

"This wasn't built by the school, or even the British despite its mock Tudor exterior."

"Wow! It's a given that all buildings with a slanted roof in the valley were built by the English during the Raj era but this one wasn't. How do you even know that?" Raul was intrigued and openly showed his admiration for her expert knowledge of buildings.

"No idea…" Una was puzzled and creeped out by her own statement. Besides studying structures for parkour purposes and seeing a few Tudor houses in Cheshire near her home she didn't know much about architecture. Nor did she want to.

"It was built by a nawab." Grace was always irritated when Raul showed interest in Una.

"What's a nawab?" Una did the usual when Grace used that particularly irritating tone and moved herself away from Raul and closer to Grace.

"It's a bit like your British peerage." Grace looked relieved and a little sheepish. She gave Una a smile of thank you.

Una was past caring about Grace's answer and feelings and just wanted to get into the building.

"Raul, can we go in?" asked Una.

"Yes, we better, we've only got access to the library for a couple of hours."

Una carefully climbed the narrow red ochre stone steps bordered by a Victorian black and white diamond pattern. The steps were built to the side of the library and were housed in a beautiful wooden summerhouse styled frame with decorative windows made of small sections of glass supported in lead.

There was no time to look at the spacious balcony. Still the little rooms, panelled not just in wood but mahogany, and cupboards with bevelled glass filled to capacity with beautiful spine bounds, were reward enough. One particular room even had a mahogany staircase leading up to the mezzanine level. In the larger, central room, a beautiful long mahogany table commanded the visitor's attention. There was a lack of seating around the table, but many cane plantation chairs were scattered around the room. Una couldn't resist and without waiting for an invitation, settled into one. She rested her forearms on the arms and stretched her legs out. She mimicked puffing with her fingers which was strange enough as she didn't smoke and never had.

"You can almost smell the cigars, can't you?" Una jolted up. She'd forgotten about Wolf.

"A cigar room in a school?" quizzed Una, narrowing her eyes. *Really?*

Wolf pointed to the name of the room over her head: Cigar room.

Opened mouthed, Una trailed her eyes across from the sign to the rest of the wall. There were highly polished mahogany and brass plaques with all the previous librarians' names neatly engraved on them. The last name she read was:

Avatar Singh Rana.

On cue, Raul handed her a ledger. "That's Avi. According to Meeru and this ledger, Avi lived here most days."

Una mouthed *Avatar* in surprise.

"Always knew he was a loser even at school." Gagan appeared from nowhere and flipped the ledger out of her hand. Luckily, it landed on a floor cushion.

"Enough!" Wolf began to pull a large book off a specially built reference shelf. Hastily, two soft-gloved younger cohorts rushed forward and carefully completed the task and carried the large reference ledger to the centre table. Wolf extended his hands and another trainee put a spare pair of gloves in his palm. Una was surprised that Wolf would care about such things.

"Come forward, Una."

She stayed put but the others meticulously filed out into the side rooms. It was as if they were primed or… Una realised, he must have broadcast his commands for them to leave through thought talk and blocked her out.

"I'm waiting."

Una shuffled forward. She was just about to put her finger on the text before her when she heard a grunt.

She looked up. Wolf signalled for her to wear the gloves on

the table. "Burfani, although a name given to all snow leopards, is specific to one in Khamosh Valley. The local indigenous Jaga tribe believe that Burfani is a half human and half snow leopard being who although suited for colder heights comes down to the valleys to re-establish equilibrium."

"So now I hope you understand why you are not allowed to show your animal self to the others, they must believe that Burfani is with us. At the moment you don't know enough to pull off the deed, they'll guess you aren't her, but after much training, I'm sure you can fool them."

"This doesn't feel right. It feels treacherous…"

"No more treacherous than Jesus deliberately entering through the gates on a donkey because it had been rumoured that the saviour would. We are just following his example. Una, you studied Greek myths and Roman and Viking invasions at school so this should be interesting."

"Are you saying that you are using the Blesseds' very own valley myths and beliefs against them…"

"Exactly. Being Burfani will save you too. I imagine you might learn that Burfani is exempt from punishment."

Wolf could see that the penny had dropped for Una.

"Remember, Gopan was a Blessed, a relative and possible successor of the Sharman. Of course, his family don't know that he double-crossed the Blesseds because he wanted to make sure it was him and not Avi that was the next Sharman."

Wolf held Una's hand and patted it. "Una, killing any Blessed is against the law and punishable by a mauling death."

Una wrenched her hand out of his and lost balance. "You knew the rule and knew he was Blessed… Yet you left me no choice but to kill him and break the rule."

Una understood the horror of Wolf's intention and she doubled over as she spoke. "You actually planned for, and wanted, me to become a monster." Una's voice trembled with fury and disgust. "You wanted me to become like you and follow through with your grotesque deeds."

"Now you are being a little over dramatic. Anyone would think I was the Big Bad Wolf. Oh wait, I am!"

Hot tears raged from Una's eyes. "Why? You already have my dad."

Wolf shifted a little uncomfortably. Tears did that to him just as Meeru's had before she died but like then the emotion passed – quickly. "You weren't exactly on the best terms with your dad. You might have refused to do my bidding and save his neck. I couldn't risk your tantrums and rashness. One has to make doubly sure when planning the big game."

Una was horrified. She picked up a book and threw it at him. "Game… you think our lives are a game?"

Wolf dodged.

Smouldering, Una screamed, "I hope you fucking die, you filthy twisted scumbag!"

"Oh, that word again!" Wolf laughed. "Save your dirty mouth, dear. You really haven't got time for this." Wolf picked up the book and returned it to the table. "Study hard because whether you like it or not, Avi and his family are out to get you."

Una wanted to puke.

Wolf smirked. "You've turned green already and I haven't even told you the best news yet."

Una gawked at Wolf as if he were deranged. His next words proved it.

"Today you are going to learn how to use Avi's charming little hobby of researching Blessed myths and his habit of writing helpful and appropriate references down in the ledger, to bring his own downfall. Bless him, he didn't even know he was Blessed at the time."

Wolf caught himself listening to his own words. "Oh, that's funny, he's BLESSED indeed."

Una spat at him and missed. Unperturbed, Wolf slipped off his gloves, flicked on the side lamp beside the ledger and disappeared.

Chapter 16

Reason to Fight

A flock of beaks snapped at her fur and tail as emerald feathered owners swooped low and chased her straight into a trap of chattering monkey teeth. A slither of hope broke through her paralysing fear when she heard Avi's voice from the shadows between the monkey bodies. "Stay calm, Una, I'm here for you." Avi's words of encouragement loudened as he approached her. Una gasped in relief, like old times Avi had come to save her. She stood still, cocking her ears, and moving her gaze slowly, looking for him. She didn't find him but instead witnessed a dark mass looming forward from the shadows. Her dread dissolved a little when she heard Avi's voice upon her. She tilted her head upwards in anticipation, her heart beating rapidly, and then stilled in terror as her eyes latched on bloodshot ones in a mass of black fur. Her internal scream dissipated into a weak and shrill mewl. A satisfied grunt resonated in her ears. Next, a wide mouth swooped on her feline neck and severed her head.

Una woke up in a sweat and in her human body. Dreamworld was mocking her, reminding her that she was now sat on the first rung of survival. Like it or not she and Avi were on opposing sides.

It was her naivete that allowed her to entertain the thought that their short friendship was strong enough to overcome the fact she had killed his cousin, Gopan. Avi didn't know Gopan per se, so would he really care?

But then could he forgive her for killing another human

regardless of who he was? Could she?

Una rubbed her brow; she would find it hard to believe he would murder someone. Did he of her? Did she really understand it herself? Wolf had reminded her of the monster she was, the one who had snuffed the life of another. Yet she had to keep herself safe just until she found her dad.

Una's quick shower was unable to wash away her filthy guilt. Distracted she pulled at the button on her combat shirt and it came away. Una glared at the innocent button. Avi was the last button on the fabric of her "normal" life that had fallen off and however much she wanted to she could not sew him back on again. Una had no choice. She was now a Forced Blessed and when the options were just "Dead" or "Alive" she chose to survive and the only way to do that was to completely accept and adopt the Forced Blessed ways even if they were monstrous. Revulsion for the loose button compelled her to sew it on fast and prick her finger in the process.

Pulling her impossibly long hair into a ponytail in the mirror, Una couldn't help but remember the old Avi who spent time with her on her grandfather's roof. The Avi who stole looks at her when he thought she wasn't looking. "Damn you!" She twisted the elastic band on too tightly and cursed. "Why didn't you just choose the Forced Blesseds like some of the young born Blesseds. You would have saved me from myself or even understood why I did what I did, or if you were on this side Gopan would not have brought my father here." Una stopped yelling and realised what she was really doing. *Was she really laying the blame of her murderous act on Avi?*

In the mirror's reflection she conjured Avi in his army gear beside her, then snapped at his imaginary presence despite her disgust for herself. "But really, why didn't you join the Forced Blesseds when you seem to prefer uniform to feathers? It's pretty obvious that you are ostracised from your Blessed side…" She cattily added, "…Nothing changed there for you then, did it?" Incensed by her wrath at Avi but really at herself, Una threw her wet towel at the mirror and his imaginary reflection. With a pleated face, and lethally tight and painful ponytail, she marched down to the gymnasium. *Heaven help whoever tangles with me.*

***

Sitting on the bench in the gymnasium in the same building as the dormitories, Una's eyes wandered over the fifteen seasoned and younger Forced Blessed recruits as they scaled the slanted climbing wall and worked on apparatus such as the vault horse and practised manoeuvres like backflips on the floor mats.

Eventually, her eyes found Gagan's menacing pair.

"Looks like he still hasn't forgiven you for humiliating him in front of his friends on Meeru's wedding day," chipped in Grace as she placed a towel around her nape and collapsed on the floor near Una's feet.

Just like balm, the memory of sitting over Gagan as he held his bleeding nose with marigolds haloed around his head, soothed her anger. "I guess Meeru told you about that."

Grace's forehead furrowed as they both watched Gagan do some of his kick moves whilst holding Una's gaze. "*Uh-oh!* Watch out, Una, he's ready to erupt. He's just waiting for you to light his spark."

Una uttered a gruff sound in answer. Grace was genuinely worried and forcefully held Una's chin and turned Una's head from Gagan to her. "Seriously, Una, I would stay away from him and save your fights for the Blesseds."

"We are both on the same side. He wouldn't dare strike me down. Wolf won't have it."

"That's true but Gag wants to finish both you and Avi off. It's the only thing that keeps him going."

"What about you?" enquired Una.

Grace looked away. "What about me?"

"I know why the Blesseds and even Gag want to kill me. But how do you want to take revenge on the Blesseds?"

"I'm Forced Blessed, and we want to conquer the Blesseds."

"Why? For their land?"

Grace pulled herself onto the bench from the floor and this time confidently returned Una's gaze. "Land… not really. We want to be in charge of the jungle and break the Blesseds' pact with – your and Avi's grandparents – the bastard property developers."

Una had forgotten about her grandparents for some time since she saw the fake news about herself. "How do you intend to break the pact?"

Grace looked directly at Una and in a casual tone whispered, "By killing the property developers and any family that chooses to live on the land."

Una pulled away from Grace and her words in shock. *Was Grace playing with her?*

"But Meeru was your friend and you helped with her wedding…" stuttered Una. "I mean you sat in my grandmother's house and bantered all the time with both household members as if you were very fond of them." Exasperated, Una added, "Uncle Sid even took Tommy for walks."

"Meeru was a friend and was on side…" Grace tailored off.

Una felt some relief with the possibility that Grace cared. That is until she saw Grace's chilling smile. Una's innards shivered as Grace carried on.

"Meeru took care of killing herself before we had to make a decision on her. The rest are worthless and killing the scum will do everyone a service."

Una's tongue froze in her mouth as Grace's contemptuous words of hatred sank in.

Grace took one look at the impact of her words on Una's demeanour and paused. Then with some obvious reluctance to correct herself she asked in brittle tone, "You ask about their lives but what about ours?"

Una's thawing tongue had no answer.

"We were sacrificed for their greed. Where is the justification for that?" asked Grace.

Una was unsure if there was one.

Grace continued, "Anyway, I thought you would understand considering you killed Gopan for the very same reason."

Una was aghast. It was true. Who the hell was she to question Grace when she had intentionally killed another?

Yet another niggling question popped into her head. "If you don't wish to harm the tribesmen then explain this…"

Una had Grace's full attention.

"I saw your brother and some of the lads present in this gym today come to my grandfather's rescue with knives when the tribesmen came for Avi and me."

Grace laughed. "Oh, that was just letting the Blesseds know how organised we are. We're not mercenaries as everyone perceives us to be. They are not our target. We see ourselves as ideological warriors against the injustice done towards us."

Una was confused. "Are you saying that you don't see the Blesseds being at fault?"

Grace nodded in agreement. "They're not at fault. They were clear about what would happen if the jungle land on the left side of the path was developed. The property developers shouldn't have bought the cursed land from the tribes when they knew the folklore and they definitely shouldn't have sold the land to my papa on the wrong side of the path."

"How is it worse building the house on your side of the path?"

"Seriously, Una, haven't you noticed yet?"

"Noticed what?"

"Wolf isn't the only one who was forced to be Blessed."

"You said you weren't Forced Blessed when I asked."

"That's because you wouldn't have understood. My sister and I are tainted but don't hold Forced Blessed animal forms. However, we are part of his wolf pack and are anatomically altered to hear and obey his command."

Una didn't have any siblings, but she could imagine how siblings would hate to give up their will to their eldest sibling.

"It wasn't just family but his classmates who were close to him that were impacted too. The poor buggers who were firstborn even have the animal forms."

Una felt compassion for Grace and Alice and the Wolf's loyal friends. They and Wolf were truly innocent.

Una didn't know what to say but, "I didn't realise."

"Granted, the Forced Blesseds' strains are weaker in my sister, and even less in me and in his friends, which means if any of us leave the area, we do not feel the pull of the animal side and can live normal human lives as long as we live away."

Una now understood why she hadn't seen the other sister yet.

"Alice doesn't want to be here, does she?"

Grace's face dropped a little. "Well, she comes during the day sometimes if she isn't too busy at college."

Una was still puzzling over the Blessed and Forced Blessed separation. "So, if the Blesseds are not your enemy then why are you separate?"

"Because we are brighter, and we don't believe that the hereditary-born Blesseds have the right to decide how we live. Worse still, they expect us to honour the agreements they have with the property developers."

Grace slid across the bench and put her arm through Una's. "You have to agree that we are more educated than the Blesseds and thus far superior. It was their backward ways that compelled the newly converted Christian tribesmen to move after selling their land to the greedy slugs who put you and all of us in this situation."

Una wanted to know more but their conversation was interrupted by an announcement. "Una and Gagan, it's your turn to spar together on the central floor mat."

Chapter 17

Unpopularity Contest

Una could feel the tension and static generated by the distrust and loathing between herself and Gagan. After the full realisation of what a low life she had become, her dejected self-preferred to surrender and let Gagan finish her off.

The announcement of their names came again. Grace patted Una's back and motioned her on. Una nodded, made a meal of taking her trainers and socks off and listlessly made her way to the mat.

She had barely straightened after their customary bow when Gagan slammed into her forcefully with his fists. He was fast and correctly predicted all her moves, landing his punches effectively on her increasingly sack-like body. Several spectators winced, perhaps with animal hearing they too heard more than one of her ribs snap.

"Una, collect yourself!"

Wolf's timely invasion of her mind brought her attention back from some dark place.

Gagan had her on the ground.

"Una, if you don't come back from this, I don't think Gag is going to let you ever get off the floor again. Remember your rage towards him, his grandfather, Major and..."

Una blocked Wolf out. She didn't need his words, she remembered Major's last conversation with her grandfather. He had made a deal to sell her to the Blesseds for a paltry sum of money, for a timber merchant investment.

If I hadn't run away, Wolf wouldn't have me. If I'd not been caught, I would not have murdered Gopan. If I had not murdered Gopan I would not be hiding, and my life would not been in danger. Even if I still landed here, I needn't have killed Gopan. If Gagan hadn't picked Dad up from the airport. If it weren't for Gagan, I wouldn't be riddled with guilt and be so fucking beaten. No, instead, in this instance I would be beating the crap out of him like I'm going to do right now.

Una's mindset shifted in time to lock on to Gagan's bloodshot eyes. He was so sure he had her. He raised his arm to deliver a blow to her head; shouts could be heard from the spectators, and then…

It became quiet, so quiet. Not a single voice or thought could she hear. Her limbs, without any instruction from her closed off brain, responded well to the danger. She rolled and caught his arm and then he was the one on the ground, receiving her silent punches and kicks. Although her brain was switched off and she felt nothing, Gag's senses were linked to his brain and registered every single one of her blows, obliging her by writhing and screaming on the floor. Even so, she didn't stop… not until she was picked off Gag's bloody body by several arms.

Back to her senses Una found all in the gymnasium staring at her with mixed looks of horror and disgusted awe.

Grace aimed a face towel at Una. "Wipe off the blood spots on your face."

Una caught the towel by flinging the person holding her arm down easily.

A gasp was heard.

Una wiped the blood off while she studied Gagan's distorted face.

He was bleeding profusely from his mouth, skin, and nose. Una checked her ribs, but they seemed to be fine. Perhaps one had not snapped after all.

Grace was black with fury. "You didn't have to humiliate him again and make a permanent enemy of him. The others don't know about the earlier incident between the two of you and the brutality you executed in a training session is beyond anyone's comprehension."

Una thought: *if I were them, I would think I was a psycho too. Correction... I AM a psycho.* Una's body was still strumming. It was taking all her strength to normalise the furious pumping of blood in her body to a natural rhythm. She was out of control.

I still want to kill Gagan!

Her confession hit her between her eyes and toppled her into Wolf's arms.

"Get a handle of yourself," whispered Wolf. "You're too late with your femme fatale act."

Una straightened herself.

"Now, both of you bow!" commanded Wolf.

Una reluctantly stood on the mat while two others brought and held Gagan in position on the mat opposite her.

Una bowed; Gagan fell forward. Two volunteers picked him up and carried him out. Everyone else left but Wolf and Una.

"Don't waste your time worrying about what the others think."

Una looked up, surprised.

Wolf handed Una a mop and a bucket of soapy water. "They aren't to know that Gag intended to finish you off first. It's just that you turned the tables on him."

"Are you going to set the others right so that they understand too?"

"Why should I?" Wolf smirked as he walked away.

Una didn't look up; she mopped the mat and the surrounding floor in silence. Her thoughts however were anything but quiet.

I almost killed a second human being, actually another Blessed being! Images of trying to explain how she accidentally killed two Blesseds to the Sharman sprung into her mind. He wouldn't buy it, nor could Una.

Am I a rogue killing machine?

Alarm raged through Una and she was forced to prop herself steady on the mop handle, using both her hands.

Is my body going to easily trip to survival mode at the slightest provo-

cation and block my human brain of reason? How was she going to stop herself? Could anyone?

Tears rolled down her cheeks.

"Get yourself together and head for the medical room. Those bruises need some attention, or they will take too long to heal," barked an irritated wolf as he slammed the gymnasium doors. This time he really left.

Bruises – she didn't feel any pain.

Curious, Una examined her arms, the bruises were fading fast before her eyes. Una lifted her tank top. Her skin was unblemished. Not only that but her ribs no longer hurt either.

Una ditched the idea of going for medical help and opted to stay in her room for the rest of the day. She felt no remorse for what she did to Gagan but was regretful that the others had witnessed her monstrous rage.

Lying on her bed Una trained her ears to listen into the conversations happening in the boys' dormitory.

Surprisingly, they weren't talking about her, but they were involved in role play instead. The scene was set for a major road accident. She now understood that the role plays were not auditions but were practice sessions to imitate and understand the nuances of "real life" roles such as doctors, army, police, and road safety personnel. Previously, Una was asked several times to join in especially as she had little experience of living in India, but something held her back and she felt uncomfortable about it. Nonetheless she swung her legs over the bed, put her combat jacket on and crossed the hall.

"Perhaps I'll join you this time…" Una's sentence tapered off.

It was as if she had shouted "freeze". None of them spoke or moved until she stepped back from the threshold. As she left the dorm entrance, she heard them continue with their role play as if they hadn't been interrupted at all.

Back in her room Una slammed and locked her door. She slumped on the edge of her bed. Her whole body was shaking. She was in shock. She'd just witnessed Raul in a police beret wrapping a blanket over a younger boy who was acting as if he were paralysed with shock. The scene was familiar, no it was identical. Instead of the young boy she kept seeing flashes of her father. Another youth was playing dead in a chair with a steering wheel jammed to his chest by another chair. There was something in Raul's expression when she paused her glance over his beret and attire. His usually honey-toned face was chalk white. The scene somehow looked familiar, but she couldn't remember why? Straining to unlock the memory only caused her to rush to the toilet seat and puke volumes of bitter bile. Wiping her mouth with the back of her hand, Una sat shivering under the cascading shower fully clothed. Police outfits didn't usually have any effect on her. Definitely not the Manchester Metropolitan Police ones, when she had been picked up in police cars due to trespassing. So why did Raul's?

Chapter 18

Scented Message

Una awoke on the bathroom floor ravenous. Hunger was magnified in her snow leopard frame, killing all other thought. Luckily for her a lack of thought resulted in things like hope and guilt being removed. For now, all she had to engage in was kill, eat, and sleep. Food was her priority; she hadn't eaten for a couple of days. Wolf made it a rule for newbie Forced Blesseds, that they ate the majority of their food by hunting for it in their animal form. If they were unlucky for three days, they would be provided with animal kill. Eating food prepared for humans was disallowed. It was a great relief when darkness drew over the skies. Una only stirred when the stratosphere shed little to no light thus enabling her to escape her quarters unseen through her open window. Sid Rao made sure the OTHERS, the non-Blessed students, were kept locked in their dormitories just in case they became suspicious of the whereabouts of their senior dorm-mates. Although Una was sure they were all sleeping deeply after their compulsory amber tea nightcaps.

Evenings and nights were growing colder which meant Una's insulated coat was becoming more comfortable. While she now understood why this guise was chosen for her and how she was transformed into a snow leopard, she wished she had been a leopard instead. Her white coat was too warm and two white. Worse still, in the moonlight, it made her conspicuous when it reflected it brilliantly.

The pitch-black night brought Una a stealthy kill on a cliff deemed too precarious for training. She'd surprised the poor horned goat from behind without disturbing a single loose rock. Belly full and heavy, she dozed happily until she was drawn to the scent of an animal. An animal she was sure Wolf was unaware of and wouldn't believe existed on his turf because if he did, she was superfluous.

Since the first night Wolf threw a pole in the manhole, Una's snow leopard instincts had sharpened. It wasn't very long before it became mechanical practice for her to know where to make a kill and what to eat. Tonight, however, she stumbled upon her new natural without any practice or introduction. She circled the hanging rock before her reluctantly, trying to hold back from what her body was intuitively telling her to do. Her human sense of self held her momentarily hostage while making her feel disgust, embarrassment and even intrigue at how her animal body found it so hard to walk past the overhanging rock. She could appreciate that it was a good ledge to sit or stand on, but her head was reluctantly drawn to a pungent smell on the vertical face of the ledge. The overpowering fresh odour that pulled her in to investigate would have her gagging under "normal" circumstances.

Alas, her strong animal instincts pushed her feeble human ones aside and she involuntarily rubbed her face on the urinated rock, startlingly setting off territorial signals in her. She deliberately stepped forward and for the first time since becoming a snow leopard, audaciously lifted her tail to spray it. Next, on instinct she rolled on the ground near the rock and sprayed it again. She couldn't say how but she knew what she first smelt was the scent of another snow leopard. She was further shocked when she pictured a male snow leopard. Una shook her fur body in relief. Did animals pursue Blessed creatures? It wasn't far enough away according to the fresh odour she smelt. Snow leopards were solitary creatures according to the research she found in the library. She wondered if it was a possible threat to her or if she was one to him. Then Avi's face came to mind.

Was Wolf wrong?

Was Avi the male snow leopard after all?

If so, was he a threat to her existence directly or indirectly?

Una had another thought. *Whoever the snow leopard was, he would read the animal urine identification she'd left behind on the rock face.*

She decided to move to safety while she mulled over whether she should tell Wolf her news.

Una scaled the terrain quickly to get back to where she knew the wolves roamed. When she picked up their scent, she halted.

How was Wolf going to react to her news? If the snow leopard weren't Avi then would Wolf hunt and capture the snow leopard and use it instead of her?

Her blood froze despite her fur coat.

The fact the snow leopard existed in the area and not in the preferred colder altitudes logically meant the snow leopard had to be Burfani. Wolf was cryptic about Rosetta still being alive therefore Avi had to be the new Burfani.

Alarm bells rang in Una's head.

Wolf only required one snow leopard and if the male was Burfani then she was doomed.

Una didn't care about her own life; it was already compromised but she needed to find her dad and get him to safety.

She could be wrong of course about the young snow leopard. It could be a leopard or if it were a snow leopard it might just leave the area on its own accord and go back to higher ground soon or risk being hunted by other animals. She doubted that an unaccompanied cub could fend for himself.

Una decided to not share her findings with Wolf or anyone else for that matter.

With her decision made, her body lost its restlessness and she was able to hanker down for a short nap under the stars. Short but deep, for she missed the scent of a black mass lurking in the shrubs.

⁂

Avi's jaw dropped. His weak eyes had to be fooling him. *He nerv-*

ously moved backwards on all fours. He was sure that the odour was that of a snow leopard.

Avi sniffed the air again. *He was sure it was a snow leopard's but remained confused. The odour was similar to his little Burfani's yet not quite the same. Was it because the snow leopard was an adult instead of a cub or could it be that the snow leopard was actually female?*

The Sharman had said that only one snow leopard ever existed in Khamosh Valley at a time. Yet he'd just left a sick snow leopard back in his cave.

Avi had only come back to the spot to mask the juvenile's spray after it mischievously crossed over to the Forced Blessed side. Avi had been troubled by little Burfani. The poor thing. Instead of growing it was becoming sicker day by day whilst dwelling in the cave. It only seemed to perk up on the rare occasion when Avi sneaked him out against the Sharman's instructions to keep the little cub in the cave.

Although he was strict, the Sharman actively avoided Burfani and only visited him to gauge his progress.

Avi was already suspicious about the Sharman's attitude towards the little thing, but now that he could see a snow leopard's profile rising and lowering with a light purr, he knew he had to investigate how the two could exist in the valley at the same time. The problem was the information was in St Anthony's library on Forced Blessed territory.

What did he remember about Burfani?

Avi wandered closer to the purring body and from behind a tree peered at the magnificent cat sprawled on the ledge.

The Wakhi tribe who lived much higher than Khamosh Valley in upper Pakistan, Afghanistan, and China, believed that supernatural beings called "Mergichan" sometimes took on the guise of a snow leopard. These beings were very holy, powerful, and dangerous. The tribe of Khamosh Valley and his grandfather, the Sharman, believed Burfani to be such a being.

Avi was sure the sleeping beauty was female. He had thought the Sharman stayed away from the snow leopard in his cave out of reverence, but he now wondered if he stayed away because he knew there was something wrong with the snow leopard and was suspicious of it not being Burfani. He couldn't take a risk and tell the Sharman yet because he didn't know how he would react. He would kill the male snow leopard. Avi was already very fond of the snow leopard living in his cave. It was the only one that didn't fear him. Their solitude from the others suited both of them. No, he hoped this snow leopard he'd discovered left soon. It was a good possibility that she would. Plus, of course, in daylight she could be another species, perhaps just a leopard…

Anyhow the smell of the half-eaten carcass of the goat overpowered him and he had eyes for nothing else. Whatever she was, he could drag the rest of the goat's carcass to his cave to feed both himself and his Burfani. Perhaps it might make the little blighter feel better. So far, the cub had begrudgingly eaten the ants and foliage he had brought back to the cave. Avi slowly dragged the body away. The snow leopard on the rock did not stir. Sated and asleep, or so he thought.

Chapter 19

Rendezvous

Una's ears twitched irately to a shuffling sound on the ground. The scent was new, but it was moving away from her, as was the fresh meat aroma. Una snapped awake to find her half-eaten goat gone. Drat, she would have to hunt a day sooner than she would have liked. The wolves often tried to steal her kill as did the jackals, but their noisiness gave them away. She should have been angry or followed the scent, but her hunger sated, she had other things to do. For instance, check if the male snow leopard had returned to the rock. Una, much to her chagrin, smelt the rock again. She was still the last snow leopard to have visited it. The faint smell of the male snow leopard was still there too. She hadn't been mistaken earlier, which could only mean that she had a limited amount of time to find her father before the male snow leopard realised, she existed.

Wolf had her father and was not likely to release him or even let her see him until the Forced Blesseds were victors over Khamosh Valley. For the Forced Blesseds to be victorious, Una had to find out where the majority of the Blesseds lived. She hadn't found anything yet, like an ordinance map in the library to help her with that. Una mused, perhaps the only way to speed up the invasion was to scout the Blesseds' area.

Una chided herself, *and how was she to do that? The boundary was heavily patrolled.* It would have been convenient if they all lived in one big building like most of the Forced Blesseds, but they didn't.

No one even knew how and where the tribesmen lived, let alone the Blesseds. They all knew the Sharman lived in the temple, but the steps were enchanted and none of the Forced Blesseds or anyone else beside the Blesseds could climb them without permission granted by the Sharman.

To learn more about the Blesseds and tribal dwellings, she had to go back to the library and find out the information quickly so she could bargain with Wolf. The allotted times in the library were not enough. That meant she would have to cut short her sleep and enter the library at dawn when the school was sleeping and all the Forced Blesseds were asleep after their long night in the jungle.

***

It was strange to make her way out of her bedroom window during daytime hours and that too in human form. It was a total drag climbing onto the dormitory roof without her padded feet. Still, she was able to make the least amount of noise as she scaled her way to the skylights of the library with the precision and control of her feline self, whilst still in her human form.

Several times she stopped and crouched as school servants hurried around the campus getting the dining room ready for breakfast at 8am. Luckily, they were occupied with their grumblings of being awake whilst others were still in their beds.

She had an hour before the bell rang to wake the boys for their morning athletics.

When the coast was clear, Una opened a skylight without much sound, crossed her arms and wedged her body through its narrow aperture. In one fluid movement she speared down through the sunbeam dust before she landed on the marbled floor below.

The room was magical in the mornings with the sun spotlighting the floor in several pools other than the one she had landed in. She followed the spotlights in an almost straight line to the largest pool of light which made the gilded edge of the library ledger shine bright. In the ledger she found Avi's handwriting and carefully read through his references.

It took her a while to find the large green A2-sized book embossed with gold topped pages, an intricate gold lace pattern on the front and a beautiful pinecone hanging on a single pine branch. Excited she pulled out the book and carried it to the wide table where the ledger sat. There was a thin film of dust on the mighty cover and a few spindly cobwebs. Una was too impatient to care to dust the book off but did manage to put some gloves on and turn the pages carefully to the page Avi had referenced.

The indigenous people of Khamosh Valley, the Jaga tribe, are a highly mobile community. They are descended from one mythical ancestor called Abu Tami who taught them how to cultivate rice, which is their main staple food. They have no tribal organisation and are led by a Sharman. The jungle dwellers and their settlement are completely reliant on wood and bamboo for their utensils and long house buildings. The tribe do not believe in land tenure and maintain that no one has individual rights to land or animals such as cattle.

Due to the timber industry and the building of an army cantonment, the area they live in has been restricted to a small area.

The tribes' people believe in mystical creatures, in particular in the folklore of shapeshifting. Their folklore suggests that a section of their society can shape-shift to protect the natural habitat. The shapeshifters are led by a snow leopard called Burfani who can take on a human form when necessary. No conclusive evidence has been found of her or any shape-shifting behaviour.

Christianity has impacted the area and the converted Jaga tribesmen live in a separate area. There are tensions. It is alleged that the new converts did not wish to live in the houses of those who followed the old faith and animal sacrifices. They have moved out and abandoned the elderly.

Forestry Report 1912.

Interesting as it was, it didn't have the information she required.

"You must be really disappointed."

Una swivelled her chair around.

Avi was sitting in a dark corner on one of the plantation chairs. Slowly he arose and appeared in a spotlight stream. Amongst the dust particles his face and body looked ethereal.

"You're looking for the elusive map of where the tribe or the Blesseds live, aren't you? I did the same and looked and looked, with little luck." Avi chuckled. "You could have saved yourself time if you had finished reading my account in the ledger."

A breath hitched in Una's throat. She hadn't seen him close up for a long time. The boyish lankiness was replaced with a muscled body. Realising she had been staring for longer than necessary, she asked her own questions instead of replying to his. "Clearly you are trespassing since you no longer go to the school?"

"Trespassing… Me? Never!" replied Avi with a fake tone of bewilderment, whilst wagging his finger at her. "I came to read like you. But unlike you who broke in, I came through a door using a key." Una's gaze fell on the skylight she had used to trespass. *Trespass... not entirely true... she could come here but he on the other hand...*

"The library is out of bounds for you Blesseds…"

"Quick as ever, it seems. I never said the key was not forged." He smiled one of those smiles that didn't reach the eyes and then posed another question.

"You are allowed to use the facilities so why such a novel way of entry?"

How did he know? Oh, he was tapping into her thoughts...

"Still a little slow in the head, Una."

Una chose to ignore him and continued the conversation by voice. "Yes…"

"Just answer me – why are you breaking in?"

Avi raised his eyebrow and glanced over at the skylight she came from.

"You saw that!"

Bemused, Avi answered, "It was difficult to miss the 007 move through the skylight. I thought it was very impressive once I got over the fright you gave me."

"I have much to catch up on in comparison to the others. Even Gag knows the area better than me."

"You're lying, Una, it's more than that." Avi moved forward

a step. "It's interesting though that we still have something in common."

Una was nervous. "Like what?"

"Like Gag getting under your skin. We all picked up the tension between the two of you when he appeared. How is it that you already have an unpleasant history between you?" Una's colour changed when she remembered how she had, as recently as yesterday, become a pariah amongst the Forced Blesseds because of Gagan. Watching her discomfort, Avi changed tactic. "Be careful of him, Una, he has a tendency to hold grudges and despite his vileness he has a talent for bringing the others to his side." Avi's voice was gentle and full of concern.

Una twitched uncomfortably. *Avi had first-hand knowledge of her antagonist.*

Avi didn't say anything but her twitch must have given away the status of Gagan and Una's relationship. He clenched his fists protectively towards her and then unclenched them.

Una understood. Her woes were of no concern to him anymore. Instead he would be thinking of how to take her to the Blesseds to be punished for killing another Blessed.

***

Avi was finding it difficult to be aloof and was quite taken by the cobwebs stuck in her hair. He wasn't sure what to do and then he remembered the book she was reading before he interrupted her. *She wanted to come to the Blessed territory, so perhaps he could trap her there and find out what really happened to Gopan for starters. His investigation into the female snow leopard would have to wait.*

"I'll give you a helping hand with your research just to give you a fair head start." He smiled, taking Una by surprise as he swivelled her chair round so, she was facing the table again.

"I didn't know we were in a race or something?"

"Really, what do you think all the strutting and the expansion of his group in numbers is about, if he doesn't want the Blessed territory?"

Una didn't wish to talk any more on the subject and was quite relieved when Avi stopped talking and walked over to the glass cabinets and opened one. Una watched him "home in" on a book, a cartography of geographical maps of the eastern hills of the Himalayas.

"You'll have to go to the Cartographers of India for new maps. But this will give you a good idea of the land the tribe operate in."

He carefully used the index to find Khamosh Valley and then moved himself and the book closer to her.

Avi watched with interest as Una's cheeks heightened in colour.

She moved an inch away from his body but paid attention to what he was showing her.

"The land you see is only the outer edge of the tribal area, but as they move around, their houses disappear overnight and are camouflaged by a deep jungle. The Blesseds live on the outskirts to protect the land from the Indian commerce and government and keep the number of animals balanced by safeguarding them from hunting and poaching."

"Poaching?"

"Yes, certain animals are used for their medicinal value and furs. Tigers, leopards…"

Una interrupted Avi, "What about snow leopards, what about Burfani?"

Avi flinched this time. "Why? Have you seen her?" *Or is it that you remember the day you saw Rosetta, my mother?*

"Umm…" Una looked up at Avi.

Their relationship had changed. Avi tried to read her thoughts but she'd learnt how to block him thanks to him. Idiot! It didn't matter, his body was still attuned to hers and he could read that she was hiding something.

Avi was concerned. She was lying. Yet, he knew Burfani had remained in his cave most of the time and only left it when the Forced Blesseds were involved in their training.

"So, we are the gatekeepers of the jungle?" asked Una, changing the subject, and glancing back to the text she had read earlier.

Avi was confused by how much she had changed; he was Blessed by blood and had not yet integrated with the rest of the Blesseds and yet she who had found much to be offended about not that long ago, had seemingly accepted her fate. He had expected her to be broken. When she first came to Khamosh Valley she had been so adamant about "going back home". Paradoxically, he felt a sadness for her, that she no longer wanted to go back to England and leave him behind. It was like staring at the ghost of someone he once felt strongly about. *Was she so changed?* Or was she putting on an act like him?

"How is it that you have taken your Forced Blessed conversion much easier than you did being left in India in a posh school?"

Una shrugged. "It's not like I can change back to complete human, is it?"

He nodded his head sideways in agreement. It really rankled him that she was content to be a Forced Blessed. Was he jealous of her or was it that she didn't need him to survive?

"How are they treating you, Una? In fact, how are they treating both you and Gag?"

"Fine."

The answer was too short. She wasn't giving anything away.

"I'm just wondering, because you are both grandchildren of the Forced Blesseds' arch enemies."

"That hasn't been mentioned, maybe it's because we are just as much victims of our grandparents as they are." Loyalty to her new cohort sprung up from nowhere when she unconvincingly said, "But they are on the side of the property developers… remember, you saw them come to the rescue of our grandparents when they asked for us in payment."

Avi snorted. "Don't kid yourself, Una!"

"Fine, you don't have to believe me, but can I ask you a question too?"

Avi was intrigued to know what her question would be. He nodded in agreement and gestured with his hand for her to ask him.

"Did the Blesseds get their leader?"

The colour left Avi's face. "Yes."

"Is it you? You are Rosetta's son and she was…"

"You remember meeting Rosetta, my mother…?" Her remembering dissolved his shield and he felt her rush of blood. In her unprotected state, across the library walls she projected the day they kissed, when she thought he had survived death, to the tell-tale bullet dropping and his body miraculously healing, and then his mother arriving in her snow leopard guise.

RRRRingRRRing! The school riser bell had Una coming out of her projection trance. Avi gently pushed her back in the swivel seat.

"Catch your breath, I'll tidy up," said Avi, leaning across her to close all the open books gently.

Una agreed and watched him put the reference books carefully in their rightful places.

A key turned in the lock. Avi crossed the room and pushed them both under the long table.

The *chowkidar* – the caretaker – walked in with his ring of keys and noisily began to unlock doors and open them wide.

He stopped at the table and wondered at the pencil and note-book left there. He tutted and then muttered something about careless students and walked away.

Avi pulled them both out from under the table when the coast was clear. Seconds passed. Both stared at their joined hands. Avi gently held it and peered into her eyes. "I won't be giving any more pointers for you to try and find our main territory. So, the next time we meet will be on opposing sides again. Do you understand that?" Una blinked. He drew away from her and let her hands go.

Una grabbed Avi's arm. "Avi, can I ask you another question?"

Avi looked down at her fingers round his black denim shirt and nodded.

"Why did you join the Blesseds and not the Forced Blesseds when you obviously don't fit in?"

Avi was impressed that she had picked up on his isolation just as he had picked up on hers.

"First, I will say, despite you choosing the Forced Blesseds you seem just as isolated, otherwise you would be legitimately here in the evening…" He paused, waiting for her to react; her wide eyes were enough to tell him he was right. She had begun to climb the top of the cupboards to get to the height where the short rope of the skylight ended, and he followed. "And the reason I joined the Blesseds you already know, but just to remind you about that something else…" He caught hold of the rope and dragged her head down. As her hair cascaded around them, he kissed her. He reasoned that shock had left her immobile even though his lips still lay settled on hers. Staring up with mirth into her wide eyes, his lips curved at the edges, he parted her lips with his tongue. Her eyes drifted shut and her body awoke, and she was kissing him back furiously. Lost in their passionate exchange, he rested his gaze.

The shrill bell rang again.

Una pulled away.

Avi's eyes shot open. Una was gone.

Chapter 20

Resurfacing Connections

Why did he go and kiss her? He could feel her heart beating, even though she was no longer present in the room, drumming alongside his own pounding heart in his chest. Was this a human or Blessed connection, or something else? The something else they had had before they were even Blessed. Avi grasped the back of the chair he had occupied earlier.

"Get a grip on yourself," he ordered.

The last thing he wanted was this connection with a possible murderer.

Avi was desperate to get away pronto. If found by school staff in the supposedly locked library with a key there would be trouble, but much worse if discovered on forbidden territory by the Forced Blesseds, especially as he held the secret – a book with all the information they wanted; he and the Blesseds would pay with their lives. Knowing all that, Avi slumped in the chair he was leaning on weakly until now. Their connection had robbed him of any strength. Holding his chest, Avi vowed silently: if he could just unclasp her from him, he promised to stay away from her and never connect with her again. His heart violently tugged, drawing pain. Under his breath he cursed her. *Damn you, Una, let me go!* Wherever she had gone to was not far enough.

He slapped the side of his head with his free hand. *Remember, she possibly killed your cousin, brutally, and even if she didn't, she is a menacing, she's...* The way his blood surged when she was close... *she's irresistible.*

"Aggh!!" Avi thumped the armrests with both hands. He had existed for so long without connecting to her... Avi grimaced at his reflection in one of the library book cabinets. Who was he kidding? He had felt her in the rains, months ago and most recently when the Blesseds wanted to hunt Gopan's killer.

Avi shook his head and ran both his hands through his hair and roughly tugged at it.

Even across the path he had been able to connect to her, until the Sharman had wised up to their connection and fortified the enchantment to the walls and roof walls after Meera's suicide.

At first, Una's return to the jungle during her summer holidays had brought him thrill, a feeling in such contrast to his deep despair and self-hate caused by his ambiguous fate. However, he was soon swamped with fear. He didn't want the same for her and he could see the desperation of both Wolf and the Sharman who were both accelerating activities to bring her over the path to their respective quarters.

He repeatedly warned her through thought talk, but she was downright flippant. In sheer desperation he involved Kulkil to intercept her when she made her way, laden with marigold garlands, to Major's in preparation for Meeru's wedding. His unstable Blessed state at the time made it impossible for him to engage with her in person.

At the time Avi was still naïve of the Sharman's abilities and stupidly believed he could persuade Una to leave Khamosh Valley, but the Sharman caught him and spoke to Una himself. Still undeterred he was able to reconnect with Una later, almost too late, that same afternoon. Through Una's eyes he'd witnessed Meeru's expression when she recognised his wedding present of the cigarettes. His heart had gone into overdrive when Una volunteered to go to the Modern Ruin and get the extra film for Sid. There was no opportunity to thought talk. On that occasion Avi somehow wrenched their connection and dashed to her aid in his unstable state. The Sharman was no fool and used his powers to still Avi before he stepped onto the path. All Avi was able to do was warn her… with a message, a lame message on a mango.

Their ability to connect troubled the Sharman. Their connection was rare and usually only happened between a Blessed parent and child and on the rare occasion, between twins, like the Sharman and his great Uncle. The Sharman could not have his own grandson warning Una and jeopardising his plans to transform Una into a Blessed. To kill all connections between them, he strengthened Dev's roof walls to keep the Blesseds out. For Avi, the Sharman came up with some cock and bull story that he had fortified the walls to protect Una from experiencing the pain during his body's distortions and of course from Wolf. Avi was no fool.

The protective walls didn't work during the monsoon. Avi had tried so hard to stay away and block Una but he always found he was drawn to Dev's property just to capture her faint heartbeat. Luckily or unluckily for her, he had been there on the day the river broke its banks and swallowed the boundary between the OTHERS and the rest of the jungle. Una had been instructed by Dev, her grandfather, to secure the property's gate. She would have been fine if she had but no, she stupidly stepped out onto the path and walked beyond where it was safe to observe the fast-moving river. Wolf and his cohort saw the opportunity to snatch her. Avi had to see them off. Without a backward glance at Una he chased Wolf and his pack away from the boundaries of Dev's house to protect her. Yet he'd put her in more danger.

While moving his focus from her to Wolf he had somehow brought her with him. One moment he felt she was with him just like he had felt Rosetta while he was running to the Blesseds, but in the next when Wolf made it to the Forced Blesseds' territory, he lost her. Panicked he ran back to where she had stood. He found her there, but something was wrong. Avi remembered that her body was undulating like she was breathing but he knew she wasn't actually in there.

Avi recalled how helpless he had felt when nuzzling and poking his rain drenched body, trying to stir her heartbeat, thinking it was lodged in him. He remembered the agony of when he thought Wolf might have connected to her instead. Avi felt a gush of relief again when he remembered how Dev's shouts had brought Una back. He was still haunted by her words, "My days are numbered."

Which she uttered before her body collapsed with exhaustion into the shallow new river path.

After the rains he'd sensed Una again, or so he'd thought. Avi pulled at the chain around his neck and opened Una's locket, which he'd kept on his person since finding it.

Aggravated, he pulled the thing off his neck and flung it onto the centre of the wide polished table in the room, hoping to be free of his turmoil and Una.

Noises of staff coming up the stone stairs alerted Avi. He had to hurry. He didn't have time to put the cartographer treasury of maps away. Avi sniggered. He'd lied when he said there were detailed maps of the area. The law had safeguarded the tribe and its locality which meant that even though they were the official Cartographers of India maps they were at best sketchy. The tribesmen knew of the map but only because they had learnt to walk and had their own posts and handmade markings to suggest routes to their fellow tribesmen. Closely holding it to his chest, the book that he had saved from Una's eyes before she came in, Avi struggled to lock the glass paned door. Perhaps because he was distracted by the glint of the tarnished silver locket. A groan slipped from him. Helplessly he looked over to the stairwell. He recognised the old heads of the library staff emerging as they nearly reached the landing. Avi slipped the key back in his pocket, rushed back into the room, snatched the silver chain, left the door unlocked and darted past the staff, purposefully toppling the books in their hands as a diversion.

Chapter 21

QI

Avi navigated back to the safety of the Blessed territory without raising any alarms in either camp. He had learnt to sleep for fewer hours – a survival instinct due to his mainly vegetarian diet, therefore he was not particularly tired despite the hectic activity of the night and early hours in the library. However, devouring the substantial meal the night before had made him sluggish. Funny that. In the confusion caused by meeting Una, he had forgotten about the presence of a female snow leopard and the goat remains he'd stolen for the cub.

Avi pulled himself up on a high perch to rest. Something jarred his hip bone. Grunting loudly, he tilted his pelvis and pulled out the reference book he had "borrowed" from the library from his jean's waistband. The book filled him with nostalgia for the antiquated library he still missed sorely and for the hours he was able to spend poring over the glorious maps.

Completely wrapped in the maps in his head, Avi, without consciously realising, projected the maps onto the existing terrain. Thus, casting a virtual reality web over it with labels. In the past when he had pored over the volumes as the student librarian, he had never dreamt that he would become part of the legend and walk through the named parts. The increasing glare of the late morning sun made the vision harder to keep. With great reluctance Avi pushed off the cliff and strolled slowly back to the cave whilst still maintaining the vision cast markings on the landscape.

Avi hadn't found a clear answer in the library book he held. It was true that snow leopards were solitary beings and in Khamosh Valley, according to the recordings, only one at any time had been spotted and that too rarely over an expanse of years. It didn't say it was impossible though. When he thought hard about it if Rosetta had survived, she would have helped his transformation and there would have been two snow leopards on the same land at the same time. He did find, in the section that discussed legends, that it was unusual for Burfani to live in Khamosh Valley permanently. So perhaps Burfani would have left eventually. Legend or not that made complete sense to him – *snow leopards don't exist at low altitude naturally.* Which brought him back full circle. If they didn't exist naturally in the low hills, then why was there an ordinary snow leopard in the vicinity when it wasn't cold enough for them to run out of food at a higher altitude?

His dwelling was soon upon him with its vision cast title placed over it – Robber's Cave. The British loved naming things. Avi let go of the casting and stumbled into the mouth of the cave.

Chapter 22

The Sharman Suspects

Weak from vision casting, Avi slumped against the rock by the cave's mouth. His relaxation was interrupted by voices coming from the heart of the cave.

Other than the Sharman, himself, and the cub no one else ever entered the place. At first the voices were barely audible but then they picked up in volume and soon a heated exchange bounced back and forth between the rock corridor walls all the way to where he sat. One of the voices expectedly belonged to the Sharman, and the other…

Avi sat bolt upright. *He had to be mistaken.* He nudged closer to the corridor. *He wasn't!* Avi pinned his fringe back over his forehead, which he did when thinking. He shook his head in disbelief. *How was that even possible?* Anxious to know if he was right, he listened carefully. The intermittent mention of his name left him in no doubt that he was not meant to have discovered the truth.

Desperate to know what he was being excluded from Avi nearly climbed a rock nearby before he corrected his folly. If he took his normal route into the cave by scrambling over the dry rocks on the side leading to the concealed dry ground behind the waterfall he would be spotted. Avi grimaced as he took in the crystal-clear stream. Nevertheless, it had to be done. His human heart almost stopped when he slipped into the freezing waters. A moment or two later after the shock, and with warm blood once again pumping through his veins, he waded stealthily through the deepest part of the stream. Deep but at its narrowest the stream veered to the left between two jutting walls.

The Sharman stood under the arched rock connecting both walls. Avi ducked his head in the water, freezing his brain, and swam underwater until he found large boulders in the darkness. He pulled himself up and away from the Sharman in the shadows. The Sharman in contrast was in full daylight.

Avi wasn't sure what he expected. Perhaps he expected to see the Sharman talking to the cub, who according to the voice projection should have been in front of him but instead the cub was asleep at the Sharman's feet nowhere near the projected voice.

Avi glanced over in the direction of his dead mother's voice and stumbled. His mother wasn't there nor was another woman, nor even the shape of a human. Instead of a concrete shape and form, the voice vibrated from a cluster of tiny blue stars at the furthest end of the cavernous dwelling.

Avi squinted and realised he was looking at the shining outline of Rosetta as she had looked like a snow leopard, dispersed like a star constellation across the dark boulders that formed the cave roof. Her ethereal vision was intensified by the waterfall falling to her right, gleaming white due to a hole in the rock roof.

"Rosetta, you can't carry on like this. Can't you see that?" pleaded the Sharman with the spirit of his daughter.

"Why not? You managed to live with my ghostly existence when I was stuck on the roof?" Rosetta's voice was changed after all, it was shrill and lacked body.

"I didn't know… not until it was too late. Rosetta you can't live confined in this young body… You have to give it up and move on to the next plain."

She didn't agree and desperately tried to free herself from her confined spot.

The Sharman's gaze stayed steadfast, holding the luminous corridor from him to Rosetta's form despite her continuous shifting and ebbing, trying to unlink his communication channel.

"Papa, I'm not going to do that!" she screamed. "I will never do that. Put me back in the cub. I need him, so I can stay near my boy."

In anger, she swirled the air between the electromagnetic outline of her snow leopard to change her shape into a comet-like structure and dashed between the boundary confines, along the perimeter of the cave, momentarily disappearing when the water from the waterfall interfered with her.

Frustrated, she wailed, "Why can't you let it be?"

Nonplussed by her antics, the Sharman uttered, "Let the innocent be! You are killing it. He still has time to survive." He took a long pause and then added, "Let me take it back to the Valley of Flowers and hopefully find its mother."

Rosetta was livid. "How dare you care about him and his mother. My Blessed body aged on the other side of the human path unlike yours on this side. Still, I would have happily withered and died to keep my son protected from the others. All you had to do was keep us safe on his way to becoming Blessed. Why didn't you and your monkey army protect us from the Forced Blesseds' scheme?"

The Sharman's head hung in shame. But he knew one wrong could not absolve another.

In the gentlest voice he could summon he tried again to appease his deceased daughter. "Rosetta, please be reasonable. Remember, it was you who made me promise not to interfere with your in-laws in any circumstance. Whether that was when they married your husband to another or worse still when the butchers mercilessly killed their own granddaughter, Avi's twin sister. You begged us to return to the jungle and leave Major and his family alone. You pleaded with me and the jungle ensemble to do nothing and let Major and his family treat you as they felt fit." Tears soaked his white furry cheeks and chin. "How was I to know that the Forced Blesseds knew the importance of Burfani, the snow leopard, and that Meeru, the very person you saved when she was a young girl, would lead you to your demise when she grew up."

Rosetta fashioned her snow leopard shape again and seated

herself mid-air with her paws ahead of her and her head muzzled in a defeated posture. Hurt, her voice wobbled. "It always comes down to my faults and stupidity, first my marrying Avi's father and then leaving my daughter in the care of my mother-in-law. I really believed the soul of Burfani, which was encased in her, would protect her."

The Sharman held out his hands and blessed the essence of his child. "None of us could have predicted that. Still, Rosetta, you rebalanced it by allowing the essence left in you from carrying the new reincarnate of Burfani to transform you into a snow leopard instead of your daughter. You accepted the burden even though you knew the transformation would and did completely finish off any hope of you being treated with kindness by your in-laws. Instead it gave them further leverage to humiliate you with brutal cruelty and separation from your own child. You endured them turning you into a living punchbag just for sport."

Rosetta's face lifted from her paws. "So, Papa, let me live in the cub. Can't you take comfort from the fact I have finally come home, to you and to the jungle. I couldn't have left Dev's roof without its body due to the prayers and enchantments you put on the roof walls. If Gopan hadn't put the cub in the truck I wouldn't have made it here."

"Gopan?" uttered the Sharman in shock. "Are you sure?"

Rosetta nodded. The Sharman slumped in response and muttered, "If he knew… then my brother did too." Upset, he snapped, "I don't know Gopan's motives, but you shouldn't have come…" Catching himself off balance, he paused and then in a neutral tone said, "I can't allow you to stay."

Rosetta's starlit head spun back and speared forward, almost touching Sharman's nose. "Can't or won't? I've been so lonely for so long. All these years I consoled myself that Avi was near and I knew my banishment would end. Through all the old age pain and the whipping and cruel conditions I comforted myself that my abuse and separation was for a finite time. But now that I am finally with him, you say you can't allow it?"

Rosetta's wounded outburst bounced around Robber's Cave, waking, and scaring the poor cub from his slumber.

"You can't allow it..." Rosetta's second cry of outrage was brought to an abrupt end by the cub who tried to run out, but Rosetta stamped her electromagnetic paw on its tail. The poor cub yowled in fright. Avi was conflicted. He desperately wanted to interfere, but it conflicted with his need to know more. Mouthing sorry to the cub who glanced at him with pleading eyes, he made a silent promise to himself to somehow make it up to the cub later.

"Rosetta, let him go. Don't be so wretched," cajoled her father. "Remember you are now free of this cursed death and birth cycle. That is the gift for your great sacrifice promised to you. GO now, my daughter, it's time to become part of the collective consciousness."

Rosetta protested. "I don't care for any of that. Why don't you become part of the consciousness and leave me in peace?" Her voice became more agitated. "I want to stay here with Avi. Papa, do you remember how I was separated from him when he was just three?" Rosetta waited for a reply that didn't arrive. "Well, do you?"

Avi found his grandfather's silence unbearable and so it seemed Rosetta did too.

"Father, you owe me this, vision cast what happened, I want to see if you really bore witness and were there as you promised for my son."

Pop! Her snow leopard outline disappeared again and as a single point of light she climbed to the height of the roof and reformed most of her molecular cloud into a tall sheet, illuminating the top of the cave roof and the dark walls while she still kept the outline of her head. Avi stifled a cry and nearly gave himself away as he watched himself at three years old, screaming as she was dragged away from him. Next came a barrage of memories of the times he called out for her and how his wailing increased her suffering and beatings in Major's outbuilding. He saw himself a year older perhaps running to his father's second wife and calling her ma. Finally, he was a six-year-old standing at the post which separated Major's compound from the outbuilding and with Gagan and his uncles Riki, Niki and Chaz he was shouting out, "Crazy! Crazy…"

"Enough! STOP IT! STOP PLEASE!" Avi came out of hiding, holding his hand in front of him so he could no longer see the vision cast.

Rosetta abruptly halted the images and her own ethereal form dissolved and dropped onto the floor of the cave.

Its tail free, the cub jumped into Avi's arms, almost knocking him down.

"I didn't know…"

He squinted his eyes as he looked at the Sharman. "Nana! You knew all this time… why didn't you say anything?"

Avi dragged his eyes from the Sharman to Rosetta's form.

He held the cub by the scruff of its neck, making it yelp in protest. "So, this cub is just a cub not Burfani?"

Rosetta rose again into her snow leopard form. "While I am still in a body, in this case the cub's, I remain the essence of Burfani. Hold it tight, Avi, so I can…"

The Sharman butted in and moved towards Avi, stretching forward to grab the cub from him. "Rosetta, I cannot allow you to take over the cub's body again. Avi might not know or understand it yet but you know you do. You are too far advanced in this transcendental state. You know you will kill the poor cub eventually if you stay too long in him."

Avi pushed the Sharman back with unintentional force with his free hand. "Nana, you don't have a choice. You are going to have to allow my mother to inhabit the snow leopard."

The Sharman protested.

Avi just ignored him and continued, "The tribes believe Burfani is back… they believe their bad luck will change. More importantly the Blesseds deserting us and joining the Forced Blesseds have dropped. If you look carefully all the tribeswomen have begun to wear magnolia buds in their hair out of respect.

Everyone feels rejuvenated. My mother as Burfani will bring order. Besides, I saw…"

"What did you see?"

Avi was glad for the interruption. It allowed him to check himself. He had to work out what impact the news of the female snow leopard would have on the two individuals present. Moreover, the consequences to the three of them if the Blesseds found out that they had been tricked into thinking the cub was Burfani. The Sharman's brother was already stirring matters as it was. With the defections to the Forced Blesseds Wolf would no doubt be alerted to the snow leopard's existence and if he found the snow leopard then they were all doomed.

Avi wondered who he was really protecting. After listening to the confessions earlier did, he trust his family anymore.

"I've kept an eye on the border and I have seen increased exercises close to the imaginary line." It wasn't what he was originally going to tell them but all the same it was true.

The Sharman knew he was hiding something but the cub in Avi's hands had all his attention. "Her staying in the cub's body will eventually kill it, if not the people will become suspicious of the lack of growth spurts. Her continued occupation of his body will stunt him completely."

"Yes, but we need to concentrate on what we are going to do about Wolf and his rule breaking. The consequences can be more immediate than the cub's death."

Without planning it, Avi had finally become a Blessed. His nana noticed that too. He could no longer be on the outside anymore. "What if Rosetta only used the cub's body a couple of times a day when it is essential to interact with the other Blesseds and tribesmen? The rest of the time she remains in her ethereal form here in the cave."

The Sharman pondered over Avi's request. He was outmanoeuvred.

"I can follow those rules," agreed Rosetta most earnestly.

"*Daikhing gai.* Let's see how you do," muttered her father. He abruptly retracted and smothered the gateway of communication with Rosetta.

Rosetta pranced forward towards the cub. The cub yowled and tried to hide in Avi's hoodie. She still advanced. The cub hissed and jumped from Avi's protection. Rosetta chuckled and speedily enveloped the whole cave by elongating her form. The cub had nowhere to run, yet Rosetta could not enter him.

"Nana, you just said let's see how she does so let her enter the cub's body," requested Avi with some trepidation.

The Sharman shrugged and removed the protection from the cub. Rosetta wasted no time and the cub squirmed and hissed on the floor of the cave until its body stilled in exhaustion.

Avi was sickened by his own insistence that his mother inhabit the cub's body and put its life in jeopardy, but he promised he would safeguard the cub as well as he could. Avi felt strange. His loyalty lay with the cub and not his mother even though she sacrificed so much for him. *Shouldn't he automatically love her more than most?* He knew he didn't. She made it difficult. He couldn't comprehend or respect her judgement for staying in the body of the cub. Paradoxically, however, her greed to live was the only thing maintaining the fractious stability of the jungle. He had no real choice. Drained from all that had happened in the last twenty-four hours Avi greedily helped himself to the water from the waterfall.

The Sharman intuitively thought talked as he left. *"Today I am both saddened and proud of your commitment to your mother and the jungle. Finally, you have become a true heir of mine. I know I can trust you."*

Avi stopped drinking the water and gazed to where the Sharman had stood and where the cub lay in exhaustion. Trust? He wasn't worthy of either of their trust. Disgusted with himself he stepped under the waterfall and splintered its spray, hoping to be washed clean.

Chapter 23

Recruitment Drive

Someone was banging frantically on her bedroom door. Peering between her entangled hair, Una realised she'd slept through her alarm clock and missed the martial arts completely. She covered her head with her pillow. Her head was sore not from underage drinking like the old days but for taxing her brain in the early hours. The stupid complicated map drawings of the antiquated maps had confused her and left her clueless and sleep deprived. The river course of yesteryear was different, and the map was lacking landmarks such as houses and paths to help her. Yes, thanks to Avi she now understood what the buildings might look like if she got to the tribesmen's village but after studying the maps several times, she wasn't any further in her quest to finding directions to the tribesmen's dwellings and main hold.

"Una! Get up! It's your assessment day and you are already late!"

Una jumped out of bed and rushed to the door. She had bolted it because Grace had slept over at her parents. "Assessment day?"

"Questions later, toilet first, brush your teeth with water, and the pine toothpaste in the closet. Don't use soap please and absolutely no deodorant, especially not the vanilla essence one you favour."

Grace barged right past her, flung opened Una's closet, and rummaged through her things, making an absolute mess. Una began to protest and before she could even open her mouth, Grace shoved her into the en suite. When she arrived back in the room, an outfit hung on her cupboard door. *Oh,* thought Una. That was the one she had placed several clothes on due to the shortage of hangers. No wonder her room was a mess, Grace would have had to strip the clothes off the hangers to find that outfit.

"It was lucky that I had placed the outfit in the cupboard myself, otherwise I would have sworn it wasn't here." Grace tossed the offensive garment to Una.

It was very different from her usual T-shirt, jacket, and cargo trousers uniform. The outfit was a type of jumpsuit with a combat pattern different to the usual with splodges of darker hues of brown.

She was glad she hadn't bothered wasting time on brushing her tangled hair because she first had to wear a hairnet and cover it with the jumpsuit's hood which, when zipped up, covered her face and fitted her skull precisely. It even covered her eyes and mouth too.

She didn't like the feel of the cotton and lycra material of the jumpsuit but the ingenuity of the finely netted material covering her eyes, ears, and mouth so she could see and breathe, did impress her. The suit had streamlined shoes built in. Astonishingly, the shoes still had the same amount of grip and protection as regular boots.

Grace was in a hurry and brusquely turned Una around to inspect her outfit. She was smouldering but said nothing. Una was sure that whatever was eating Grace was much bigger than her being late.

Was Grace envious of her? "How come you aren't in special gear."

"I'm not being assessed and if you have paid attention to those around you, you would have noticed that I am barely Forced Blessed. I have to feel immense emotion from either side of the spectrum to be attuned to my Forced Blessed self."

Una couldn't believe what she was hearing. Grace was actually feeling sorry for herself and was despondent that she wasn't a firstborn!

Una was glad to leave Grace in her hissy mood and join the

other's in the gymnasium. All of the candidates wore similar jumpsuits to hers except that they were dressed in combat colours and shades according to their natural hunting grounds. Una was unable to tell who anyone was except for Raul and Gagan mainly due to their height. Gagan being the shortest was at the opposite spectrum of Raul. She was sure she was just as conspicuous to the rest of them, judging from the amount of interest she got. No loose garments here.

Attention!

Una didn't remember Wolf making an entrance and was sure he hadn't been in the room when she appeared. He'd snuck up on them. She quickly fell into her place based on her height.

Legs apart they all stared ahead at him.

"Good to see all fifteen of my old recruits and the two new ones here. Today is about recruiting new members from our martial arts beginners' group. This session is to promote interest to boost numbers and show the wannabes from the main school a taster of what they must be desperate to join. To keep them engaged the youngsters will monitor your progress through feeds on their computers from the expensive camera drones we recently purchased."

All of the team looked sideways at each other. Before they could engage in any conversation the assembled were split into two teams. Gagan was not in her group, but Raul was. *Thank God!*

"Both teams A and B will start on their own side of the terrain. Your goal is to get to your oppositions' starting line. The team with most members standing on their enemy's side will be declared the winners."

It sounded simple enough to Una.

"Remember, this exercise is to show our new candidates our scouting, hand-to-hand combat and our ingenuity to use whatever we have to hand. Also remember, the task is to not be eliminated before the end and to sustain the least amount of injury. Be warned, the worse your injury the longer your body will take to self-heal. After the exercise we will not set your broken limbs or do anything much beyond cleaning your wounds. Also, we will not use any pain relief because pain is the best deterrent from getting hurt again in the next training session."

Una missed most of the warning as she was still fixated on the word eliminated. It sounded ominously final.

As the groups began to move out, Wolf cleared his throat. "Oh! I forgot to mention the twist to the exercise." Everyone stilled in their places. "The juniors have been given an interactive part too and have been split into groups A and B to complement your groups. They are in control of the cameras on the drones which also happen to have lasers attached to them. If the laser hits you, it will release a chemical into the folds of the material you are wearing to make you luminous and the game will be over for you. If this happens to you, don't move until you hear the 'end of prep' bell.

"No one is allowed to use weapons so make sure you leave all your personal weapons on the table in the hall. Not even a nail file can be used."

A little gasp left Una's mouth when she looked at the table piled high with all sorts of combat weapons. Where had they been hiding them on their person? There was enough for an army and yet there were only seventeen of them. Worse still she hadn't learnt how to use any weapons yet and didn't even have one of her own.

Both groups marched out of the room using opposite exit doors, passing a control room of their own. Group A's team juniors were in royal blue T-shirts, whilst Group B sported red ones. Both sets of supporters gave their team a mighty cheer and tried to drain out the cheer of their opponents.

Raul took charge of Group A by roll-calling them into a line based on order of experience. The more experienced ones were put in the front, and she was last.

Raul hand signalled them into a huddle. When there was no space left between them, he cleared his throat and began his game instruction. "Okay! So, this is the plan: the captain, which is me, will place his team members, that is you, into your own unique and individual camouflage spots, where I will clip you in. From then on no one will be able to move until Grace releases your clip remotely from the control room. Only one team member in any team can move at one time. You must move in the direction of the enemy camp and not be sighted. Where necessary you will have to attack a member on the opposite team when moving forward but you will most definitely attack an advancing opponent to stop them from making it to your base camp. The lasers that the opposing team have on their camera can only work if the object it is tracking is moving and their juniors like ours will be looking for their opponents, and will stop them with the lasers so they can help and support their teams effectively. This is the most important advice I can give you. When you attack your opponent make sure you are effective. A wounded enemy can still hurt you. Remember your wounds will heal according to how long you have been a Forced Blessed, but there is no one here who will be able to heal before the end of the exercise as none of us are original Blessed stock."

"Is that why the Blesseds who have come over to our side are not taking part in the exercise, because they will be able to heal and attack again?" asked one of her team.

"Perhaps, plus they are not part of the training, just in case they are double agents."

The enormity of the exercise hit Una. She nervously asked, "Does anyone die in this exercise?"

"No. Una, this is a training exercise which is designed to be as real as possible, to help you pick out your weaknesses to improve. You have heard of self-assessment and targets in your school no doubt?"

"Yes."

"Well that's what you are doing. You are setting targets for yourself so you can improve on those weaknesses in your next training sessions."

Oh boy! Una wondered what her old school sixth-form tutors in Manchester would have thought of this novel idea of target setting.

"Any questions?"

"I take it the camera drones aren't released until the exercise begins and only after the prep bell for the rest of the school is sounded?" another boy asked.

"That's right."

"What is the success rate of getting to the enemy's side uninjured?" asked Una.

"Slim."

Five minutes later, when Raul was satisfied with the solemn and introspective silence that followed, he began.

"Looks like we are ready. Now, I would like you to do an about-turn."

When they had done as instructed, he continued.

"I will place the newest team member on the terrain as a marker and then the rest of the line will progress across the width of the start line. Each one of you will be placed at the start line in an appropriate terrain based on your hunting ability." Raul took in a deep breath and then set his eyes on Una. "Follow me!"

Una was impressed that her orange and brown splodges matched the rock formation on which she lay down, including the clump of shrubbery her shoulder pressed down into. The outfits must have been digital carbon copies of the landscape.

Una lay down and Raul moved her arms, legs, and head in an awkward fashion, so the landscape was unbroken. Once he was happy, he whispered into her ear, "I'll let you into a secret. Wolf lied when he said the lasers don't work if you are stationary."

"I figured that was a possibility."

"But did you predict that the lasers are really tasers, and that they will keep firing until your body is completely luminous?"

Una's body squirmed and then stilled completely after remembering her taser experience at the hands of the UK police when she refused to cooperate with them.

Fifteen minutes later, the shrill sound of the prep bell filled the air.

The game was afoot. Una hoped her whole team were in place

before the bell went. But she couldn't be sure. Nothing could be assumed when it came to Wolf. Her last thought was: *did the students in the control room know what they were playing with?* She was sure Wolf would have forgotten to tell the students the lasers were not just coloured beams of light but pain-inducing lethal machines. She did have one happy thought though. *Thank God Gag is not in the control room.*

Chapter 24

The Game is Afoot

Una could hear the grunts and tussles of bodies moving against the rock and in the growth near her, and a little further away. The thud of something or someone hitting the ground grew amongst the torturous wails and flashing red and blue beams.

She herself hadn't even moved yet, when she caught something on the periphery of her vision, stirring. Una held her breath as a drone hovered overhead. It jittered forward and backward, scanning her chest and shoulder. She tried not to flinch; she could tell the rookie manoeuvring the red camera suspected she was there. She couldn't hold her breath any longer. He fired. The beam hit the shrubbery above her head. Acrid smoke emanated off the tips of its leaves not far from her netted face. Una stayed still. Moments later the camera moved on but not far enough.

Una, still close to her starting point, realised that the drone wasn't the only danger. Something else was moving nearby; she was sure of it. Their movement was painfully slow and was coming from the opposite direction. She wasn't sure what to do. If she moved, she would give her position away to the drone and to her opponent but if she didn't, even if he didn't see her, he would be on the other side of her team's starting point.

Una never liked long drawn-out games and thought she would have a cleaner fight with anyone but Gag, and the elongated body coming towards her was definitely not Gag.

Decision made she hawk-like watched his minute movements

as he approached her. The front of him, his head she presumed, was at a tilt. There was a good chance he hadn't spotted her possibly because there were no tell-tale human moaning sounds after the laser singed the bush nearby. He would have noticed the drone and thought the area was clear of humans. Gritting her teeth, Una slowly edged her shoulder in line with the singed bush and then headbutted the opponent's stooped head. She could only surmise that he'd been looking down at the time, expecting his opponent to be at a lower position. She expected him to drop down and be safe from a drone attack but instead he jerked his head up and a blue drone camera from her team spotted his movement and made its way to him and attacked. The cry from his body was excruciating, the liquid took too long to swim through the material to illuminate it. Una remained silent and did not move, because a second drone and red camera checked the same shrubbery again but this time thought better than wasting its laser despite the probability of her being there, which told Una that there must be a fixed number of times it could be used.

On several occasions she heard movement below or above her, but never abreast her, possibly because the lasered area would show anybody up. Her first movement had been a better tactical move than she had thought possible.

Dusk arrived, which suggested the prep bell was going to ring soon. Una wondered if she was the last person to move forward in her team. The opponents' drone above kept her in place. Still, either she was desensitised to the moans and couldn't hear them any longer, or the darkness hindered the camera's efforts to detect movement. It could also have been that the teams were tired and were no longer picking each other off.

Una had almost given up hope about moving before the bell when her clasp opened up, releasing her from her fixed position.

Una's vision was changing. Whilst she could, will her body to stay in human form, she was still able to stay on the cusp and use her enhanced senses to hear all movement. Her vision had turned to pale greys and blues and she was able to make good ground as the smallest of movement alerted her.

She was speeding up but stopping instantly before the drone cameras came. The two cameras where crossing each other's paths like they would in a kite race. They were distracted by each other and she was distracted by them and nearly missed a flicker of steel hovering over her chest and then the red camera tried to taser her, but she could tell it was jammed. A blue camera hovered over her next trying to pinpoint her attacker, but it too was jammed. The knife however had no such problem and, undeterred, mercilessly ripped through the material of her suit, skin, and sternum.

Cool air turned her warm gooey blood cold as it seeped out of her body. Her unsteady head slumped to the side as she stared into Gag's exposed face against the purple twilight. But still the prep bell did not ring. Gagan chuckled then deliberately and clumsily climbed over her to her starting line.

If she was going to die, she damn well wasn't going to let Gagan get to the end as well. With a roar which her snow leopard body couldn't produce she drew the knife out of her body and with her hand tightly fisted around the helm, burrowed it into the cliff rock. She then twisted her body to the side and followed Gagan. Gagan dodged her up and down the rock surface. She knew he was close to his finish line because she could see it herself. However, he wasn't there yet. She hovered her eyes over the scorched area she had first inhabited. She could see the familiar edge of the shrubbery but rather than the shape she expected it to be, it seemed smaller. He had to be lying there and covering it. She could make out the outline of an arm. With surprising ease, she grabbed hold of the arm that was splayed towards her and with all her strength rolled onto it.

He yelped in pain and thrust his legs to try and kick her, to loosen her grip. All those hours of parkour taught her how to crouch her legs so he couldn't do it and then she put one of her legs between his and kicked under his thigh. Then with lightning speed rolled off his arm and held on to the surface of the cliff with her fingers. She felt great satisfaction when his body rolled past her. Unbelievably, the prep bell still hadn't sounded. She made her way back in the opposite direction to the other side. Just as she did, flood lights blinded her.

In the sharp light her startled eyelids remained open, but she had lost her vision. She felt people on either side of her grab her arms, while one of them closed her eyelids for her. Thankful, she collapsed into the arms holding her. Whilst they carried her, she thought she heard muffled cheers from behind a glass. It must have been "A" team's control room. She was placed on a bed, not her usual one. The pungent odour of disinfectant stung her nostrils and mouth, letting her know she was in the medical room.

"Am I blinded?" She tried to open her eyes from under the weight of another's hand.

"Hopefully, it's just temporary." Raul's voice was not completely devoid of emotion. Una bolted up and pulled out a drip line attached to her and something else when Grace was called for on the intercom. Una wondered why a drip line was attached to her at all when Wolf said there would be no help with wounds.

Grace couldn't have been far away because she suddenly appeared. Una recognised her by her distinctive footsteps.

Una heard curtains being drawn after the footsteps of the others backed away. She heard a clink from a nearby table and then a tear. Grace noticeably gulped as Una's arms protectively covered the upper half of her body. She was, after all, naked under the suit.

"But there was so much blood left on the rocks..." exclaimed Grace in shock. Someone drew the curtains back. This time Una only heard two sets of footsteps, the other Forced Blesseds must have left. She hoped her arms covered her well enough... but then Grace grabbed her arms away. The shock of being exposed jolted Una's sight back to normal. Not surprisingly Una wished she hadn't quite recovered it.

Both Wolf and Raul were staring at her chest as though they had just seen an alien bare herself. Una pushed Grace's hands away and slid off the bed. She held her torn suit as best as she could together and walked into the bathroom attached to the medical room. She almost fainted when she opened the flaps as she faced the mirror to examine herself. There was not a single scratch on her chest where the knife had cut through. Had she imagined the stabbing? No, her clothes were red and damp and smelt of rusty iron, so how? When had the pain disappeared? She'd been too distracted by her lost vision to notice. Una collapsed to the floor. She kept her eyes closed when she heard the door open.

"Looks like she has passed out…" Grace whispered.

"Well… That's something," Wolf replied, both perplexed and angry.

They had hoped for her to heal but not so quickly and not after the amount of blood she must have lost. Were they scared of her?

Someone, Grace, Una hoped, put a dressing gown around her and then someone else raised her arm, rolled up her sleeve and injected her with something. They were not taking any chances.

Before she slipped away, she asked, "Did the blue team, my team, win?"

Chapter 25

Caved

Avi in his human guise played with the cub, much to the annoyance of his mother's ethereal self who was relegated to staying put behind the waterfall at the back of the cave.

"I have listened to you and allowed the cub to be on his own for long periods of time, which leaves me unoccupied, doing nothing."

She was exaggerating. Yesterday, cub hadn't been out because Avi had spent the evening sat on a ledge in forbidden territory spying on the strangest form of training. It was more like a "Call of Duty" game, but not. He couldn't tell where the participants were on the terrain. With his naked eye he only managed to spot where they were when they were hunted and found by drones. He had thought them to be harmless drones but then he began to hear the moans and squeals. *Was Wolf really using weapons on his own?*

Avi wanted to intervene, but then checked himself. Why did he feel or even care about them? His attention had been brought to himself when he felt his sternum ripping. Only it wasn't. It was red and bruised but the skin was intact. *Was Una in trouble?* I need to… Holding his hand over his sternum he faintly heard his old school's second electric prep bell ring in the distance just as he slipped into an unconsciousness state within the Forced Blessed territory. Hours later, when he woke up disorientated, he almost fainted again when he clocked where he was. How did they not find him? *Was Una okay?*

"Avi, are you listening to me?" Avi looked up at his mother's imprint. "Chalo, I've got your attention. I need to be able to do more and I can't unless I'm in the cub's body."

"That's not my fault, you could transcend if you feel you have no purpose here."

The waterfall's rhythm wavered, capturing Avi's attention. Dispersed sparkles of light emerged and regrouped to make a new form, a cleansed form of a tall woman with flowing hair, an image of the mother he had seen in the projection of a two-year-old Avi. She must have been beautiful, and he could see why his father's head might have turned. He wondered why she punished herself living on the other side of the water because the water appeared to disperse her. He noticed that when he went into the water his own electromagnetic field outline became less visible.

"I will make a bargain with you, let me be a mother some of the time, and I will leave as soon as you are able to find Burfani."

"…and where would I find Burfani? You are just buying time… if there was a Burfani she hasn't surfaced since the sister I never knew I had died. That was nearly nineteen years ago."

"What about Una then?"

"What about Una?" asked Avi.

"Nothing really… I just wondered where she was."

Avi knew his mother was lying but at the same time he didn't want to let her know that he had seen Una on the Forced Blessed side.

"Your library might help you perhaps? I know you have been there several times," continued Rosetta.

"How do you know that?"

Rosetta's image flew to the waterfall, parting it to reveal the map of the Valley of Flowers on the wall behind it.

"You couldn't have retained that detail and knowledge from when you were at school."

Avi shrugged his shoulders. Rosetta laughed lyrically. "*Beta*, Ma knows all!"

She flew back to Avi and hovered over him and ruffled his hair, accidentally touching the cub on his shoulder, who drew his claws and pounced at her, unfortunately clawing Avi instead.

"Ouch!" Avi removed the cub by its neck, whilst trying to relieve his arm from the claw. Blowing on his arm, waiting for the blood to congeal, scab and disappear, Avi asked, "Can you please stop tormenting the cub."

"I wasn't tormenting him, just stroking your hair in a motherly way."

Avi gave a wry look.

"Ask that boy Kulkil to come with a knife and a comb."

"Fine, but I'm really fed up with everybody's obsession with my hair since I was young."

"It's not an obsession. Tidying your human form might help your Blessed one."

Avi was fed up with the conversation and did as she asked.

While Kulkil chopped his thick hair and nicked his face with the knife while giving him a shave of sorts, Avi watched the cub, who although had grown a little since he was no longer inhabited for long periods, was still traumatised. Avi had to find a way to release his mother from the cub permanently. *But how?* He had to do it before the tribes noticed the stunted growth of the cub. It was time to go to the library. Avi wasn't sure if he was finding excuses to go there because of Una. He hoped she'd recovered enough to go to the library to find the map reference book, and him.

Chapter 26

A Trap is Laid

Una awoke with a dry throat. She stretched her naked body as normal, placed her feet on the floor and, instead of her flip-flops, felt cloth underfoot. Una bent down, fisted the stiff material, and brought it up to her eyes.

"Ugh, ugh!!" Una threw the bloodied jumpsuit and scrambled off the bed, pulling the bedsheet with her. Blood streaks between and below her breasts reminded her of Gagan's attempt to maim or kill her.

Una scratched at the bloodstains expecting scabs, except she found nothing but smooth skin. There were no scabs, stitches, or any lines, not even sleep induced ones. How? Her mind raced back, and she remembered Grace's shock.

This isn't good! She had to get out of the medical room, have a shower and make a plan. Una looked down at herself and thought: *clothes and then plan!* Nodding yes to herself, she clumsily tied the sheet still entangled around her and shuffled to the door with most of the sheet dragging behind her.

The doorknob didn't budge whichever way she tried to twist it.

An ominous feeling came over Una, but she didn't have any time to ponder on it.

Click!

Una scarpered back to the bed, sending a kidney dish flying off a trolley left at the end of it onto the floor. CRASH!

The door pushed open.

Una hastily sprawled her legs on the bed and placed her foot on the trolley.

"She's still out… looks like she slept kicked a dish onto the floor. No biggie. I'll put the quarantine board up on her door and lock it. That should keep everyone away." Grace sounded smug.

"You must have overdone the dose. Still, it works for us. The boys will just think she's out of action like all the rest with their injuries," agreed Raul.

Una waited until the door closed again before she wrapped the sheet around her properly, picked the lock with her trusted hairpins, and stealthily made it from the medical room to her own. After the shower she didn't know what to do. There wasn't much she could do as she shared the room with Grace, apart from climb out of her shared room's window.

***

Una entered the library by the high skylight using a short rope, as she had the day before. Perched on top of the cupboard, she scanned the room carefully making sure there was no one around. This time she was alone. Surprised by her disappointment she tutted and silently made her way towards the central reference table and then balked.

Several large books were opened and arranged on the table ready for her. They were the same volumes Avi and Una had briefly studied together the other day. The maps were not there though. Her rationale argued that anyone interested in the tribes could have chosen those books, until her eyes fell on the request forms. Neatly placed on each book was a request form with the title of each book and then the requester's name – Una.

There was one book she didn't recognise. In its centrefold binding sat an ornate, Victorian key and a request form. Una picked up the request form and recognised the hand it was written in. It matched Avi's handwriting in the ledger. It read:

Request By: Ms Rao

How did he know that she was called Ms Rao?

Title: The Myth of Blessed Creatures – Centaurs of the Jungle

Keywords: peaceful centaurs, healing powers, telepathic pain.

Why was telepathic pain heavily underlined? It couldn't be that he... he had felt her pain when she was stabbed.

Una pushed the captain chair screeching backwards. A flash-back to the inexplainable pain she'd felt when Avi was whipped by the Major and his uncles hit her between the eyes. Telepathic pain… It had to mean that the two were still joined even though they were meant to be enemies. Enemies across two camps but right now he was somewhere close. Avi had to be in the room – he wouldn't be so stupid as to leave evidence of breaking in so close to opening hours. She checked the interlocking library rooms to no avail and returned to the central room with the reference table, perplexed. She grabbed the request forms Avi had left.

Something flickered above in the balconies. She rushed up the wooden stairs and walked against the walls close to the ceiling, nervously holding the banister, not sure of the reliability of the ancient two-foot-wide balcony. She approached the staircase without encountering anyone from the opposite direction. But just as she took her first step down the staircase, she noticed one of the bookcases glass doors was open, which she hadn't noticed when she had walked past it at the start of the walk around. On closer inspection Una found one of the books was oddly placed and hence was jarring the door. She opened the glass door wide and pushed the offending book back against the cupboard back and realised there was an empty slot. A book was missing but then it was a library. Even reference libraries had books withdrawn. She had wasted enough time already and was determined to get on with learning the geographical terrain. Shrugging off her apprehension, she firmly closed the glass door and caught the reflection of someone sitting and reading in the captain's chair she had recently vacated.

It was Avi, a shaven Avi.

"You didn't have to shave for me."

"I didn't."

"What was the request form ab…"

"A reminder to not hurt yourself selfishly," cut in Avi as he took several steps at a time up the staircase to the balcony.

Avi closed in on her and placed his hands on her shoulders, then scrutinised her body up and down. "I say that but there is no way you could have applied the pressure to stab yourself. Where are the bulges of the bandages? Why did someone in the Forced Blessed stab their own on an exercise?"

"You know about that then."

"Why would they hurt their own?"

"It was just training." Una dismissed his concern.

"What possible purpose can there be for you to be in such intense pain that you were unconscious. It was too near my heart; I thought the phantom pain was going to kill me."

Several emotions crossed Una's face but all that she was able to squeak out was, "Sorry. Fuck, sorry!" Avi was not pleased to say the least and couldn't help but shake Una. "How can you stay on their side? You've got to leave the Forced Blessed mercenaries and come to the Blesseds."

"No!" Una shrugged off Avi's hands.

Avi roughly caught her again and searched her face as if she'd lost her mind.

"Why not?"

"I can't…"

Avi raised his eyebrow.

"Can't or won't?"

"What difference does it make." Her defiant directness smashed into him. "You know why I can't," she continued.

"No, I don't, spell it out clearly." Avi backed her up harshly against a glass cabinet.

"I… because he… my father, I…" Una didn't know where to start and what to say.

Avi didn't want to hear what he thought she was going to say. "Wolf has your father?"

"I think so." Una was scared.

The school's first morning bell rang.

Avi moved off her. "We haven't finished this conversation, but we've got to go."

Avi took the request forms from her and put them in the old fireplace, and from a cupboard took out some matches and lit a fire. "I can't leave evidence of our meeting here or anywhere. Neither side can know we have met, both sides will not listen to reason and will make examples of both of us."

"I believe you, The Forced Blesseds are already wary of me..." Avi had been avoiding eye contact with her, but her admission caught him off guard and he looked up, surprised.

"Why, you passed your initiation test and you won the training task for your team."

"How do you know I won the competition?"

Avi raised an eyebrow. She knew why, she was sure her side of the Forced Blesseds probably had lookouts too.

"You really are on the opposite side." Una sat on the chair near Avi.

"Undoubtedly, but you need to explain why you think they are suspicious of you."

Una didn't think words would make a stronger case than showing him.

She walked over to Avi and dropped down as if she was going to tie her laces, but instead she took out the knife rolled up in his trousers. She gasped when her fingers contacted his flesh. Red streaks on his cheeks told her he was just as affected. He was watching her intently as she placed her hand on the desk, palm faced up, then gently placed the tip of the knife on her palm and drove it down with her chin, stabbing her own palm brutally.

"What the...?" The spell was broken. Avi ran over and placed his hand over her palm to stop it from bleeding. He teethed at his sleeve to tear a strip off, all the time glaring at Una.

Una pretended to be unaffected. "Release my hand, I want to show you something," she said without any trait of emotion.

Unwillingly he complied. He expected to see a clot forming

on her palm at best, based on her Blessed infancy. He was dumbfounded to find a smooth palm of unbroken skin. He was a Blessed from a long line and he didn't heal as fast. Yet she did… Avi's whole body began to shake. He pushed away from her and stood as far away as he could on the chequered marble floor.

"They reacted in the same way as you have," Una hurtfully muttered. "Why is it a big deal?" she asked.

"…They reacted like me…" It sounded like the beginning of a question and a statement to Una. "They reacted like me because it means you are Blessed; you are Blessed stock not Forced Blessed. For your body to heal so quickly you would have to have generations of Blesseds on both sides of your family."

"But that's not possible… I even look like my parents and one of them was Irish!"

Una was shaking. Avi wanted to cross the room but he couldn't. He stamped on the ashes in the fireplace to make sure they were completely out. "You are in a great deal of danger. The best scenario for my side would be that the Forced Blessed kill you for this, or they use you against us." Avi absent-mindedly smeared soot into his forehead as he pushed his hair away from his eyes so she could see he was serious. "Your father would want you to stay safe. You have to come to the other side."

Una shook her head in disagreement. Avi thought about dragging her out with him, but the bell had already gone.

"For now, I'll put the books away, and you need to leave before I come to my senses and realise my folly…" Avi realised he had left sooty fingerprints on the ancient date ink stamps. He used his T-shirt to wipe them and then stopped. He muttered something like, "It could help you fool them…" He rushed to an ancient davenport writing desk she'd not noticed before and from a drawer removed two ancient tins, with sepia and Spanish moss on them, and along with his knife and the Victorian key, pressed them into the cup of her hands and then grabbed her arm and pulled her to the door.

"Avi, what animal form did you take on, just so I know what to avoid?"

"Una, I can't tell you that and you shouldn't tell me yours until we have a plan."

"A plan?"

"Yes, because both sides are capable of cruelties and with your father missing, the Forced Blesseds have leverage over you. And because we have been close..." Avi paused and then spoke the next half of the sentence very quickly.

"Friends, the Blesseds can use you as leverage to bring you in, they might even suspect you of killing Gopan." Una tried to interrupt him, but he shook his head. "If we don't know what we are, we won't be able to divulge information to compromise the other. Una, it seems the only answer is for you to find your father and for me to find what I came looking for."

The fire alarm interrupted them.

"Oh shit, someone must have seen the smoke coming through the chimney."

He ran back and cleaned the table by pulling his shirt off and wiping it.

"That'll have to do," he said as he pushed his T-shirt into his pocket. Despite his ability to heal he still had a whiplash line tattooed on his back.

Una's breath caught in her throat.

Avi flung the library door open. They both sneaked out and then he removed the key from her palm to lock the door, and then gave it back to her. Before she could ask why she needed them he said, "The skylights are locked in the winter – bats like to hibernate in here if they are left open." Outside, both of them scaled the walls and then the roof and ran in two different directions.

Chapter 27

Show and Tell

Last night was an exception, it almost mirrored the confusion of his first night as a wolf. Then like last night the lack of attention mangled the images sent by his pack of possible kills and he found he was sending them in all directions. Of course, he put it down to poor communication, hindered by their tiredness and less than optimal bodies after yesterday's task. They even believed him because they didn't know that despite his calm persona his mind was trying hard to keep them out of his head as he couldn't stop thinking of what Una's healing ability meant.

He didn't know how he had refrained from stabbing her multiple times with one of the scalpels in the medical unit to see for himself how quickly she healed, and then he remembered Grace had stopped him – reminding him that injuring her after the concoction she was injected with could add complications. But now he wished he'd taken the risk. Anything was better than being riddled with the questions and possibilities. He wanted to go and check now but wasn't expected on the campus until later.

Tired of pacing up and down the camouflaged steps of the Modern Ruin, he entered his mother's kitchen and morphed. Rarely did he take on his human form if he wasn't training his cohort in martial arts, but he had to be sure he hadn't missed anything. He unlocked the room at the top of exposed stairs and headed straight for the desk. Grace was sitting at his desk. He didn't need to ask how long she had been there. She was still in yesterday's clothes.

Wolf looked over to the shadows. "Is he asleep?"

"Yes, his body is too weak for anything else."

"Why are you here and not sleeping in your room at St Anthony's?"

Grace raised both her hands in frustration. "For the same reason you are… According to Meeru's notes, yours and our logs of transformations, there is no way Una can heal this easily without interference. The only person who came close to her rate of healing was Avi, but he had Burfani genetics and even he took longer than minutes. Even then, he had to turn eighteen first. And Una…"

Wolf swiped the sheet in her hand. "Is not eighteen yet."

Wolf stared at the black printed words in the cream parchment. It was there in bold letters. Una Dev was born in Wythenshawe University Hospital, South Manchester, in the UK. Her birth date told him she was not yet eighteen.

"The British organisation of records is too accurate to question, there's no chance of tampering with the year to get your child into school at the most favourable time." Wolf gestured for Grace to give up his chair.

Grace nodded and stretched. "It was pretty easy to order her birth certificate unlike her school grades and juvenile police records. I scoured through them but there was nothing beyond the mundane and ordinary."

Wolf wheeled his chair over to the wall with Una's family tree, which he had created when he first began to plot his revenge against Dev, her grandfather, and Major, Avi's father. He found she came from an Irish mother, Alice Saoirse O'Reilly, who had lived in Belfast most of her life until her parents moved to Manchester. Una's father, Vivek, was born in Burma while his father, Dev, was posted there with the army. Una's parents were married at a Manchester registry office. Dev and his wife were originally from Ambala in Haryana. Wolf was able to get Dev's records from the Indian Army and Cartographers of India records.

He traced her lineage and stabbed his thumb on her school photo. "Looking at that, Una at most is a first-generation Anglo Indian as opposed to us who are third generation Anglo Indians. None of them were even born in this state or came from lineage from Uttarakhand. If anything, we are more likely to be Blessed than her based on our families always having lived in this area."

Wolf threw a dart at the Sharman whose face adorned the door he'd walked through. "I can't even say it's something to do with him. I'm the only one who has been in contact with her except for him saving her from the taxi driver I organised. Even then I was the one who drove her to Dev's house."

Grace picked up a photo of her brother and Meeru, from when they were both still in high school. "Do you think Meeru told you everything she knew?" Grace stroked Meeru's face. "I still can't forgive you for not giving her an alternative but to hang herself. Do you even miss her?"

Of course, he missed her, who didn't like the feel of a beautiful woman and he would have rescued her from her wedding, but the foolish girl sent Una to him and made her virtue expendable. Wolf grunted. "Only that if Meeru were alive, she could have manipulated Avi to get the information from the Sharman… Aggh!" Wolf threw a dart at the langur's face. "It always came down to him. Even after all I have achieved, I still fall short of the Sharman…"

"EXCEPT THIS TIME!!" Grace interjected. "You could expose her ability to the Blesseds."

"NO… not yet." Wolf mulled over his sister's suggestion. "But you're right, I could use her against them. But somehow at this moment that would be giving up a significant secret that could be advantageous to our cause." Wolf stilled, assessing what he just said and gave a half smile.

Grace trembled. "Just like the strategic placement of Gopan's body so the Blesseds would find it. Again, did you have to go so far? The poor girl only took a bite, she only wounded him but to date thinks she killed him."

"Grace don't go soft on her like you did with Meeru. The frenzied mutilation of his body by our cohort was necessary." Wolf relaxed and leaned back in the chair. Satisfaction pinned on his face as he remembered the horror on the Blesseds' faces.

He studied his sister's pallor. Was she thinking she was expendable like Meeru and Una? If so, she was so right. His half smile turned to a full one. This wasn't his animalistic wolf side that found delight in her predicament as they were loyal to family, but his human side. Power was such a dizzy aphrodisiac.

"In that case, we should go and check on Una in the medical centre before the others wake up." Just as she finished her sentence, they could hear the school's fire alarm go off in the distance. Wolf's euphoric bubble burst.

By the time the siblings arrived on the school premises, students were running out of their dormitories and making their way to the emergency point. Grace deflected a teacher who tried to herd them too. Wolf ducked and made his way to the Forced Blesseds' isolated dormitories and building. It was important the official Forced Blesseds stayed in and the uninitiated students made their way to the emergency point to be counted.

There was utter chaos when he got to the dorms. His dad and Grace were trying to pacify the youngsters. Raul had kept the Forced Blesseds in, but he couldn't see Una… she was still in the medical room. It was locked. He banged on the door vigorously, and just as he gave up finding Raul, a sleepy Una came out with a sheet wrapped around her. "I had to lock up, you didn't expect me to leave the door open when I realised, I was naked."

Relief rushed in; she hadn't taken this opportunity to run away.

"Just ignore the alarm, it's just a fire drill for the school."

He walked away, thinking he had seen something odd and then he realised, he hadn't seen anything odd, he had actually smelt something – blood. He turned around.

"Una, I forgot to ask, how are you feeling?"

"Fine… Why?" Had he imagined Una's pallor fade further.

"It's just that you have blood on your sheets, which is odd."

"I was knifed yesterday what did you expect?"

"When we left that sheet was clean and you had no injuries let alone blood on your body."

"No injuries? Then where did these scars come from?" She lowered her sheet a little to show discoloured bruised skin between and on the peeking mounds of her breasts, with a couple of deep knife cuts that looked…

Una cleared her throat. "Don't mind me…"

Wolf averted his eyes in embarrassment.

"But you haven't self-healed?"

"No, it's still bleeding in some places, if I squeeze them when I lie down like this…" Una began to squeeze her breast.

Wolf's eyes enlarged and then when she raised a sardonic eyebrow, he belatedly averted them to his shoes. As soon as he did so he realised his error. She had expected him to do that. Clever girl! He looked up again, but the aged bruising was still there. She couldn't have cut herself again to fool him. The shades of bruising on her breast's surface looked like a healed wound had reopened. This time he jolted her when he automatically raised his hand to touch the area.

"Wolf… what are you doing?" Raul interrupted. Una quickly pulled up her sheet, faking mortification.

He would have to keep an eye on her. Perhaps Gagan had not lodged the knife as deep as they thought, and she bled only when pressure was applied. The actual blood on her clothes could have been Gagan's. He did have a gushing nose afterwards.

When Wolf arrived back at the boys' dorm he couldn't explain or prove it, but he felt like she had played him. No one played him… No one.

The junior potential recruits were coming back. It seemed the chowkidar found evidence of a midnight feast in the library. The contents of the librarian's snack stash had been raided and because the bins were still in the recycling shed, the students had stupidly decided to burn the evidence, making everyone believe the library was on fire.

Chapter 28

Truth Sucks (Avi)

He couldn't breathe. He went looking for answers but not the ones he found. What a fool he was. First Wolf and then Nana had implied that she'd killed Gopan. But he hadn't believed that. He should have let her finish her sentence, but he didn't. He allowed her to change it. Did he really suspect that she had killed him? Did he know she was going to say what he didn't want to hear? Avi was so frustrated with himself. Why didn't he think she wasn't capable of it? Another more sinister emotion came over him – did he really care if she had killed him… knowing Wolf she would have been pushed to do it… Gopan was no one to him so was it bad not to care… Aggh! The horrible truth stamped on his face was reflected back to him in the ripples of the water. He averted his eyes.

"Avi?"

Avi physically took a step back from his reflection, which had contoured into Una's. "Leave me alone!"

"I didn't have a choice."

"How could killing him have been your only option?"

Avi destroyed her watery image by splashing it with his feet. She reappeared; she was looking through him.

"Avi, he led my father here, I thought he had my dad set on and killed..."

She held their connection tightly. Her thought words were garbled, almost like she was swallowing her own words. She tried something else that he couldn't ignore. She spilled her emotions into him, stirring his physical body to respond. Both rage and exhaustion fatigued him and then she opened her gates of utter despair with a single question.

"Are you going to tell the Blesseds...?"

"About you being Blessed?" Again, he cut her off. *"I don't know."* Avi closed his eyes. Big mistake.

Her trembling defences opened her up and he was there looking through her eyes at her reflection in a sort of medical room. Her face was ravaged, she had scars on her body. Scars she had painted on according to his thought talk advice.

"I used the knife and inks so I could recreate my injuries..." He was relieved. *"I fooled Wolf as soon as I got back."*

As soon as she got back? It rankled him that she was in danger even from him...

"Am I to safeguard myself from you too?"

"I don't know, perhaps."

Avi felt Una's shudder.

"Una don't get caught in your animal form because unless you are a top predator you could be killed easily. If Wolf is shielding your Blessed animal, then let him. It must mean he is not sure of your safety. Una, Wolf keeps your father close to him."

"You're sure he is alive?" Una asked excitedly, forgetting how scared she had been just moments earlier...

"Don't tell me you were staying on the Forced Blessed side without being sure?"

Una went Quiet.

Wolf keeps her dad close. Where... she'd searched the dormitory block and training rooms, even the Modern Ruin...

"How about the top room?"

"I... Wolf has sent someone to call me... I've got to go; I was meant to meet him half an hour ago."

The delicate thread between them snapped and Avi's reflection was his own again.

Chapter 29

Hot Seating

Una's nervousness and sensation of being a prized prey were back with an additional chilling feeling. Una ghosted her hand over Avi's knife, lying on her side table, until she rested her index finger over its sharp tip. The one thing she was sure of was that he wouldn't tell on her. Why did she feel that? She couldn't say except that it was her gut feeling. Una placed the knife under her pillow, then hesitated and picked up the knife again. Wolf had lied to her when he said it was common knowledge amongst the Blesseds that she had killed Gopan. Otherwise Avi would have said so rather than be cryptic, and then shocked. Una raised her trouser leg and placed Avi's knife like he had around her shin. She was sure Wolf was still suspicious of her and based on where she was summoned to go to, a knife would be handy. Her minor scars makeover had brought her a little time but that's all. Avi's knife on her person not only provided a weapon to save her from others hurting her but also for deliberately hurting herself should she need to re-cut herself. Una blushed. More than any of those reasons it also meant Avi's knife reduced some of her loneliness; he did give it to her… That was something, wasn't it?

Una smacked her face as she walked out of her room. At this moment she had to concentrate on the dangers nearer to her. Gagan already showed her he wanted her dead and given the truth of her rate of healing he would happily sell her out unless he could find a way to kill her himself. Perhaps she should check with Wolf about how many knew about her animal form because if what Avi said about animal forms making it easier to hunt down then she needed to know who knew her secret.

She arrived at her destination. Una stood just outside the noisy gymnasium and in complete fascination watched the potential recruits innocently greet each with high fives for passing the laser test. Una shook her head and looked at Wolf. Time to test if he was always listening. *"I wonder..."*

"You wonder what?" Wolf's eyebrow arched.

"Oops, did I think it aloud?" Una faked surprise.

"Stop acting coy, it doesn't suit you."

Una placed her hand on her chest as if to say – what me?

"You've only just put your shield down. What do you wonder?"

Una smiled. *"I wondered if Gag knew what animal form I had."*

"Not a dumb question judging there's 'no love lost' between you. The answer is no, he just knows you are not a wolf and believes he is ahead of you in the chain."

"Why does he believe that?"

"We've told him and the Blessed defectors that you are not initiated yet."

Una hadn't expected that answer. *"So, you don't trust them."*

"Only the original Forced Blesseds know that you are a snow leopard and they are bound to me, so I trust them."

"Bound? What do you mean?"

"It's funny you ask that because I'm hoping you learn that today during the tests."

Tests of allegiance? Una reacted by raising her thought barriers. Wolf chuckled and motioned for her to come and stand with him. She reluctantly stood behind the glass double doors. Wolf cleared his throat and brought the room to a murmur, and then to complete silence. "Today's session is called 'Hot Seating' which Una, our victor, will lead."

The Forced Blesseds' task under the camouflage of a taster session of jungle survival had been a test for the young martial arts recruits too. Without seeing the paperwork or design of the task,

Una could see what Wolf was looking for. At minimum they were junior martial arts students who were able to successfully laser the Forced Blesseds. They also had a streak of something mercenary. Una somehow didn't think it would horrify them if they knew the truth of the pain they had inflicted if it meant they were chosen to remain in the dormitory.

Una wondered how many of them would accept authority from the wounded seniors they defeated and successfully maimed. Of course, the juniors were not privy to the injuries. Instead they were disappointed when told that most of the Forced Blesseds were on a trainee expedition away from campus. Although they did perk up when they realised, they had the whole gym to themselves.

Una and Raul were the only ones who were unscathed and therefore they were designated to running the trials for the new recruits who wanted to join the "Wolf Gang". Wolf Gang… A juvenile name perfect for Disney not the jungle and Wolf.

Una took a deep breath before she walked through the double doors of the gymnasium where testosterone was flying high in the room. "Here comes the victor of the taster session."

Una plastered on a smile and pretended to hold her ears as she received a foot stamping ovation.

They should be on the tribe's side instead with all that stamping.

"Before you start your own trials, we thought a Q & A session with the victor would be a great treat especially as she herself is a new recruit in the Wolf Gang. The room broke up in cheers. *This is ridiculous,* Una thought as she tentatively seated herself in the chair Wolf pointed to before joining the clapping.

Una felt sick. She moved uncomfortably around her seat when the previous day's trial session appeared on the pull-down screen. Although she knew where she was, she couldn't find herself, until Wolf used an integrated board pen to outline her body. He barely put the pen down when a voice broke out above all the surprised murmur, "I knew she was there, but I just missed her, it was the shrubbery camouflage, it looked so real."

"Well done for shooting your laser, do you have any questions, Vibu?"

Vibu gloated and then asked, "How did you know how to place your body?"

It was time to make the young realise their true part in the task. Una cleared her throat. "Well, the pain from the scorching of a laser would make anyone of one you lie still too."

A hush fell over the whole group. *What is wrong with what I said?* Una glanced over at Wolf. She didn't need to read his thought to know how he felt.

"They don't know the lasers were real, they assumed that they were just beams of light that could trigger a luminous liquid on the suits. Make a joke of what you just said. That is an order!"

Una's perused the recruit's incredulous faces and Raul and Grace's worried ones. Wolf's skin was stretched taut.

"Oh, I was just joking, but we had to make it…" Una used her index fingers on both hands in the air to make speech marks, "…'real' for you. But seriously the reason I didn't get hit was two-fold – one, I observed the rock pattern before I was placed and secondly, and most importantly, Raul placed me well. It felt very odd to be sprawled in that awkward position and without guidance I'm not sure I would have managed it."

One of the trainees said something rude and Una just laughed it off.

Raul beamed in surprise at receiving praise for her win and was happy to reciprocate the juniors' high fives. Una couldn't help but smile until she picked up on Wolf's nod towards her. He was assessing her… had he just ticked "team spirit" off her list?

"So, Ms Rao, how did you decide to remove the captain of the other side. It couldn't have been out of defence because we were told you would have been spared by the other Wolf Gang as you were new. You only had to fight the new recruit from the opposing side."

Una was stumped. She looked at Raul, who looked a little sheepish. He had forgotten to tell her that. She couldn't land him in it now. It possibly explained why Gagan was still in the game when they both met on the rocks.

No wonder the coward was still standing, so to speak.

Una returned her attention to the group and spouted a team building spiel she had learnt during her explorer scout days.

"It's quite simple. Who likes charity here? In real life no one is going to say here is a chance. Plus, truth be told, the other team's captain would expect to be allowed to pass because of who he was. He wouldn't expect me to ambush him when I did. Surprise is the best form of attack."

"Quite right, Ms Rao. In fairness you did him a favour," Vibu shouted in agreement.

"How?" Wolf asked. He rewound the footage of the trial to when the captain of the other team was ambushed.

"He won't be so complacent next time," replied Vibu, and because he had Wolf's approval, he became cocky. "According to the footage, it seems like the laser hit him badly. Look at him." Vibu pointed to the footage. "He's very dramatic when he falls down, a little unbelievable if you ask me."

Guilt riddled Una. She hadn't asked after Captain Christopher.

"Don't worry, all the wounded are recovering well at my parents' house."

"That's why they weren't in the medical room when I was brought in. Why aren't you telling the juniors about how I got wounded... shouldn't they know that Gag was punished for ignoring a direct order from you?"

Wolf didn't say anything.

"You are going to punish him, aren't you?"

Wolf smiled infuriatingly, leaving Una agitated. She brought the question and answer session to an end. Nonplussed, Wolf began to explain the trial tasks to the eager trainees.

Una walked over to Raul. "I don't understand why anyone would want to join the Wolf Gang after what they watched, even if they believed it to be a game."

"Don't you play PlayStation or Xbox games?"

Of course, she did, and knew it wasn't the violence of the acts that excited her and others but the thrill of outsmarting the supposed enemy.

"Did you volunteer because you thought it was like Xbox?"

"That's crazy. We didn't volunteer. We were transformed because of our existing friendship ties to Wolf, who called us into the jungle. Unlike you, him and Gag and the rest of us can live normal lives if we move away from Khamosh Valley. We have no property here so we have no real links with the earth, which means as long as we don't come back to Khamosh Valley we can live quite normally as humans but..."

"But? How can there be a but?"

"But we are proud to be part of the Forced Blesseds. We have a purpose."

"Aren't you describing the army?"

"No, we are more like brothers who love and respect each other. We believe we can make a real difference here. Better than the greedy property developers and even the unrealistic hereditary Blesseds who think they can keep people off their land when the human population of this valley, like India, is increasing."

"If that's so then why don't you just tell the trainees what you are."

Una felt smug.

"We might not tell them straight away, but we do give them a choice. You'll find out for yourself in a few days."

Their conversation came to a natural end. Just as well, as Una, Grace and Raul were called upon to take part in the trial activities. Una wasn't surprised to find she was used as aggressor on the mat and the students had to defend themselves. Despite Wolf's goading she went very lightly on them.

Raul was teaching the others how to climb a wall during a pursuit.

Una was intrigued by Grace's lesson. She was teaching a group how to throw a dart carefully on the boards ahead. *Why darts?*

"We can't really give them daggers at this point, can we, Una? Actually, I think you should join the group, it might improve your curved trajectory."

Una knew she was still goading her, but actually it wasn't a bad idea. She bowed at her disappointed opponent and left the mat to go and stand in queue in Grace's line. Grace shot Wolf a look and he just smiled and bowed at her abandoned opponent and began to spar. Wolf's opponent could not hide his absolute delight and pride that he had been chosen.

What a mug, Una thought.

That evening, Una didn't feel like going out, she had really enjoyed learning from Grace and had enjoyed Raul's company. But most surprisingly of all she had enjoyed Wolf's banter and sparring.

Perhaps it was the team camaraderie. An elite team at that. And that's how she knew why the others stayed. Wolf made them feel special.

Late in the night she went with Grace to her parents' house and helped give out amber tea to the ones who were taking longer to heal. Other's just wanted to be fussed over.

Una had to cover her mouth often when she saw gauged or bloody wounds. Sheila, Sid's wife, took pity and asked her to sit down.

"Poor thing. Is the sight of blood making you heave?"

Una nodded in agreement. It wasn't the reason. She wasn't heaving. Instead, her mouth was producing copious amounts of saliva. She wasn't hungry and definitely wasn't a man-eater.

Una smiled weakly.

"Perhaps she could kiss me and make us both feel better. Especially my face where the laser hit before I fell." Captain Christopher didn't look too unhappy to see her. Una found the camaraderie of the group quite comforting. Light-heartedly, Una gave him a peck on his bruise and then pulled away. Her lips stung from a faint electric current from when her mouth had connected with his injured skin.

Captain Christopher's eyes sparkled. "Oh, I already feel better. Do you want to give a few more? I've got a cut on my mouth."

Una was still in shock.

"Don't look so surprised, Una, you don't have to."

Una carried on staring at Christopher who was already bantering with Grace shamelessly. Even in the poor lantern light of the evening, it was plain to Una that the area of Christopher's face that she had kissed had already cleared. Her kiss had healed him. Her saliva build-up now made sense. The injuries had brought on the saliva.

Chapter 30

Where's Gagan?

Several amber drinks later, Una's inhibitions were gone. "Hey, Christopher. Seriously, how can you guys even talk to each other, let alone be dope about what you guys did to each other?"

"Man, we're brother's in arms – a tight lot." Christopher knuckle bumped several of them. Una laughed and shook her head at all the grimacing and moaning.

Raul fell in between Una and Christopher and grabbed his friend in a headlock. "We have to practise our hand-to-hand combat during the day tomorrow."

"Hand-to-hand combat. Poor Gag will miss out."

Christopher freed himself from Raul, looked first at Una and then at Raul before asking openly, "Why?"

"Because he used a…?" Una's frown bridged her nose. She looked around. Gagan was missing, which she had expected because she thought he would be isolated somewhere due to his punishment.

"Because he fell badly when Una defeated him and broke his arm," Raul jumped in, leaving Una with an open mouth. His cold stare made her shut her mouth.

"He's upstairs sulking because he lost. Wolf's up there with him," said Christopher while yawning. His interest in Gagan had petered out.

Something was afoot. *Why was Gagan's offence a secret? If so, did it mean that the Forced Blessed core didn't know about her bleeding too?*

Una turned to Raul who was mouthing words to Grace. Strange when they could use thought talk. Una was sure she heard the pack talk when she was hunted down, when she escaped on her first day in the Forced Blessed jungle. Perhaps it was Grace who couldn't. It didn't matter, their distraction ploy was soon evident. Grace tottered over with a thermos. "Una, these guys mustn't transform tonight so we need to make sure they've had enough amber tea to keep their Forced Blessed guises subdued. Can you fetch me a couple more flasks from the kitchen?"

"Oh, does that mean I can't go out? I was hoping…"

"Una, you've not had enough amber tea to knock you out. It's only working on them because they are not fighting fit."

Relief washed over Una's face. Grace chuckled. "Never thought you would prefer your Forced Blessed self when I consider how you tried to run away from Khamosh Valley."

Grace's words niggled at Una. She was right. Una's mindset had changed. Perhaps she could also feel differently about Gagan as he was in the same pack as her so to speak. Fat chance of that! Una placed her empty flask down and picked up one more and a tumbler. Perhaps she should check on Gagan anyway.

A strangeness overcame Una as she climbed up the outdoor steps leading up to the sisters' room. The one she hadn't inspected yet. Her apprehension grew when she tried to turn the knob. The door was locked again. Yet she could hear muffled voices.

She tried to think thought to Wolf, who she was sure was inside, but he blocked her. The other person seemed to have no ability. Like Grace, Gagan seemed to be unable to think thought too.

She might not have read or been able to communicate with Wolf, but she knew she had got his attention. She had begun to notice the subtle shadowing of Wolf when he tried to eavesdrop on her thoughts.

She heard shuffled feet behind the door before Wolf opened it.

Una barely had time to look inside. All she saw was a mirror and some sort of dresser…

"Una, why are you here?"

Una was troubled by the mirror but whatever it was remained on the edge of her mind.

"I've brought amber tea."

"I didn't get hurt."

"But don't you need it to remain human in the evening?"

"No. As a firstborn nor do you. It's a mindset thing."

"Well, I actually brought the amber tea for Gag. Is he in there?"

"No, no one is in there."

"But I…"

"NO ONE is in there, UNA!" Wolf fired her a warning glance.

Una nodded. She was quiet for a few seconds and then opened her mouth again to speak.

"UNA!"

"It's just that Gag was injured, and I wanted to see if he was okay. After the pep talk about the tight group and loyalty, etc., I wanted to make a fresh start with Gag."

"Una, did you think I would have him in the house when he defied my rules. He's in the cooler."

"The cooler?"

"Cooler… where you were… the manhole. He will have to stay there to learn a lesson, plus it keeps him out of the way of the possible new recruits too. Now, let's go over tomorrow's training with the new recruits. We are going to take the trials outdoors."

Una wished she hadn't come upstairs and had remained with the others and the fun. She slumped down on a chair on the roof.

Una could feel her body transforming. Wolf remained in his human form.

"Time to let you go… you will have the whole of the jungle – at least the Forced Blessed part – to yourself."

"Why, are you not changing?"

"Nope, not tonight."

Wolf pointedly hinted at the darkening sky.

"Una, you'd better go down quickly, you are going to need your hands to take the thermos down."

She was too late; she had begun to transform. She dropped the thermos and the glass. Wolf caught them mid-air and pointed to the ledge on the side. He was right. If she went down the stairs she would be seen. Una was sure they knew her animal form but perhaps they didn't all know. She never expected to be one of the many secrets, if not the biggest, kept from her own Forced Blessed compatriots.

Still on the roof, Una was sure she could hear a faint thumping. It reminded her of the sound she used to make when she rocked her chair backwards and forwards out of boredom in her classroom back in Manchester. The thumping was to a rhythm. When Wolf returned to the room, the rhythm ended sharply. Una was in mid-air when she realised why the rhythm was familiar. It was "Glory, glory, Man United", Man United's and her favourite football team's chant.

Like a key it unlocked the vision that had been at the edge of her memory and cast it before her. She was looking at a mirror but instead of her reflection it was Wolf's human form and, on the dressing table, was a comb. It was the time she had temporarily been pulled into his body during the monsoon when lightning had hit her as she stood in the flooded path that divided the property developers from the jungle. She recognised the comb as her father's. There was something else strange about the reflection. In the bottom corner she saw a hand stretched out. It looked familiar. She looked carefully at the ring mark on the wedding finger. Una saw the chain Wolf was wearing. It had her father's ring attached to it like a pendant. Una fell to the ground. She called out in thought, *"Avi, I have proof that my father is alive!"* But then came the sinking terror. She had killed Gopan for stuttering…

Chapter 31

Should She Stay, or Should She Go?

Una fled to the cliff. No other animal from the Forced Blesseds would be there but what about Wolf? He was too clever. She had felt his intent eyes on her and even now she knew he was prodding the edge of her mind. The knocking of "Glory, glory, Man United!" was familiar all around the world and even if it weren't, Wolf would know it. A shiver went through Una's furry body. It was no accident that he had surrounded her with things she loved, down to the toothpaste brand she used. He would know she was a through and through Man United supporter. Sometimes he fell in line with her far too easily. It was almost seductive, but she knew it was only due to their thought reading. It wasn't like what she and Avi had before they even knew what it was… *Had?* Did they still have it?

Was she safe in the jungle? Una wondered where she could go.

Minutes later she cursed herself. She hadn't consciously decided to come to the familiar gates, but she had. It was strange to be looking in rather than out. She wanted to see if her grandparents were about. If they were would they know it was her. Undaunted, Una placed her snout forward to look between the grills just as Tommy, her dog, used to before he was killed. Unlike his, her snout did not make it through the grill, instead it was cushioned by a plasma mass. Una scrunched her face and tried harder to no avail.

"I should have had an inkling a few days back. But I didn't.

You are pretty stupid to give yourself away so easily. It has to be you, Una, because why would a snow leopard that is elusive come to check out a house that is padlocked?"

Una cocked her ear and stepped her four-legged body around. Avi was in the Blessed territory behind the rhododendron bushes where she first met Kulkil, when he spied on her.

I could hear your thoughts, so I followed... I was coming here to find a way to protect you after what I heard about what you did as revenge. I suspected you killed Gopan but this... I was ready to even overlook it, but this...

"Avi, you told me not to tell you what I had become..."

"Yes, but that was before I knew." Avi's voice broke off. Una heard the agony and wrath but was equally perplexed, especially when he shouted. "How is it even possible... why you?"

Why not me? What was happening? Wasn't it a big relief for him? Una's own confusion was moving up the Richter scale of anger. How dare he think it was something she wanted. Meeru was the one who gave her Cat. His aunt! Shouldn't he have been pleased... even as animals they were...

"Are you sure of that?"

Una groaned; he was reading her mind. What else had he read?

Una's fur shook; he was furious.

Avi chose that moment to step forward so she could see him. Una's internal mind walk instantly came to a halt. Avi cast a large shadow... only it was not his shadow, it was him.

In animal form. All at once she could see they were not compatible.

Minutes passed before Avi broke the silence. "Nothing to say..."

Say? What could she say, she was still reeling from shock, but she knew she couldn't just gape in silent horror at his fate? "How did you become this... your mother was a snow leopard and she would have been affecting you."

Avi growled and stretched to standing position and edged towards her with his claws out.

Una retreated.

"Ask Wolf."

"Wolf caused you to become a bear?"

Avi pounced forward. Una moved to the side but still found herself corned between the plasma wall and him.

His matted fur squashed her whiskers.

"Avi, stop…" He did but only after making her tumble sideways and then backwards, past the rhododendron bushes and into Blessed territory. He loomed over her. She was no longer helpless, but she was furious. She hissed at him, baring all teeth with her ears pulled back. How dare he treat her this way. Una locked eyes on him, but he was staring ahead.

She heard her very own British accent. Una twirled her body around to look.

He was vision casting!

Una's temper vanished as she watched Avi save her… save her from a hulk of fur bolting towards her.

Then she saw the claws come down on his skin.

"It was me; I did this to you!" Una choked out. Repelled by her own sixteen-year-old self in the vision, her hind legs gave in.

Avi's eyes bored into hers and his next words broke Una's heart.

"I carry your curse; it was just about bearable but not now." There was pain and repulsion towards himself in his voice as he first looked down at himself and then at her.

Una welled up.

"Avi, believe me, I didn't make this snow leopard thing happen but if you want to finish me off, then do."

His anger dissolved into something else…

Avi was silent for some time, then in a subdued voice asked, "How did it happen?"

How did it happen? Una was puzzled. What did it matter, it's not as if she wished for it? What was he implying, that she had a choice or had taken his?

"How did it happen?" he repeated, threateningly.

"I don't know I was thrown out of a moving vehicle over the bridge. When I climbed down a tree that broke my fall into the river, I found I was a snow leopard," she shouted out, annoyed.

"The river, the bridge..." They must have all arrived on the same day. Before he could ask if she knew, Una sprang up. "Now, when I think of it, I was changing before that. Cat was sneaked into my wedding clothes by your aunt on her own wedding day and he brought on the change. You should know this, your aunt, Meeru, was working with..."

"Wolf."

"The Sharman."

Both said simultaneously.

"Why would it be Wolf?"

"Why would it be the Sharman..."

Both spoke again.

"Does it matter now? I'm a snow leopard and you are..." Una lowered her head, stopping herself before she stated what was painfully obvious.

"Not?"

Una jerked her head up warily. In their animal guises she couldn't read his expression. He also kept her out of his thoughts. He was so still. He reminded her of Wolf. This new Avi scared her.

Avi gave her a long look and then stepped back between the foliage and disappeared.

"Wait," Una cried. He couldn't leave it like this. Una felt like a large portion of her heart had disappeared along with Avi. Her heart ached... It was amazing that he had spoken to her in the library considering the fact she had forced his initiation by a bear and killed his cousin, Gopan. The third thing, the snow leopard thing, was not her fault, but it was the thing he couldn't forgive her for. It was then that Una realised she had lost something extraordinary before she had even recognised it. She wanted to follow him, her heart wanted to risk being discovered by her enemy and being killed but she couldn't allow herself that gruesome indulgence either, she had to find her dad. For the first time she knew he was alive. Wasn't that the reason she had come to the house. She had thought seeing her grandparents' house might give her some ideas. With a crushed heart she began to creep away from the path and the perimeter of the Blessed territory before she was seen. She rubbed against the trunk of the mango tree used as a watching post by Kulkil in the past and looked up. Something tweaked. Was she being watched? Una left.

***

Rosetta had to be careful not to be seen out and about in cub's body. She had promised Avi after all. But then if she had been obedient would she have learnt that Una had made it and was a snow leopard?

It was a shame for Una and a blessing for her that she wasn't alone. Gopan's grandfather was with her. This was a situation that allowed her to kill two birds with one stone. Only in this case it was a snow leopard. There could only be one power, one snow leopard… convincing the Sharman's brother to go against his own brother for a share in power will keep him quiet. Rosetta forcibly shrugged the cub's shoulders. There was no place for father-daughter sentimentality here.

Chapter 32

Breaking Point

The Sharman tried again. "Avi, where have you been? The cub is not in the cave and nor is your mother."

Avi didn't even look up, he just stared at the worn temple step underfoot.

"Did you hear what I said?"

"You said the cub is not in the cave and nor is Rosetta," Avi repeated impassively.

His mechanical tone made the Sharman nervous. As did the fact that he was in his human form and sitting in the temple. He needed the whole night to feed his bear self to keep his strength.

"Why aren't they with you?"

Avi looked up and stared straight at him. He didn't say anything. His face was hard and tight with bitter helpless anger. The Sharman made to move forward in compassion, however Avi's scrutiny held him captive.

"Neither do I know, nor do I care to know. I've had it with snow leopards." No explanation of why was granted.

The Sharman found his words bewildering.

"You've had it with snow leopards… why? What happened with the cub and Rosetta?"

"How should I know?" he answered and then went back to staring at the steps below him.

Horrified at his cavalier attitude, the Sharman raised his voice. "You should, you were not meant to leave them unattended."

"I left the cub with Great Uncle, your brother," Avi lashed back. "I wasn't talking about them anyhow."

"You weren't talking about them?" Avi caught the Sharman's attention. Instead of surprise he sounded cautiously anxious. "Then where did you see another snow leopard?"

"At her grandparents' house." Avi rose his head stiffly and zeroed in on the Sharman. "Don't even deny that you don't know who I'm talking about."

He waited for contradiction but his elder had read the challenge in his words. Instead his nana sat on the step just above his grandson.

"There was so much I wanted to tell you but..."

"You didn't know how to tell me that she was a snow leopard."

"Yes, no... it wasn't relevant."

Avi turned his body and grabbed his nana's hands and explored his face. "It wasn't relevant, *really*?" The Sharman didn't flinch but instead watched his grandson's face bear the unbearable pain of betrayal. He was making no attempt to hide it. The worst of it was the Sharman knew he was to further disappoint and let down his grandson and daughter in the future if it meant that equilibrium in the jungle was kept.

"Was it relevant that Rosetta might have had a hand in changing her? I thought it was Wolf and she thought it was you but we both know it was her, Rosetta, when she was Cat."

The Sharman shook his head.

"Not then?"

"She didn't..."

Avi jumped up and walked up the steps and turned to face his nana's back. "No, you're right, it's before that, I should have realised it... if Rosetta could impact me then she could impact Una too." As he uttered the words and mulled over the possibility, he remembered Una talking about meeting a strange woman when she first arrived, when she was looking for her father after the curfew. She had tried to show him a scratch that wasn't there.

"Did you encourage Rosetta to scratch Una?"

"What are you alluding to?" the Sharman was genuinely confused.

"She scratched Una before I was scratched by the bear."

"When?"

Avi retold Una's story.

"It sounds like your mother got a fright and scratched her by mistake. Avi, you are reading too much into this." The Sharman sounded so sure about that.

Why? Avi was surprised at how easily his nana dismissed his words. He would have expected the opposite.

The Sharman noted his grandson's piercing, watchful eyes over him and in the most neutral voice he could muster he said, "Avi, it's done."

Avi shifted his body off the temple pillar and straightened himself and put his laser focus on the Sharman. The Sharman flinched under Avi's cruel smile.

His voice was oddly serene. "Shouldn't you be worried? Wolf knows what he has. He's been upping the trials." Avi paused as he watched the many emotions race across his nana's countenance. "What if his big reveal brings doubt about our dear Burfani's abilities and we lose the Blesseds to the Forced Blesseds' camp?" Avi's face broke into a smile and his hands fondly rearranged his nana's scarf across his shoulder, preoccupied and distracted. Not fooled, the Sharman stilled Avi's hands. Avi's smile dimpled and with swirling mercurial poisoned eyes, he whispered, "Before Wolf reveals her to the rest…" Avi's breath blew his nana's hair as he spoke, "…we should do away with the charlatan."

"Do you want to kill her?" choked the Sharman.

"I have to."

"How can you say that… even when she couldn't see you and just sensed you, she tried to engage with you… for heaven's sake you saved her from Wolf when you were on the river."

"If you want to go over history, do you remember that Una was looking for her father?"

The Sharman nodded.

"About that..." Avi paused to make sure he had his nana's complete attention, "...she's found him."

"That is a disaster. If she confronts Wolf, he will toughen and implement whatever plans he has."

"Exactly." Avi breathed out as he let go of his grandfather, who swayed. His thoughts immediately turned to Una once again. Now she was a snow leopard she would be the target of all, even his mother and him.

"Breathe, Avi!"

Avi's body shuddered. He hated the treachery of his body as it trembled, and his heart raced. Why did his body fail him? With determination, he collected himself and in a voice that no longer knew of a past, he said, "Perhaps it's a good thing Wolf accelerates his course of action."

The Sharman looked up, horrified. Avi's cold heart grew in proportion to the many furrows on the Sharman's already creased face. "Without too much preparation, we could target and expose Una to quash his plans. Let's give Wolf a dose of his own medicine, of being a 'sitting duck'."

"Avi..." Whatever the Sharman wanted to ask remained unasked as they both witnessed leaping and menacing shadows cast by the diya light. Avi tensed as he watched his great uncle leap up the temple in his rhesus negative monkey guise with the cub at his heels.

Despite his great uncle's presence, Avi continued in an offhand manner. "What... Isn't it the Blessed Oath to protect the jungle? If it isn't then what am I and Una doing here?"

His great uncle unfurled his fisted digits and showered gravel in front of Avi's feet. Avi didn't have to examine the offensive gravel to know where it had come from.

"Let's hope your words are not empty because it's time to balance the scales."

"What do you mean?" blurted the Sharman.

"He means Avi is not the only one who has discovered Gopan's killer," answered Rosetta. "Oh, and my secret too."

The cub pounced on the flame of the diya and put it out, leaving them in pitch darkness.

Chapter 33

Bookworm

Una was struck by the emptiness in the pit of her being. She was completely alone. Earlier, even if she couldn't see Avi, she always knew he was there – in her heart. But now?

She preferred that he came at her with vengefulness, anything, so she could react and respond. But the thread between them was severed. There was nothing. Worse than nothing. On her heart there was a large imprint of where he had been.

She wasn't sure what Avi or Wolf would do now. They all wanted to use or kill her. She was just a big dirty secret. A dirty secret that couldn't extinguish itself because it still had a living dad to rescue.

Three nights ago, Una returned to her room desolate and beaten after her disastrous rendezvous with Avi. It was a bittersweet thing to find that Grace and the other senior Forced Blesseds had remained at the Modern Ruin.

Alone, she put all her energy into working out how to use the fact that she was a snow leopard to her own advantage. For the last three mornings before the others woke up, she visited the library to learn any little scrap of information about snow leopards. Anything that would help her strategise her father's escape. She began by hunting through the reference books for more information on the tribe's people but there wasn't much more than the information in the books Avi had entered in the ledgers.

Walking past the reference cupboard she came across a volume purposefully placed flat between vertically stored books. Avi had done that. She remembered how Avi had put a book back very quickly when they escaped the library last time. It surprised Una that it was still there. Had Avi put it back deliberately for her to find during her next visit. The answer was yes. It was the first volume of myths and legends around the world. She would have walked past it only because it was mainly about the Greek, Aztec, Aboriginal and Nordic myths. Flipping through it she did find the usual Indian myths and legends – stories of Brahma, Vishnu, and Shiva but then she found a green parrot feather lodged between myths of Pakistan and Nepal and other Himalayan legends.

Surely Burfani had to be mentioned there? Una didn't know how long she had in the library, so she found a book of the same weight and size from a dusty cupboard and put it at the far end, pushing the rest of the books together to remove the gap left in the "Reference Only" shelf.

Back in her room Una greedily opened the book to where the feather poked out. It was the wrong page. Frustrated she riffled through the contents page, then the many pages of the thick volume but couldn't find anything. She placed the book down and pushed it away from her. She hated research at school. She could still hear a teacher whining about her laziness for not using the index provided. The index! Una scoured the index and sure enough she found "snow leopard". There were two pages about snow leopards. Greedy for information she read the first page. Apparently, the Tibetans believed that snow leopards were lamas in disguise, so they could find medicinal herbs, but worryingly the Nepalese believed that spirits chose to be born as snow leopards to remove their past sins or the sins of the humans, and killing one meant all their sins would be transferred to the hunter. Did that imply that anybody who knew this would not try and kill her? It was what she was looking for, but she didn't know how to use it. Absent-mindedly, Una turned the pages to a print of figures and animals, but before she could read them in detail, she heard the dormitory's wake-up call. It always rang too soon for her.

Involuntarily Una began to look for a place to hide the book. She didn't want anyone to discover the information before she could work out how she was going to use it. She scouted around.

Cupboard?

No, Grace was always in there making sure she had the right clothes.

Bed?

The dormitory staff stripped the beds, so she couldn't hide it in the folds or under it.

So where?

Bookcase? Too obvious… or was it?

Una quickly slipped the cover off an encyclopaedia – nobody used those these days in the world of Wikipedia and covered the myths book with it. She then placed it back amongst the books Sid had put in as props to make her look like a college student.

Just as she fixed the book neatly amongst the shelf of books over her desk, a stabbing emotion attacked her, forcing her to slump forward and press her chest against the edge of her desk.

It was stupid. She was back to hiding things like she had since she found out her mum was ill. She hid things from her father, grandparents, the Blesseds and Forced Blesseds, but now once she worked out what to do, she would be hiding things from Avi too. Ever since she had come to India, she had got used to having Avi… in her heart… and now?

Pain of fear, greater than her body and mind could comprehend, screamed through her. Normally she overcame fear by taking action and that was just the problem.

What action could she take?

Wolf was treating her with kid gloves, he was waiting to see if she had heard the Manchester United thumping. She had to purposely carry on as normal and avoided visiting the older Forced Blesseds at Sid's house as they recuperated so it looked like she had no reason to go there.

Being hyper vigilant allowed her to not dwell on her bottomless pit of guilt towards Avi.

Avi's bear curse ate at her the most. Unwittingly, she'd pushed him to the bottom rung, in a worse situation than he had been on the OTHER side, all because she couldn't follow rules.

Una felt a hopelessness, a desolate loneliness of a kind she had never known before even when her mother fell ill and passed, and her father had left her with his parents.

Wiping her tears with back of her hand Una knew there was only one thing for her to do.

She was to do nothing.

To carry on as normal – for the moment – and wait to see what happens.

Chapter 34

Turning Point

A couple of weeks later

A thick trickle of resentment, hurt and anger bubbled through Avi's veins, congealing his heart. Avi tried and failed to quantify whose treachery – Una's, Wolf's, or Rosetta's – hurt him most.

Finally, he decided, it didn't matter. Not anymore.

He was done with the dark Blessed heritage. He knew there was no quick exit from his tangled and ugly existence and if there was, he wouldn't take it. Not now that he knew he had to take out Una, whether that meant killing or kidnapping her. Rescuing her father had already proven difficult and it would take more time the Blesseds just didn't have.

Innocent or not Una was a weapon Wolf was likely to wield with great vengeance. Now that he suspected she might have Blessed healing abilities; Wolf was going to strike soon.

Mind made up, Avi explored his course of action. He skimmed past the "today" to plan his ambush. At dusk Una would most likely be in her snow leopard guise. That was perfect. Seeing her in snow leopard form instantly triggered his hostility and annihilated any tender feelings he had towards her while her human self-did quite the opposite. He was digressing. It took him ages to learn what it meant to be a bear and he suspected she wasn't at full snow leopard capacity yet. He was banking on the fact her snow leopard instincts would naturally back off from a foe whilst his sloth bear ones went on to full-blown attack mode at the slightest provocation. Avi's choice of weapon were his bear claws and teeth. He hoped he could hold back from killing her but could not guarantee it. Whatever the outcome, today had to be the day, he'd been watching and eavesdropping on the Forced Blesseds training and it looked like Wolf and his pact were preparing for something today. Something that would happen when they were sure Una had left the low ground and disappeared in the opposite direction to go to her favourite ledge and higher feeding ground. The ledge where he first spotted her was the most likely place to ambush Una. He had to hurry; dusk was coming soon.

In his haste to get on with the mission, Avi made a foolish mistake and forgot his own rule. For the first time ever, he transformed into his full shabby sloth bear form whilst in view of anyone looking up or near to the temple. Until this day many of the Blesseds suspected he maintained an erratic snow leopard form, but most didn't know that he had abandoned that unstable form for the lowliest permanent form of the Blessed animals. If only he had hidden behind the pillars or gone further into the temple during his transformation. Instead, he was distracted by a coach horn as it drove by on the bridge and then began its descent down the hill.

Oblivious to his onlookers, standing on his hind legs, Avi lifted his eyes, past the snaking dry river, to the dirt tracks behind the tree foliage. With his poor eyesight he could see very little, but his nostrils did not fail him. The transport coming down the hill ponged of young human sweat. After lifting the dust from the flying gravel, the coach's occupants' yells in his old school's slang and its own heavy braking squeals, it came to a screeching stop. Avi could not see but he heard St Anthony's old reliable coach stop on the distant gravel drive of the Modern Ruin.

The temple bell's furious clanging made the temple pillars tremor thus bringing his attention back to where he was and the fact that his transformation had not gone unnoticed. The Sharman deflected their attention when he ferociously swung off the bell, signalled and led the charge of the Blesseds in their animal avatars on the ground, through the trees and in the air. All made their way to the Modern Ruin. Furious that his plan was foiled, Avi raced ahead of most to finish Una off at the Forced Blessed fortress instead.

Chapter 35

The Crossing Over

Ten hours earlier

High up, while inspecting the climbing holds, Una barely clocked the returning Forced Blesseds below. Her annoying cat attributes now meant she fell far too easily into an anally retentive preoccupation with whatever she was doing. A far cry from when she used to be distracted at the back of the class and looked for constant adventure.

For a couple of weeks, since meeting Avi, she didn't have time to think of him and spent all her time being inconspicuous. Una had lost herself in training and maintaining the climbing equipment. She was careful to maintain her behaviour in accordance with how she was before her miraculous healing. Too much enthusiasm or lack of it would have Wolf paying greater interest in her. As it was, Wolf and Raul spent a lot time together away from the main group. The rest of the group minus Gagan had fallen into a rhythm of some sort of solidarity. It was a relief to no longer be the newbie. The power of the collective mind of the wolves, which she now was allowed to connect to temporarily – Wolf had stressed the "temporarily" – lacked conflict unlike her lonely snow leopard mindset. Stilling her hand with the screwdriver in hold, Una wondered if she might have been better if Cat had not scratched her because then she would have been a wolf as Wolf had met her at the river. A wolf?

"An interesting idea. Perhaps you might have been more receptive to the

fact we are all waiting for you to bring your 'feline self' down. The selective hearing of cats is definitely true."

Looking over her shoulder, Una noticed fifteen pairs of eyes on her. Without a thought she leapt into the air to catch the rope hung centrally in the room and shimmied down to wolf whistles.

Una took a bow and sat on a block left for her.

Wolf began, "Now that we're all here, I've come to a decision about the trainees."

Christopher asked, "How many made it?"

"After much deliberation or perhaps none," Wolf smirked, "all of them."

A collective gasp of surprise rippled through those assembled.

"All thirty?" Una swung to catch Raul's attention. His expressionless eyes met hers with an added mechanical nod of agreeance.

"You guys must have really trained them up in our absence, I thought a handful perhaps but…" Christopher dropped off in response to Wolf's raised hand.

"They are good enough. We need the numbers. Anyhow we can always 'let go' of the weaker ones after the initiation."

Silence. In collective agreeance the unit began to prepare for the initiation process. All except for Una. She stayed put on the block, wondering about Wolf's ominous words "let go".

Ten hours later, Una and the rest of the Forced Blesseds stood on the oddly laid out steps leading to Agnes and Grace's room, dressed in tawny and tan camouflage outfits sporting netted camouflaged legionnaire caps. Una focused on the space ahead of her. She worked hard to not look into the room on the roof from where she had heard the Man United thumping chant. All the time Wolf edged and tried to access her thoughts. It was tiring Una. The best way to distract him was to thought talk deliberately.

"Who knew there was such a large choice of camouflages? The army on the other side of the bridge would be jealous."

"Possibly."

"Why are we waiting for the initiates here? Don't all initiates come through the quadrant of the river?"

"No, not all."

"Surely the Blesseds must witness..."

"Yes!" Even in thought wolf sounded agitated. *"They think they should... but they won't be able to do anything about it... Stop with the prattle, the new crop is here."*

Una glanced towards a rumbling sound further away.

A laden coach groaned downhill over the uneven dirt track. Una was confused. *Why couldn't they have just come through the boundary hedge like she did to get to the Modern Ruin?*

Wolf was no longer listening to her thoughts.

The coach nearly nosedived several times as it sped down the gradient of the hill it came down. The groans and creaks loudly announcing its arrival to the Blesseds, advertising Wolf's intentions perfectly. When it finally halted outside Sid's house its occupant couldn't get out fast enough. A couple of them heaved over on the path, amongst others sprawled around them. "Ughs" were added to gravel noises as they reshuffled to clean spots.

Unmoved, the Forced Blesseds watched in continued silence.

"I thought we were going to a hall in the town or even to a hotel for a celebratory meal."

"Perhaps Rao sir should have used his money on this place, instead of donating it to the school." The boy was kicked on the shin by another.

Wolf emerged from the kitchen door and stepped up three steps on the staircase. All grumblings and chat ended with a single flicker of Wolf's eyebrow. Without a further command the initiates stood to attention.

"So, here we are at Mr Sid Rao's home for your graduation and..."

Una darted her eyes to the boys to see what had interrupted Wolf.

One of the initiates was straining his neck to look above Wolf and the Forced Blesseds.

"What is it, boy?"

The initiate's horrified eyes swung back to Wolf. "Sorry, sir, but what's up there, sir?"

"Just a room."

"But why are they all guarding it?"

"Guarding… there is no one there…" The rest of the initiates began to murmur and stopped midway when all the Forced Blesseds walked down to an unheard command.

Una began to file down too.

"Ms Rao stop where you are and step aside. We need you to be a lookout."

Una stopped. She was fuming. She couldn't possibly have trained to just be a vanguard.

Gagan elbowed her as he walked past her. "*Chori* girl! You didn't really think you could be one of us!"

She ignored him and called out to Wolf, "Lookout for what?"

Wolf held his arms open wide. "For our audience of course. They will be making an appearance anytime now. An old langur should arrive sharpish."

Una squinted ahead. "A langur and a troop of rhesus monkeys and parrots are already here." *Not a be... thankfully.*

"Oh good, the rest will follow. Alert me straight away if a bear appears." Una lifted the visor of her cap. Even amidst an event such as this he was eavesdropping. *"Why a bear, Wolf?"*

"Because he is dangerous."

"I'll let you know."

"Be sure to."

Una contemplated the Blesseds in their animal and bird forms perched on the trees butting up against the invisible barrier keeping them in check.

Wolf, triumphant, commanded, "Wolf Gang, move in between the initiates! Lock arms! Move closer – there should be no gaps between you! Wolf Gang seniors, forward march!"

A resounding "Oss" was shouted.

"Eyes right," barked Wolf from the centre of the line-up.

In horror the trees came alive, with squawking, screaming, and howling. The cacophony of distress instantly took her to the day when she first arrived in Khamosh Valley… nearly a year ago… it was the same distressful clamour she had heard on her grandfather's roof on the day Meeru, Avi and Major had hastily called their visit to an end.

"So, you converted someone on the day I arrived…"

"Yes, in celebration of the elusive firstborn arriving from Manchester. If you must know."

Her innards knotted, and her heart began to pump with a louder beat. Her claws came through her hands and her incisors grew. Her snow leopard vision blurred and then…

"No, Una, you must calm down, it's not time yet."

They should have been Wolf's words, but they weren't. They came from the furry head of the langur. The voice belonged to the Sharman. The langur's face belonged to a fuzzy memory, of a dream, of such a face trapped underneath a taxi on a sharp bend. In her dream he had saved her. Saved her…

Una snapped back to the present day. With great effort she stabilised her animalistic instinct to not react to danger and by a fingernail's grasp kept herself human. It didn't make sense that the Sharman wanted her safe from exposure, Gopan was his great nephew after all. Surely if he knew he would command the Blesseds to hunt her down?

Her instinct was true. From nowhere she saw a shaggy body spring forth. The bear is here. Raging mad, he covered ground rapidly. In nanoseconds his two-inch-long teeth and three-inch-long claws swiped at one of the Forced Blesseds on the edge of the line-up. The invisible barrier kept him at bay. Defensively, the Forced Blessed drew his combat knife.

"Put it away, you'll tear the protective layer!"

A contorted sloth head growled contemptuously in her direction. She was sure it wasn't the Forced Blesseds he wanted to kill or maim.

Unperturbed, Wolf, centre of the line, guided his troops in military fashion to the edge of the jungle outside the property and stopped.

The male sloth bear veered his body and bounded away, no doubt in the hope of finding another entrance.

"That was close!" one of the initiates exclaimed.

Wolf turned around and all of the cohort did a hundred and eight degrees turn too.

"Do you know why sloth bears are the lowest on the chain despite their size?" Wolf asked the initiate to his right. "No?" Facing Una, he carried on, "In India there are more human deaths from sloth bears, and they don't even eat humans. They don't warn or disappear when they hear human activity, instead they sleep and lie in wait where humans might appear. When one tramples it awake, it mauls the human to death and then walks away."

The new initiates shifted nervously.

"So, if you see one don't engage, play dead on the ground. Easily fooled it will walk away."

"Oh, man! Getting to learn real hardcore jungle stuff." The initiate on the right was thrilled.

"Talking about what the bears don't eat… didn't Raul say something about our graduation meal being a true jungle feast we will love and appreciate after our initiation exercise?"

Una smirked despite how she felt. God knows what it was about boarders in general, they always talked and thought about food at every opportunity.

"Do you think he means a campfire meal? I love those," asked another initiate.

Una was stumped by their innocent chat in Wolf's presence. Clearly, they weren't yet ready to be part of a Forced Blessed army.

"Halt, initiates! Speak out of turn again and a mad sloth bear will not be the death of you, I will be!" The message was clear. Wolf expected them to do nothing but breathe and follow instructions. The brats were silenced. She could smell their fear and anxiety from where she stood. She feared for them. They really had no idea where their Pied Piper was leading them to. She had trained and bonded with these brats and thought hard of a way to stop them from their horrible fate.

"Incorrect! With a slim chance you might stop them momentarily but the Forced Blesseds will kill you. The young souls are doomed to this fate. Una, your empathy is unnecessary and too late."

"Sharman get out of my head! I don't know what your game is but I'm sure it's not about helping me. You want me dead. Give it up!"

"Is that what Wolf tells you? We are all Blessed so why would I want you or even Wolf dead? These youngsters, however, are not. Who knows if they have been prepared enough? From what I can tell they haven't been prepared at all. Anyhow, it seems Wolf is determined for us to find out soon enough."

"Why are you risking being heard? Wolf or Avi could be listening."

"They're not. I've put a wall around us, especially you. If Avi could hear you, you would've heard his angry requests to tear the protective shield with your knife and then he would..."

"Kill me? I know that! Sharman, get out of my head."

He did.

The first scream came as the Forced Blesseds in Wolf's line proceeded a step at a time and changed into their Blessed forms. They packed themselves so tightly that the new recruits couldn't break rank. Una stayed on the steps, watching the backs of the Forced Blesseds, with twisting and struggling bodies amongst them. The terror on the few turned faces of the young riddled her with horror. Human cells in her body responded in anguish. Bile filled her mouth. Her body wished to keel over but remained standing tall. Memories of how her human bones melted away and joined with others as they were repositioned, haunted her. The change in her spine had been the most dramatic. Yet she didn't register pain, strangely. These creatures evidently did. The worse screams came when their faces were squashed, flattened and sockets were moved and reshaped. Why didn't she feel pain? Had she been prepared for the transition by Gopan and his drinks or had her body changed over time on its own. The growth spurts which happened to her over several months happened instantly for them before her eyes.

Una could hear the shared feelings of disgust, horror and distress reflected in the animal calls from the Blessed camp. Red beaks opened and closed sharply letting out shrill cries, the rhesus monkeys screeched whilst they pulled the branches of pines almost to the ground, only for them to snap back. There were wolves on their side too but a different breed.

Una wasn't alone for long on her side. Before she could see or even hear, she could smell the taste of fresh animal blood. Her blood sang in euphoria.

Over several hours, one by one the new initiates and their leaders appeared from under the jungle canopy. The original Forced Blesseds were in their human forms but each one had created two more of their Blessed species. Yet there was something not quite right about them. Their eyes were duller and unlike the older Forced Blesseds, they all seemed off-centre. Had she looked like them too? Clumsy and awkward, unsure of how to use their bodies?

The initiates' bellies were swollen and bloated. She surmised they'd already eaten.

Real hunger grabbed her stomach… she wanted to go out and hunt. It was such an overwhelming desire. A chuckle sounded nearby and then a ghostly female whisper tickled her ear, "A few of the Blesseds know what you have become and what you have done. Una, think hard before you take any actions. They tend to have rippling consequences here."

Rosetta?

***

Una heeded the advice even though she didn't know whose it was and stayed in for dinner. As she prepared herself some pasta and chicken, she heard a knock on the front door of her private quarters.

"Grace, just use your key, I'm in the middle of cooking!"

"Ms Rao, can you please let me in. *Please!*"

"Me" was the frightened teenager who had missed her with

the laser camera.

"I wondered if you were cooking for yourself..."

The poor boy looked pale and without any words Una beckoned him in and passed her pasta bowl to him. He must have not eaten after he was converted because he ate whatever was left in the pan too.

If Una had known what was going to happen to Vibu, then she would have hidden him or something, but she made her second mistake in the jungle. Just hours after Rosetta's whisper. How was she to know that giving a boy pasta and chicken would be an action she would come to regret?

Chapter 36

Turncoat

The horror of the forced initiations was written all over the Blesseds' faces as they huddled together centrally between the pillars of the temple. Making it the right time for Avi to catch them unaware. With a long-drawn sigh, he broke their uneasy silence and drew their attention to himself. Their customary loathing expressions for him were replaced by confusion. He was the loose cannon that had killed a young wolf cub and desecrated the River Rule initiation of Gagan. Conversely, he was the only one out of all of them who tried to stop the unholy Forced Blesseds' initiations. Their confusion was perfect. It was to orchestrate their thoughts and change the course of the Blesseds before they recalled his sloth bear Blessed form and returned to loathing him instead of listening to him.

"I know who killed Gopan."

His stark words echoed between the temple pillars, igniting the anger of the Blesseds standing between them. Avi's eyes darted along the assembled body of people until he laid eyes on the Sharman, the cub, and his great uncle. All three of them, in contrast, were frozen with incredulity. The Sharman's expression was as expected, but his great uncles was decidedly odd. Holding his great uncle's eyes, he continued in a levelled tone, "My old friend, Una, killed Gopan hours after she was initiated into her Blessed form of a…"

His great uncle's face reddened, and his eyes bulged out as if he'd eaten chillies. He was livid but somehow contained it and said nothing.

"Surely my great uncle would want me to announce his grandson's murderer?" The Sharman didn't thought answer. Not surprised, Avi continued, *"I suppose not if he intends to blackmail and manipulate Rosetta in her Burfani guise."*

Avi glanced over to the cub. His knowing smile was wiped off his face when a furball came hurtling towards him. His instincts were quick as he fisted the cub's neck by the scruff whilst it was still in the air. "Burfani, even you can't interrupt and stop me from finishing my sentence."

An angry roar erupted.

"Put Burfani down NOW!" the Sharman shouted. Avi hesitated, the cub took the opportunity to struggle out of Avi's hold by scratching him before finding a high perch greater than an arm's-length away from Avi.

In the meantime, two Blesseds tried to grab hold of Avi but he was too strong for them and lifted them up.

"How dare you disrespect Burfani, especially after she chose to live with you!" one Blessed cried out.

"Your insolence is worthy of death," the other cried.

"If there will be a death, it will be Una's."

Avi dropped the two Blesseds. As he offered his hand to one to help him up, Rosetta continued.

"It is best that Una is killed by her close friend and the lowest grade of Blessed animal. What could be a more dishonourable death than that?"

Avi reeled from Rosetta's words. His cheeks over his taut face flared red.

Rosetta continued, "Knowing what Una's Blessed form is really not important to us because her forced transformation like all those we saw today away from the riverbed will grade her even lower than the new incapacitated wolf initiated by the River Rule last time."

By the time she finished he'd turned ghostly. Gobsmacked,

Avi searched the faces of the Blesseds. They were completely bewitched with Rosetta's words and looked at the cub adoringly.

"Una is ours to kill!"

Avi's great uncle came forward. He didn't address the cub based on how the crowd had felt about Avi challenging her and instead stood in Avi's space and talked directly to him. It was no accident that his back was to the rest of the Blesseds but the cub and Avi were able to read what he truly felt via his menacing eyes. Leaving Rosetta in no doubt that whatever he said was addressed to her too. "Don't even suggest that you will do it, Avatar. You are too close to Una and when she still lived with Dev you tried to warn her to leave the jungle and India on several occasions."

"Avi, I was there when you sent her a message through Kulkil," his great uncle whispered.

Avi said nothing.

Satisfied, the uncle triumphantly declared aloud, "You know I'm right; you aren't even trying to deny it!"

Avi was not going to let his great uncle win.

"Deny it? Why? My past friendship will lure her in. It's the very reason why it can only be me that kills her. I know her, she trusts me, and I am the only one who can draw her out and trap her easily."

Rosetta, aka Burfani, aka cub, laughed. "Avi is right. Hasn't he already shown his will when he tried to claw the protective membrane of Wolf's territory recklessly?" She looked at Avi's bloody, injured claw. "An injured bear is dangerous, but he is ours to use." Avi's expression remained impassive.

All in the assemble turned to Avi. After a long silence he said, "Thank you, I think? Surely you would like to instruct me on how you would like me to kill her too."

"How you do it is up to you, but when? Well, as soon as possible. You can see how Wolf is increasing his group numbers so easily," replied Rosetta. She then addressed the rest. "Before they get any larger, we must kill her."

"Kill! Kill..." Avi raised his hand and stopped the enthusiastic Blesseds before he had them all chanting or stomping.

"Just wait a moment please. We understand that we must avenge Gopan's death, but I think, Burfani, you must explain to us all how killing Una will impact Wolf and the Forced Blessed numbers." When everyone raised their heads for an explanation, Avi, not so innocently, asked, "Is there something you are not telling us, Burfani?"

Avi suppressed his smile as he watched the cub squirm momentarily before it returned to the sycophantic audience and asserted, "Avi will deliver, I will make sure of that. The Forced Blesseds see our delay as weakness and we must not show any. They won't expect Avi to act and I'm sure they don't know he is the lowly bear and not a Blessed snow leopard."

There she goes again! Avi tried not to suppress his anger. What sort of mother was she? She'd knifed him in his heart by calling him a lowly bear and then twisted it sharply when she said he wasn't a snow leopard.

Rosetta stoked the fire further with, "She killed Gopan on the first night she became a Blessed, so..."

"A Forced Blessed..." Avi shouted, interrupting her.

Nonplussed Rosetta continued, "So he will have to kill her in a fitting manner."

"Avi, just for you I will spell it out – hang, draw and quarter her, and then maul."

Did Rosetta really mean that? Avi stumbled backwards He wasn't sure what he expected from a mother, but Burfani/Rosetta wasn't it. He wanted to love her because he felt obliged to because of the big sacrifice she made, but that sensation had passed. His heart blackened with loathing towards her.

She knew it. Sure, she regretted it but Rosetta as the cub, as Burfani, had finally found her voice.

"There is no such thing as Forced Blesseds, only Blesseds... They can call themselves whatever they want but they are Blesseds, no doubt lesser Blesseds but like us they have to follow the Blessed rules to live in the jungle and by killing Una we will teach them that."

Avi hated speeches at the best of times. In disgust, he watched her preside over and even push her father aside.

"Since I have arrived, I know that some of the defected Blesseds have returned. I am honoured by their return and therefore decree that there will be no reprimands…"

Rosetta droned on but Avi had stopped listening and was looking at his nana.

Avi opened his channel to him. *"If she's pardoned them then, where are they? It's convenient that they and their families have disappeared."*

The Sharman remained silent.

"Nana! She's lying, isn't she?"

Avi had to hand it to Rosetta, the old Burfani was a good manipulator. No wonder she was able to read Wolf so well on the day of his escape.

His attention was brought back to the audience when he spotted Kulkil making his way slowly out of the temple.

Avi followed and caught up with him.

It didn't surprise Avi when Kulkil said, "Burfani seems to resent you, despite residing in your Ma for so long. Do you think she is angry with you because Rosetta allowed herself to be enslaved?"

Avi had momentarily forgotten that no one knew that Rosetta was in the cub's body and not Burfani. It helped that the old Rosetta everybody remembered was so different to the Burfani persona she projected, so no one suspected Rosetta.

"I don't know, but we need to get back in there before they think we are plotting something. Actually, I haven't said all I need, too."

***

He cleared his throat as he positioned himself once again opposite, but below, the cub's perch.

"Burfani, I agree with the punishment you have for Una, but I still have one question to ask you, if I may?"

Cornered, the cub nodded stiffly in agreeance.

"If Una deserves a horrendous death for killing Gopan when she was unaware of the consequences of her actions, which I'm sure she is wasn't, because I've not seen or witnessed a precedent of it myself, then…"

"Then… WHAT?" Rosetta was losing her patience.

"Then how is it that Wolf who has been here for a long period, who must know the rules, has not been killed for the deaths of Tommy and most significantly, Rosetta, my mother in whose body you resided for nearly nineteen years?"

Avi addressed the rest of the Blesseds, "Where were you? Surely you all should have avenged Burfani's previous incarnation."

The group was quiet. The Sharman dropped his head in pity. Frustrated, Avi shouted out, "Come on! You lost your leader, yet you did not do anything!"

All the tribesmen and Blesseds looked around at each other. They had no answers, or so he thought.

"It's quite easy to answer you." An elderly Blessed pushed the person in front of him aside so he could make direct eye contact with Avi. "Tommy and Rosetta were found dead on Major's and Dev's property and there is no clear picture of how they died.

"But still, how dare you blame us for doing nothing. You and the Sharman were her next of kin, yet you did not bring the unlawful deaths to the council and put a case forward to avenge them."

The Sharman interrupted, "Avi, it is you and I who have not sought justice for your mother."

"What?" Avi looked at them incredulously.

Another Blessed shouted, "Why do you think, we have been impatient with you and kept away."

Avi just stared at his nana suspiciously.

"It's true, Avatar. But before I am a parent, I am a Sharman. As Sharman I did not think it was time to act in vengeance. Gopan's family do want revenge so therefore it is your lot to kill her."

"But your leader was murdered…" Avi said, looking at the cub.

His mother was warning him through her borrowed eyes.

Avi didn't care, he still asked, "Is it because you did not care for your previous incarnation?"

"Enough, Avatar, you've said enough!" bellowed his great uncle.

Avi raised his hands. "I agree. But let me tell you, you are fooling yourselves. The truth is… that it's quite easy to kill someone who is an easy target, and not so easy if you don't know how to fight the Wolf."

"As an advisory to Burfani, I will say, Avatar is right!"

The Sharman agreed with him?

The Sharman continued in a level voice, "It's time for us to fight Wolf. Not just for bringing justice for the aforementioned but more importantly for the forced Blessing of innocent children without their consent. To stop him, we will have to pick up arms."

Burfani looked furious, the revenge situation had escalated beyond her control.

"We cannot go into battle so easily without scouting…" the great uncle spoke.

"Avi, now is the time for some of us to come clean," spoke Kulkil, for the first time.

Avi nodded. "I've already been scouting them."

"But we had an agreement, why would you do that?" a baffled voice shouted out.

Avi seized the moment to quench any other questions he might be asked. "You're lucky that I have. I've watched the Forced Blesseds training. They are skilled and aggressive. We will have to train hard to overcome their skill. You see, they don't train in their Blessed forms. Instead, like me, they are using army training. Training that I have continued with undercover."

"You've been doing what?" his great uncle shouted.

"Kulkil and several others have trained with the army." Avi changed his voice and commanded, "Raise your hands, soldiers."

The older Blesseds shook their heads in disbelief when three other individuals including Kulkil raised their hands and filed to fall behind Avi.

Chapter 37

Warning: Don't Feed the Animals

Grace tidied her breakfast things away.

"Just put the dishes down, the maid will be pleased with more dishes than the usual two," Una called out from her bedroom.

"Did you have company last night?" Grace asked, holding the pasta dish inquiringly as Una walked back into the living area.

Una wondered at Grace's suspicious tone.

Was I not meant to have company in this room?

"No, it was just me." Somehow, she thought Vibu would be in trouble if she told the truth.

"So why use different cutlery?"

Why was Grace scrutinising the dishes? Come to think of it, why was Grace having breakfast here? She normally ate at home with her parents. Was she being checked on? It was probably best not to say she had company. "Oh, I'd put my stuff in the sink already when I got second wind. What's wrong, Grace, why the third degree?"

Grace picked up the spoon the newly converted boy had used and smelt it. Screwing up her nose her steely eyes fell on Una. "Una, none of the boys came here, did they?"

Una still wasn't sure why she was lying but she found herself automatically shaking her head.

"Hmm." Grace clinked the spoon back in the sink. "Because if the boys do come, send them on their way. You can't feed them anything but raw food, is that clear?"

"But I was able to eat raw and cooked."

"That's because you were changing for some time and you are a firstborn, and older than them."

Meaning: the boys were the true forced Blesseds, weak and too young thus inadequately prepared for the Blessed community.

***

"The magic was weakened by the deranged sloth's claw swipes. He almost tore through it. Only pure hatred can do that, you said," remarked Raul.

Wolf tightened his grip on the rails above the gymnasium as he watched the training below. He had not believed that a Blessed would read his magic barrier and nearly match it. "The Blesseds don't work on their hatred so have not been able to challenge us on equal grounds. We need to be on guard while the transformation for the fledglings is complete and then we need to strike."

"I thought they would come for Gopan's killer, but it didn't happen, yet something has changed. The sloth's strike shows that the Sharman is no longer in control. If not him, then who is it?"

"Could it be Avi? We haven't seen his Blessed self yet."

"Are you sure?"

"There hasn't been another Blessed snow leopard since you finished off Rosetta."

"Yet there has been an attack by her son."

"You…" Wolf could see the penny had dropped. Stunned, the second-in-command shook his head. "How did the Sharman allow it? Oh, man! That explains the pure hatred. Do you think it would cut through if he knew what Una was, and what she was capable of?"

Wolf stared down at Una's streaked hair from his bird's-eye view. She was late. As if she knew she was being talked about she looked up at that very instant. He pushed back from the railing.

Was she enough to get him what he needed? She had to be until he could shake the Blesseds' belief in snow leopards.

***

Una returned her gaze to the fast motion of swinging and striking arms and legs working through the routine gym exercises. What she had dreaded most since she awoke that morning was what she faced. An increased number of Forced Blesseds. Scrutinising the scoreboard and then the sparring partners, Una's gritted teeth opened wide as her anger turned to bewilderment. The older Forced Blesseds were no longer leading each activity. Some were easily outdone by their young protégées in their areas of expertise.

It wasn't that their accuracy had slipped it was more that the leaders were nervous whilst giving instructions.

Una's name was not up for sparring with anyone as she was late. She began to leave through the double doors of the gymnasium when she heard Wolf's bark from above in the gallery.

"Don't even think about it. Trainee or not the last person to arrive for training has to clean up." Next, a skipping rope fell at her feet from the gallery above. She heard laughter from the gallery after she shoved two fingers up in the air.

She'd have to wait for the others. Pissed off, she grabbed the skipping rope and began ten three-minute rope jumps and between them she took her frustration out by doing burpees. Still frustrated before her cool down rope jumps, she sat on a bench, placed, and cupped her hands on either side of her thighs. Soon she had walked her legs out and was suspended on her hands. She lowered herself in front of the bench and just as she pushed her back up until her arms were fully extended, Una noticed the bottom of the scoreboard. There was only one who still remained the same in ability after their transformation and that was the previously top ranked trainee, Vibu, who according to the scoreboard was now the lowest ranking by a large margin.

Perspiring, Una collapsed on the ground, hitting her head on the bench. It had to be a bad omen.

You are right to be worried, it was foolishness that caused his demise.

***

Una burst into the boys' dorms. It was empty. Una glanced at the wall-mounted clock. She would have to wait till the afternoon to see if Vibu were okay. She prayed he was, and astonishingly he was when she was later summoned to the boys' dormitory. Her hackles settled down as squeals of laughter and mirth floated through the dormitory. Several of the boys were drawing caricatures of each other whilst others were drawing animals seriously at tables. Amidst them all, Wolf sat on the dorm's table, cross-legged, as he madly sketched Gagan's face between ten second stares.

"Hey, come and join us!" Una was caught out by the boyish and light tenor of Wolf's voice. She nodded in agreeance and tentatively stepped behind Wolf to peer at his artwork. She looked up at Gagan and smiled.

"What's the smile for?" Gagan forgot his place and leapt forward to snatch the sketchpad off Wolf.

Wolf flicked the sketchpad shut covering the caricature Una had seen and threw it to Gagan who opened it and smiled. "Ah! It was an admiring smile. I knew you would make me look good." He flicked the pad around to show Una. Instead of the caricature, she was staring at a Celtic tattoo design of a hyena which strangely enough hinted at Gagan in the curved strokes.

Una felt a swift movement behind her and before she could flick Wolf's hand away, he caught hers and thrust a balled-up paper into it. Una caught Wolf's wink. The tension from earlier dissipated from her body.

She dropped the caricature in his lap and sat on the chair Gagan had vacated, in front of Wolf.

"Do I get a personalised tattoo too."

"It will take a little longer, I've not created one of you that I'm happy with in my existing catalogue." Wolf looked up thoughtfully from his sketchbook. He was already drawing something.

"Catalogue? Show me."

"Guys, chuck me my catalogue."

Una had never seen this side of Wolf before. *Perhaps art was his sanctuary.*

"Can't be stuffy all the time, can I?"

Una neatly caught the thick sketchbook flying towards her. She didn't know what she had expected, but there were hundreds of beautiful Celtic tattoo designs. They were very unique, not the usual ones she saw in Ireland or England. These were styled with the Indian jungle animals and fauna in mind. The one that caught her eye was several sketchy leopards in motion. Disappointingly though they were of the common leopard rather than a snow leopard.

"Did you study art."

"Art, particularly Celtic art to back-up my interest in World, Indian and British history and English literature."

"Why Celtic art?"

"Why not? You've already commented on how my formations are Roman. Do you remember the Greek historians writing that, then they feared the Celts with tattoos? They were written up to be barbaric and illiterate but, on the plus, they were seen as fearless and having magical strength. The Celtic women in blue paint baring their tits at the Romans had them more scared."

"Don't expect me to go that far."

"Spoilsport."

"Can I create my own? I dabble with art too."

Wolf handed her his sketchpad and pencils, and Una quickly began to doodle a snow leopard using the Celtic knots she had studied in primary school.

Engrossed, Una murmured, "I suppose the tribal tattoos are based on Indian mythology?"

"Not really, they're based on Himalayan artwork influenced by tribes from neighbouring countries."

"Really?"

"Who etches the tattoos?"

"I do."

Una put her pencil down in surprise.

"Fortunately for me the Blessed who converted me was the tribe's tattooist. I was given a choice of occupation in the tribe and I chose to be a tattoo artist. Lucky for me it was a trade I learned easily. After a short time of learning how to survive the jungle, I left to use my new abilities, skills and knowledge of their greatest weaknesses and moved back home."

"What is their greatest weakness?"

"They are trusting and forgiving, which reminds me…"

The temperature dropped in the room. Old Wolf was back.

"Those of you who have agreed on your tattoo designs line up in the medical room. Let's get going. Don't even consider getting in line if you are not showered and clean." Ominously, he added, "Don't forget to bring your scorecards with you."

Una packed away her sketch to leave the boys to it but was stopped by Raul.

"Una, Wolf wants you to come watch."

It was nearly twilight when Vibu's turn arrived. Several times she had caught the boy's desperate eye as he lined up. He had been reluctant to come up the line and several times returned to the end of the queue instead of moving up. Was this how animals felt as they were lined up for the slaughterhouse?

Wolf made a great show of being surprised when he read Vibu's scores out. He hadn't read the previous ones. "How could you have dropped your score instead of increasing it?" Vibu bit his lip. "Who was your leader in the initiation?"

"You," Vibu whispered.

"Speak up, Vibu."

Fear turned Vibu's dark skin pale. "You."

"Me?"

Wolf looked confused.

"If I took you then you should have been top of the leader board as you are meant to take on my skills aptitude."

Una was shocked. *Could it be that Wolf was not as strong and skilled as the others?* The whispers begun and all new recruits looked at their leader in an odd way.

"Did you follow everything I taught you?"

"I think so…"

"Think carefully, did you follow through everything I asked you to do?"

"I think so… I mean yes." Vibu was visibly shaking. Una stood to intervene.

Grace stopped her and held her arms back.

"Can all those who were converted by me come forward." Two lads came forward, Una recognised them as the top scorers. Wolf read their progress out to the others. Their scores before the conversion were a good margin lower than Vibu's.

Wolf walked from behind the patient's chair over to Vibu.

"Vibu, actually these scores might not reflect your ability. You could have been unwell. Don't worry, the fool proof test can happen now."

Darkness had fallen, all the new Forced Blessed fledglings began to painfully transform before the unchanging seniors' eyes. Even Gagan had conquered changing on demand and remained in human form.

All the fledglings changed into their respective Forced Blessed forms. All except for Vibu. His transformation was not stable. Wolf changed into his Blessed Form and circled Vibu's unstable form.

"Now, isn't this an interesting situation. When you disappeared I wondered if your oversized ego had given you enough fool's confidence to make your own kill but it seems not only did you not make a kill, which would have been okay, you would have just been hungry, but you actually went to the school's kitchens to eat. Didn't you?"

"No, I didn't, I promise."

"Of course, you didn't. You're right, the kitchens were closed at the time. So, in that case, Vibu, can you tell me where you got the food that diluted you?"

One of the seniors brought in and placed Una's pan and

spoon she had cooked pasta in the previous night, in her arms. Una dropped them. Wolf leapt forward and easily overcame her human self and pushed her to the ground.

With his Wolf body lying heavy on her lungs, Una croaked out. "We didn't know."

"Wrong, Una, you didn't know, he did. It was drummed into him."

"Wolf let him go, he won't do it again," Una gasped.

"Una, do you remember the two weaknesses I learnt?"

"Trust and forgiveness." Una tried to push Wolf off frantically, only to have him scratch her and then hold her neck in his mouth. "Wolf, no!!"

There was a scream, but it wasn't from Una. "I'm sorry I didn't like the food; I couldn't bring myself to make a kill. I'll learn." Vibu's form tried to back away from Wolf.

Wolf let go of Una's bleeding neck. "Didn't like the food? Perhaps you would prefer to be the food?"

Next, he looked down into Una's barely opened eyelids and muttered, "Have you never read the notice – please don't feed the animals."

Una heard a horrendous scream, gnarling mouths and blacked out.

Chapter 38

Action in No Action

"Is anyone near, Una?"

Una prised her eyelids open. "No," she croaked.

"Ssh! I'm in your head."

Una wasn't in the mood for the invasion in her head. *"What's with you, Sharman?"*

"Una, work against your healing ability."

"No! Why would I harm myself? That to for a Blessed enemy?"

"You mustn't let your neck heal easily. They will confirm you are unlike them."

"Unlike them?" Una remembered Wolf being suspicious of her when she did that. She needed to keep Wolf's attention from herself.

"Exactly."

Una tried to think of blood oozing, but she could feel a thin layer of blood congealing over the gaps.

"How exactly do I stop my neck from healing?"

"By poking your wound and worsening it to keep it ripe."

Her neck was caked in dried blood. *Did wolf really want to take her out and stopped himself in time?*

"I don't think so, but he must think you are out of control. Una, you need to rein yourself in."

Una dug her nails into the dried blood, causing it to disperse over her clothes as she dug her fingers deep into her neck. Fresh blood assaulted her and dripped onto her pillow. She rubbed her hands clean on the sheets she lay on.

"I'm not planning to come to your side."

"You will come to realise there are no sides. That being said, have you chosen to be on Wolf's side?"

Una ignored the Sharman's question. *"You can't think there are no sides after what you witnessed."*

"So, are you on Wolf's side?"

"No, I'm not on any one's side. I just want to free my father."

"You know where he is, so why don't you take him and run."

Visions of past cruel acts she had witnessed came to mind.

"Your fear is greater than your desire. You won't be able to do it."

Visions of Wolf torturing her father mercilessly made her whole body tremble despite the increased heat as her body furiously knit her wounds again.

"You are healing fast again; you need a little longer."

God! She was even scared of being caught because she healed quickly. She needed some control and reopened her wounded neck.

"Sharman, you obviously think I am valuable too, based on how you protected my identity against your own. Why?"

"The desire and fears of my own people who sold the valley land to the army, who in turn sold it to your grandfather and Major, have brought destruction to our community and jungle. I want you to bring peace."

"For that you need me?" Una wasn't buying it. *"You want to save the jungle and Wolf wants revenge on you and Avi and any relatives."*

"We need your help?"

"How can I help?"

By using you to embrace the destruction of the so-called status quo.

"You are just like Wolf."

"Perhaps our desire for a united Blessed is the same but this is not the time to discuss it. Perhaps you should discuss what you need."

"My single desire is to cause a diversion, a big diversion for me to get my dad out. Like a..."

Both thoughts shouted "*battle*" in unison.

Somehow the words removed her guilt about the training she did with the aim to maim and even kill the Blesseds. Once she freed her father, death would be a happy end for her. Her supposed enemy had just liberated her. She was no longer trapped in guilt and fear.

A shadow appeared outside the medical room window. "She's still not healed, and you thought she could be Blessed." Grace and someone else were just outside the medical room.

Una quickly slipped her bloodstained hands under the cover. How would she explain the blood under her fingernails?

Eyes closed, Una heard the door opening, footsteps but only one pair leading up to her and then she felt hands gently move her hair away from her neck.

"Why do you push me all the time? I never intended to let you bleed as much as this. I don't want you to fear me but stand with me. We both want to save people from our fate. Don't we?"

Wolf left the medical room, silently closing the door behind him.

Una opened her eyes. *Save people my ass!*

Chapter 39

Disarm to Arm

Just before dark surrendered to the first light of dawn, Avi and Kulkil emerged from the thicket on the edge of the remote village where the non-Blessed tribes' families lived. Avi placed himself between the long, narrow mud houses. Meanwhile, Kulkil scaled one of the roofs and slung forward a goat skin drum he'd been carrying on his back. Avi gave him a wink. And while the sun was still shy of the sky, Kulkil raised his arms and slapped the sides of the drums.

Bang! Bang! Bang!

Angry villagers rushed out of their front doors in dribs and drabs. They couldn't see Avi in the dark shadows but Kulkil was silhouetted by the rising sun.

"What is the meaning of this, Kulkil?"

"Stop before we break your arms and legs!"

Avi raised his hand, halting Kulkil who instantly stopped and saluted him. Baffled, the villagers collectively turned to see who he had saluted. Like iron ores repelled, the villagers left a clear circle of space around Avi.

"I would treat Burfani's special envoy, that's me, with respect."

Avi expected laughter, loud protests, or silence but what he didn't expect was for them to turn their backs on him and walk back into their houses.

"Wait, at least hear what I have to say," Avi shouted out in frustration.

Nothing.

"Where are you going," shouted Kulkil as he slipped down one of the roofs.

He tried to grab one of his friends. Instead he was pushed to the ground.

"Kulkil, you have many friends in your brethren but stop hanging out with this sloth loser. In fact, GET HIM OUT of here NOW."

They all left.

Silence befell the village.

"Should I bang my drum again?" Kulkil said as he slithered down to the ground where Avi had remained standing all the time.

"No, give them time," Avi said. He stretched out his hand to Kulkil. "They might have closed their doors but that doesn't mean they aren't watching our every move. "We'd better show them what Burfani's special envoys are capable of."

Kulkil pushed away Avi's hand and stood unaided. "Don't you think you are over doing it with the envoy thing."

"Nope, it's time to learn from Wolf and put on a show of defiance."

"Show? Like in…?"

Before Avi could even position himself Kulkil came running at him, kicking his legs in the air. Thud! With very little movement Avi brought him down.

"That's the spirit but remember we are just demonstrating." Avi moved to help him up. Kulkil rolled away and did a kick up movement and brought Avi down.

First came Kulkil's friends who revealed themselves as having army training and them some others. They didn't join in, they simply watched.

"Let's recruit them now," Kulkil whispered as he tried to keep Avi's head in a hold.

Avi overturned the move and had Kulkil flat on the ground again. "No, let's give them time to think."

Kulkil narrowly lost the sparring session. As Avi walked back he thought he should have let Kulkil win in front of his friends. It was never too late to show off Kulkil's special skills. Avi picked up the abandoned drum and stick and hurled it at Kulkil who had walked a few metres ahead. At lightning speed, he turned and with quick reflexes, necked it, so the drum was across his shoulders and the stick was in his right fist. Neither of them turned around but they knew if they did, they would find mouths and eyes wide open.

***

The next day, the two envoys appeared in the village at the same hour and took up the same positions. This time when the drums were sounded all of Kulkil's friends came out. Using very few words, Avi lined them up and demonstrated some simple movements. They were impressively nimble and were quick to learn.

On the third day before the drum could be beaten, the volunteers from the previous day all came out and lined up. Before leaving Kulkil gave out a bundle of regular army camouflage which appeared in a cardboard box on the temple steps.

There were the exact number of combat uniforms as there were volunteers – funny that. Kulkil had been surprised but Avi suspected a particular langur had spied on them and left the uniforms. Avi's and Kulkil's uniforms had subtle differences from the others.

On the fourth day Avi and Kulkil found the village lit up with lights and their volunteers in their ensemble teaching other older men in their twenties and thirties the moves.

"I'm not carrying uniforms for them all," Kulkil moaned. Avi shoulder butted him, he wasn't fooled. He could see the pride with which his friend perused his friends and brethren.

On the fifth day the teenage girls and slightly older ones came out. Avi shook his head. He had more than enough volunteers and he didn't want any weak chicks.

Just as he moved to turn around and start the training a knife landed between his feet. A girl came forward and although she didn't look anything like Meeru she reminded him of her.

Soon they were teaching Avi dagger throwing and how to wear their tribal wear as well. He could see the value of the free movement the skirts afforded but felt a little too exposed especially with the keen eyes of some of the new female warriors.

"What would Una say, when she notices all the girls swooning over you." Kulkil playfully elbowed him in his ribs.

Avi grabbed Kulkil's shoulders and flung him to the ground, "Nothing… she'll have nothing to say." Avi straddled him next. "She'll be dead as soon as I lay my eyes on her."

"Avi, you must know she was pushed to it. You told me that."

Avi firmly placed his palm on Kulkil's mouth. "I'm not killing her for Gopan. I'm killing her for what she took from me."

Kulkil bit Avi's hand. "What did she take from you? Don't be such a loser."

Red mist took over Avi and he grabbed Kulkil's neck with his unbitten hand and squeezed whilst whispering something in his ear. Kulkil struggled to get out of his grasp. Kulkil's eyes bulged. Avi stilled. The villagers were staring at them both, aghast. Hastily Avi removed his hand from Kulkil's neck, stood from his kneeling position, dragged his friend up, brushed him down and in a monotone voice said, "Concentrate on your task."

The lessons were soon taken over by seasoned army veteran tribesmen from the Indo–Pakistani wars. Freed from instructing, Avi trained with the gutsy girl, Leela, who had thrown the knife at him. At the end of one of his training sessions with her he paused as he picked his knife off the straw filled dummy that he had affectionately named Kulkil. Kulkil himself had shaped its hair to mimic his own hairstyle. Sadly, Kulkil had evaded Avi and the Blessed training since Avi had held him in a stranglehold. Avi knew he had humiliated and hurt his friend but hadn't banked on him not coming back even if it was only for the jungle. Kulkil was deeply passionate about saving the jungle and the Blessed way. Hadn't he pestered Avi to convince the Sharman to initiate him at seventeen for that very reason?

"You didn't have to destroy the target," exclaimed the girl training with him.

Avi was frustrated and took it out on the unsuspecting girl. "Knife throwing is all well and good, but where can I inflict the most damage?"

"I think I can help you with that." The girl picked up a conch and sounded it.

Several army personnel and Dr Verma arrived.

Avi was shocked. "Dr Verma, Dada's fellow conspirer?"

Dr Verma smiled. "I'm firstborn Blessed but due to my scholarship education like Kulkil's I was able to become an army doctor. I was sent to spy on the property developers and gain the confidence of both Major and Dev. This allowed me to make sure they would call on me if you were ever ill and not some other doctor. Who do you think told Meeru how to look after you?"

"I thought it was Wolf."

Dr Verma was seemingly affronted by Avi's explanation.

"In that case why did you call me and the others?"

"It's not enough to train our skills. We need knowledge of the areas that will allow for maximum damage, so the Forced Blessed bodies don't have time to heal. I want this region to come back to harmony, but even I know it won't happen without facing the Forced Blesseds."

Dr Verma agreed to help the Blesseds in their training and soon, along with Avi, they learnt the places where a quick knife movement would wound badly and heal slowly.

While it was wonderful that the Blessed could self-heal it was annoying that they were difficult to kill. While the purpose wasn't to hurt most of them but make them back off, Avi just wanted two Blesseds – Wolf and Una – dead.

Kulkil did not come with Avi again to the village. The villagers now fully trusted Avi but still Avi missed his friend. Once when he came back from his scouting sessions in the Forced Blessed side, he thought he saw Kulkil skulking around the area. He was looking in the bushes. When he caught Avi looking at him he ran.

Avi pretended to lose him on the chase. When Kulkil was sure he wasn't being followed Avi was stunned to see him enter an abandoned hut. He heard someone call out to Kulkil. "The teacher's here, did you get the books?"

"I couldn't get there. Avi saw me and chased me," Kulkil answered.

"Did he see you come in."

"No, I lost him."

Later, Avi went to the bushes where Kulkil had been. Avi found several entrance exam books for St Anthony's school.

Six weeks later, Avi was not surprised to hear Kulkil had left.

Chapter 40

Una Meets an Anomaly

Una smudged out her latest attempt of her Celtic tattoo and placed her sketchbook down beside her on the dorm bed vacated by the "Dilute" as he was called now. Part of her thought he was lucky to be alive to be named, but then she remembered the morning after she woke to find him sobbing alone on the bed she now occupied. She had stupidly sat next to him and he screamed, "Don't feed me, please get away, no food please." He had shrunk away from her and his fellow dorm-mates. In the end, he was manhandled by the night watchmen and transported to the school's hospital.

A month later during a rainy night, she spotted him from the library window as he was carried in the arms of a watchman into a car accompanied by his parents perhaps. Under the lamplight she could see his huge eyes darting around. His wasted body convulsed when he looked up at the library window. She shifted into the shadows, away from his sight. The watchman struggled but managed to put him in the back seat with his guardian, his mother perhaps. Emptiness filled Una from that day on. The official story was that he was suffering from extreme anorexia.

Since the day of his departure she took to spending the afternoon on his abandoned bed, keeping her stupid and thoughtless action fresh in her mind. No heroics or even innocuous actions did she take without being totally present. The Forced Blessed newbies still admired her as some kind of a hero after the assessment, but her daily squatting on Dilute's bed when she had a perfectly good room served to help them focus on what could happen if they befriended her.

"Your continued martyrdom is very amusing but get off the bed now. We need it."

Una looked around. *"Why?"* Una worked hard to show no emotion in her demeanour or thought voice. *"A new recruit?"*

"Yes, clever girl! Luckily, he already understands the implications of cooked food and has already begun his transformation."

Had Una missed something? She was sure she was told all the physically fit boys had already been recruited from the possible batches. He had to be a new boy. Since it was midterm that could only mean…

"Have you poached a Blessed?"

"Clever girl! It's someone you know."

Her animal instincts picked up on Wolf's scent. He was nearing. She picked up her sketchbook and began to doodle some Celtic fish and crosses, her "go to" when she couldn't think of anything else to draw.

"Well, here is your dormitory and this is your bed." Wolf spoke with such charm. "You might even see a familiar face here," he said, louder.

"I can smell you arriving. Seriously, you don't need to shout!" Una shrugged her shoulders, Wolf was trying a little too hard to draw a physical reaction from her, it was only fair to give him one.

Una's hand stilled with the charcoal in hand as she peered up from her sketches of Celtic symbols with a quizzical look. She didn't need to fake it.

Her insides squeezed, restricting her breath. She had expected to see anyone, even Avi. She worked hard to rein herself from staring at the sullen face of Kulkil.

Una used the now old hat trick of using different images from her conveyor belt of past experiences to still her facial expressions and her thoughts by plucking an image that would help her realistically portray the emotion she wished to feel. She had also learnt not to make the images public. In this case the expression was "lack of recognition". Wolf smiled. He wasn't fooled.

"Oh, I'm sorry, Kulkil, it seems she doesn't recognise you… perhaps it will come to her or perhaps she wasn't as observant as she thought."

Una retrieved another emotion from the "thought conveyor" – confusion.

Wolf raised his eyebrow. "Perhaps you are not as observant as you would like to think you are – Kulkil says he used to spy on you, the OTHERS and the Forced Blesseds, for the Blesseds."

Una replied, "With so many Peeping Toms it's just as well I was oblivious – he was obviously more subtle than you were on the steps that day."

Wolf's lips thinned as his eyes narrowed.

"You are quite right of course. Kulkil, tell her how Avi feels about her?"

Kulkil didn't say a word. Instead he looked intently at Una and placed a cold object in her palm and then closed her fingers.

Una slowly unravelled her fingers. Her mother's locket!

She shot her eyes at Kulkil, saw something swiftly pass in his eyes before he returned to the sullen face. Una prised the object open. On one side there was a picture of her parents with her beaming away. It was taken on her fourteenth birthday. Una no longer looked remotely like her fourteen-year-old self. The innocence was in complete contrast to her now. On the other side there was a picture of her face taken on the day of Meeru's wedding. It had to be the smaller version of her portrait that Meeru painted.

"It seems he still has the hots for you."

Una blushed a little. Finally, Wolf drew a reaction from her and so of course he had to milk it. "It also proves my point about Meeru's betrayal. I would recognise those brush strokes anywhere, they belong to Meeru."

"This boy could have found my locket, when I transformed."

"That was my first reaction too. However…" Wolf then turned to Kulkil and nudged him. "Go on, tell her what you told me; it will sound so much more authentic coming from you."

"The picture is a photocopy of a miniature painting that Avi has. I got the painting photocopied. He always wore it when he was in his human guise. I safeguarded it when he was in animal form."

"But what is the importance of the locket to you, Wolf… don't tell me… on the strength of it you've included this person in your 'Wolf Gang'." Una made speech marks in the air as she said the words "Wolf Gang".

Una gave Kulkil the dirtiest look ever. How could he betray Avi like this? It was obvious Kulkil was his only friend. But then who was she to judge? Exactly how many times had she betrayed Avi?

"It signifies many things, but the main ones are that: it shows that Kulkil was close to Avi, enough for Avi to trust him and then it shows he still carries a 'torch' for you." This time Wolf did the speech marks in the air.

"Through which you plan to manipulate him."

Una put the necklace around her neck again, nodded to thank Kulkil for it, and went back to drawing, hoping they would walk away.

When she looked up, they were still there. Kulkil was holding his suitcase in his hands.

Wolf pointed at the bed.

"Oh, you want me to vacate the bed. You should have said that before."

Una moved to the long table in the middle where the boys sat if they wanted to play cards, study, or write. The silence was unnerving when Wolf left.

From under her fringe she could see Kulkil struggling with all the bedding. Tribal boys obviously didn't know how to make beds like the good old Victorians did with the top sheet folded back on itself and then tucked in. The not so poor thing had got himself all muddled in the sheets, providing much entertainment for the rest of the dormitory. Una gave in, walked to his bed, and began to pull the sheet off him in defiance. She pushed him – not as gently as she thought she had. He practically landed in the laundry basket. She didn't care for his sensibilities. He didn't either and came back, taking quiet directions from her.

As Una left, the other boys jeered at him. She thought to go back and say something. But she decided traitors didn't need her help. Still, she hesitated outside Sid's door. She shook her head and carried on to the gymnasium to train.

Just as she was finishing her training session, she noticed several bloody noses as the boys came in – Kulkil barely had a scratch on him.

Whatever animosity had gone on before due to his backward and poor status, was over. The others were happy to spar with him and it was easy for Una to recognise that whatever happened in the dorm after she left had banished the other boys' mistrust of Kulkil.

While the equipment and training moves were alien to him, he was a quick and enthusiastic learner. His bow skills were excellent and superior to anyone else's in the Forced Blessed camp. Una could only surmise all the pebble throwing he did must have held him in good stead.

Finished with observing him Una decided she was done with the climbing wall and jumped down from a height without thinking. She heard a gasp. It was Kulkil.

"Oh, she does that with such ease, don't be shocked."

Kulkil looked like he had seen a ghost.

"And another one bites the dust, don't be shocked. Ms Rao is excellent at climbing and many other arts. She's not perfect though…"

Everyone else in the gym joined in, "She sucks at aiming!"

They all giggled and began to exchange stories of how her darts had gone everywhere and how everyone feared for their life when she practised with them.

"Luckily, she doesn't practice with us anymore."

"It's a shame… I could have exchanged my knowledge of dart throwing for climbing. I can climb trees fast but not the cliff surface as quick as that."

Una felt she'd entertained the boys enough and left. She

showered and for the first time distracted from her guilt over Vibu she lay in her bed, twirling the locket. Longing to see her parents again, she opened the clasp. It sprung open and released the photocopied picture of her. Annoyed, Una picked it up and threw it at the wastepaper basket. Predictably she missed. It landed upturned on the tiled floor near her bed. Una leaned forward to scrunch the picture into a ball but stopped when she saw some black squiggles on it. The squiggles were a binary code.

01101101 01101001 01101110 01100101

Una was sure Wolf would have seen the binary code and translated it. Later, when she worked it out, she knew why he was so sure about Avi's feelings for her. The code spelt the word MINE.

She doubted if that was true anymore for him, but she hoped and placed the miniature picture back in the locket.

Una wore her chain and patted it down under her clothes. The familiar motion would no longer remind her of her mum first but would remind her of Avi instead. She remembered him doing the same when he had it in his breast pocket on his combat jacket. It made her feel closer to him, but she wasn't sure if that was a great thing. She really ought to focus on finding and saving her dad and nothing else. Thinking of Avi, her dad and her mum intermittently she drifted to sleep.

***

Una leapt out of her window after dusk in her human form and headed for the Modern Ruin. She was sure Sid and Grace were in the dormitories and Wolf was most likely to be with his new recruits, helping them with their hunt, familiarising them with the jungle as he had done with her in the early days. If she were to ever rescue her father this was the best opportunity. On reaching the side of the house, she jumped high, grabbed a branch, and scuttled up the tree closest to Sid's house.

She stopped at a branch when Kulkil shone a torch on her from his perch.

"No one could climb like you unless they had feline blood. I saw you playing with the cat on the roof but didn't think much of it. Is your Blessed form that of a wildcat?"

Una replied, "A bit better than that, my Blessed form is that of a common leopard."

Kulkil smiled. "What else could you be. Una, why you are going to Wolf's residence instead of somewhere to feed. I hope it's not to look for your father."

Una stopped in her tracks.

"How do you know?"

"Because Avi scouted for your father after reading an article."

So, he didn't tell Kulkil that he had met me in the library. Interesting.

She had forgotten about that article. Is that why her grandfather's house had been in darkness. Had they fled or were they "assisting the authorities"? Una didn't care which one.

"I will not tell you what to do but at the moment your father is safe where he is. Gopan's family know of his existence and are looking for revenge plus he could be hidden next time, somewhere you will never find him. At least not alive."

"What do you mean?" Una was shocked.

"There are many takers for carrion meat in the jungle. It doesn't take long to clear evidence."

"How do I know that you are not working with Gopan's family."

"You don't, but that would make me very stupid because I've just come from Wolf's place after telling him I knew of your father's whereabouts."

"You told Wolf that the Blesseds knew?"

"Yup, had to prove my new allegiance. For my honesty and loyalty, he even let me see your father."

He stopped to see if what he just said registered with Una.

"How is he…?" Una shook.

"He is a captive but safe."

"What else did you tell Wolf, Kulkil! Did you tell him about Avi's Blessed sloth bear self?"

Kulkil began to nod and then in a shocked voice asked, "How

do you know that was him?" Kulkil pushed Una down. "Except for three of us, the Blesseds didn't know until after that evening."

Una didn't know what to say and then quickly covered with, "It had to be him because no one would break the rules. He's already done it once when he killed the wolf cub."

Una picked herself up and this time shoved Kulkil. "You and Avi were really close. Why are you giving Avi's secrets away?"

Kulkil said nothing and began to walk up the steps leading to the school grounds.

Una ran and caught up with him. "Why are you doing this to Avi?"

"Avi?"

"Having just met you twice I could tell how close you were to him."

"Close? I thought he and I were close too. Una, you became a Forced Blessed at seventeen, but he wouldn't even try to persuade his nana, the Sharman, to let me go through the transformation early..." Kulkil stopped, clearly still upset about it. "Transformation before eighteen can obviously happen because it has happened to you. This alone shows how weak the Blessed are. Weak due to their set ways. Expect more of us Blessed cubs here – I won't be the only deflection."

Una admired Kulkil. According to what Kulkil had said, he was a braver and stronger individual than her. She had assisted the underage Forced Blesseds to train and survive their transformation, but at no point did she rebel or object.

"So, you are just joining the Forced Blesseds because you are rebelling your ancient establishment?"

"I've watched the Forced Blesseds from above and have watched them train. I admire their techniques and their single-mindedness."

Una shook her head sadly.

"You can stop that. Your reason for wanting to stay here to save just one person, your father, is hardly noble compared to mine: of saving our Blessed existence and jungle? It really irks me to see the OTHERS walk around as if they own the land. There's talk of more land being sold by Major. We have to fight them but the Blesseds won't. The Forced Blesseds are right, even if it means we have to challenge the Blesseds. Especially as they will be leaderless when the Sharman is discarded as weak by his own."

"There is Avi…" Una remembered his Blessed form… oh!!

"Now that they all know his sloth bear form, no one trusts Avi… Even if they accepted his sloth form which they can't and won't, no one could predict him. Plus, he stays away from everyone, sometimes even from me."

Kulkil's voice petered away and then it piped up again with, "Actually, Una, I haven't told Wolf this because I stupidly feel protective towards you. But stay away from Avi, block him from your thoughts because, and it really hurts to tell you this, he spends all day and evening looking for a chance to kill you."

"I know," Una purred. Purred! She had to get out. Out in the open, in the twilight her animal instincts became stronger.

"I don't understand why he hates you so much… I know…"

"Gopan," she cut in under her breath, trying to sound as human as she could.

"Maybe, but I know him, and it's got to be more personal than that."

Una stepped into in the shadows of the foliage. Oblivious to Una's need to hide, Kulkil continued.

"It could be that your fortunes have been reversed even though you both started alike, abandoned youth and all that? Funnily, both of you are the same yet the difference is that you are revered, and he is shunned."

No answer.

"Hey, where did you go?"

Chapter 41

Ambush

It was confirmed that Kulkil was on the Forced Blessed side by the lookouts. He was sure to have told Una to stay away from the ledge because, if not, why had she not turned up there? Avi was in a bad mood. He had remained in human form at this hour just to do the job he was meant to do before Wolf had ruined his plans with his diabolical initiations.

A cold sweat began to form over his brow as he approached the Forced Blessed territory. On umpteen occasions he had crept up on her after she had sated her hunger and laid under the ledge. Thus, on umpteen occasions he had failed. He smiled a smile that did not reach his eyes. A smile of longing, bitterness, and murder. *He had to finish her today while she was still awake. In her leopard form she had slept without fear of anything to hide, she was beautiful and for him, even more difficult to forsake in her leopard form.*

"If you ask me that sounds a bit creepy."

Avi fisted his hands and hit a tree trunk. Bloody knuckles didn't remove the ache and the annoyance that they were still connected. She heard his thoughts and probably had when he trespassed on Forced Blessed grounds.

"Today, I have to kill her."

"Kill who?"

Avi felt the broken skin on his knuckles tingle. The sensation of being licked triggered horror. Rather than feeling relief for the cleansed wound, he was livid. Her trespassing on his thoughts was one thing but this connection was another.

"You."

"That's fair considering it was my fault you were scratched by a mad bear whilst saving me. Then I shun you for being Blessed. Even then you still cared, yet I refused to escape when you told me to and now..." Avi should have stopped her before she added… *"I've become what you should have been?"*

Avi lived his crappy life, he didn't need to hear about it. It was time to block her.

She panicked and blurted out.

"I've known you were nearby on several occasions."

He knew that already. In her snow leopard form she had picked up his scent several times and disappeared with her agility and prowess to avoid the eventuality. Today she was unlucky.

"I've felt your determination to kill me. Yet you wavered." Una was hopeful.

She was right. The only thing that gave him purpose and spurred him on was his fate to kill her and take back control from Wolf.

"Whatever I may be, I'm not a coward. Only a coward strikes when his prey is asleep."

"No! I didn't mean that I meant... I was hoping..."

"That I still had feelings for you?"

Una went silent. She knew he didn't want to exchange words with her but had to give her and himself this very last contact. The pull of resistance in his body submerged his intensity and lowered his thought tone to a softer tone of pure mockery.

"I do have strong feelings for you. I now know that you're cheating me of my heritage and forcing on me the lowliest blessing. It is not the most painful thing and loss that I will experience because of you. My only comfort is that even for a short while, you will share my anguish and pain knowing it is me who will rob and snuff out your life."

"I see. Is that going to be Kulkil's fate too?"

Avi closed his channel with Una. He knew what she was doing. She hoped to muddle his head by reminding him of Kulkil.

He had been just as shocked as Una to see Kulkil emerge from Wolf's house. It was incomprehensible. Oh, he guessed Kulkil had defected on that day of training. But Avi had never witnessed any St Anthony's pupils or ex pupils enter the Modern Ruin unless they were converted Forced Blesseds. It worried him that Wolf wanted to entertain Kulkil. Wolf hadn't bothered with the other defectors. Avi's only consolation was that Kulkil didn't have to go through the depraved initiations Wolf had forced on the unsuspecting martial arts students.

Una had momentarily distracted him with Kulkil but not anymore.

He took his knife from his pouch. Either she could not pick his scent up in human form or he was too far away because she stood sideways to him. Whatever the reason he didn't care. He moved to get a better aim. Her head cocked to one side to pick his position up. She decided to stay put. A big mistake. His heartbeat echoed loud, he thought it to be reverberating between the trees of the jungle, but she didn't move. Her face was obscured by her hair which helped him. He concentrated on his target, her heart. Then made an adjustment and launched the knife at her.

Kulkil yelled, "Watch out!" matching the Sharman's silent warning to Una.

Una's head turned to the centre. She jerked her body back… too late. The knife cut through her abdomen. Avi watched her eyes roll up before she fell backwards into the darkness.

"You killed her. How could YOU?" Avi stepped back from his position. Kulkil couldn't see him but he knew Avi's position. Kulkil readied himself to run at Avi but then he remembered Una. He frantically pushed back the foliage this way and that. Una had disappeared.

In disbelief, Avi tracked down close to where Kulkil stood. Both of them discovered her bloodstains – at the same time.

In vain, Kulkil tried to part the foliage where the blood trailed. He was barred.

"What did you expect? The Blessed no longer accept you,

Kulkil, as one of theirs."

"I didn't expect this..." He traced his finger through Una's blood and showed it to Avi. Avi flinched which made Kulkil even angrier. "Why protect her all this time... it doesn't make sense. You didn't even know Gopan well."

"I didn't do it for Gopan." Avi's voice trembled. The enormity of what he had done left him hollow. Like he had spirited away his soul and not hers. He'd killed Una, the only bright thing in his life. "I had to kill her to protect her from Wolf."

Kulkil angrily cried, "Liar! You bloody liar. It had nothing to do with Wolf."

Nausea rose in Avi. Kulkil was right it had nothing to do with Wolf. He was a monster. Wolf would have revered Una. Even if it was for his own selfish reasons, he had kept her safe.

Was that what ticked him off and pushed him to the edge? Had this really been about jealousy? Gripped in despair, no longer sure of his motives, Avi blindly watched Kulkil try to gain access to the foliage in the Blessed territory for a few moments.

Kulkil thrashed at the bushes and then gave up. "Help me get through, Avi! Tell me where the route is that you come through?"

Avi shook his head and walked down to the foliage.

"What the hell, Avi? She'd better survive and be back tomorrow."

"Go and report her absence to Wolf."

"I will, you bastard. And then I'm coming for you."

Avi didn't have time for this he had to find her body before the Blesseds found it.

He pushed through the foliage easily where Kulkil couldn't. Then had a thought. *How did Una manage to walk through the Blessed ground rhododendron bushes opposite her grandfather's gates? Did that mean she wasn't a Forced Blessed initiate?*

"Let's hope this realisation wakes you up to yourself and she lives."

"Lives, did you say lives, Sharman? No forced or Blessed recovery will cope with that amount of blood loss. I aimed to kill like Dr Verma taught me."

"It is possible if the knife remains lodged in her body and nothing else attacks her and disembodies her in her weakened state," answered the Sharman.

***

Una

"Don't you dare faint."

The Sharman's words forced her awake.

"I've got to get this out of me." She wrapped her shaking hands around the handle of the knife. She could barely breathe let alone thought talk.

"Don't take it out, Una, you will bleed more. Morph into your animal form before the Blessed or my tribesmen find you. They won't know you from another animal. Even in this injured state you can outpace any of them. In the twilight they will just see a leopard looking for prey."

Una wasn't sure. Wolf had told her not to show what she was… she was his weapon… she had to be loyal to him until she rescued her father.

"Never mind all of that... It's important you live first."

"If I take the knife out, I will heal... and then I will get back..."

"Perhaps but you won't have time to recover from the wound. Avi aimed to make sure of that. You are in the parts that are heavily guarded by Blesseds who are even more hungry to finish you than Avi. Before anyone finds you, you have to find altitude."

Una was barely operating. The wound was deep, and she was losing blood, but it was grief that had immobilised her. She wanted to give in but then her eyes fell on the locket around her neck. She removed it and held it tight between her teeth. If she stayed alive so did her dad.

With the darkening sky she transformed as she ran. In her Blessed form she could outrun Avi and anyone else for that matter. The only problem was that she was running in their territory and didn't really know this part.

The Sharman was right – she had to find height quickly. But Una was in agony. Fever and delirium were drowning her adrenalin rush. Una stumbled, she tried to lick her wound. Her fur was matted where the blood flowed freely. The knife was loosening but so was her consciousness.

"I don't how to get to the high ground without going through the river again!"

"Then you will have to come this way. HURRY!"

This time the riverbed was dry. She could see the boulder she used when she was running from Wolf's gang. With great difficulty she leapt onto the boulder but once there her strength abandoned her, toppling her onto her side. Her limbs, without any strength, lay in a heap. Her ears and nostrils required no such strength and picked up signs that she had company. Soon enough three animal faces peered over her. The combination of monkeys and a snow leopard cub told her they were Blesseds. Through hazy vision she noted that all three were staring at her with equal measures of awe and dismay.

The Sharman was back in her head. "Loosen your body and play dead." She opened her mouth and let her tongue drop to one side.

Small stones on the riverbed flew. A male voice close to her shouted, "She's down, Burfani! Avi *really* kept his word."

Next a heavy body pushed down on her chest. Her fading senses picked up a rhesus negative monkey, a decaying one at that. "I never thought I would see a full-size snow leopard so soon."

"I can't believe he had it in him to do this."

"Burfani, why not? You asked him to do it." Before Burfani could answer the young voice asked another question. "Will Avi be cursed because he killed a snow leopard?"

Una tried to stay awake to hear the answer, but none came before she slipped away.

"Wait, what about the knife?" the younger voice asked his third question.

"Both of you come away from her body – you don't want to be too close to it if she's dead. Her spirit could leap on you. Let's take her when she is in human form." Burfani leapt over Una's body leaving the snow leopard cub scent in the air above her, and hightailed it away before they realised, she was scared.

"This will make her strong and me even stronger." Satisfied with his own words the old monkey shifted his weight on Una to make himself more comfortable.

"Stronger only if she keeps her promise to remove her father as Sharman and put you in second-in-command," the young rhesus monkey spoke.

"She'll keep her promise especially as her Blessed form is still so young and then…"

"And then?"

"When her already sickly cub form falls ill and dies of its own accord, Burfani will have to return to where she came from – the spirit world."

"If that happens what will happen to us?"

The old monkey groaned. "Why did I have such weak grandsons?"

"At least I'm not Avi," replied the young monkey gleefully.

"True, at least you aren't that."

Chapter 42

In the Enemy Camp

Who knew dawn in October could be so warm? Una lay on her side with her limbs sprawled in front of her, on the boulder. It was the tautness of her skin that woke her up. Her head hurt. Had she hit it when she fell or was, she dehydrated due to blood loss? With difficulty she prised open her sticky eyelids and scanned her body. The blood from her abdomen painted the river stones at the base of the boulder a rust colour. The colour would fade but remain there until the next monsoon. Crusty dried blood wormed over her naked body from where her flesh surrounded the knife her animal self could not remove. First shame and then despair flooded her naked body. In the fresh daylight the horrific truth of the first dark hours of last night were difficult to comprehend.

"Avi actually tried to murder me!"

"Yet you live."

Avi? Una eyelids flickered as she stared ahead. Her retina picked up faint movements in the distance, coming towards her. Una struggled to move off the boulder, but her body hadn't healed with the knife still in her and she only managed to slide an inch. Panic rose within her – a dark moving mass was bounding towards her. The shape of the thing was obscured due to her fuzzy head. Too weak to move, Una unwillingly resigned to the inevitable. She tried to shut her eyes, but they hurt too much. Wide-eyed she witnessed the mass become a still wall of fur and teeth, standing tall on its hind legs, with claws raised. Her heart jolted when a large giant paw loomed over her and then remained suspended in the air centimetres from the tip of her nose.

Despite her brain frantically warning her of a violent end her heart only felt relief. Although she saw him as her executioner, even after him attempting to take her life, he had been her only light. She had succeeded to snuff that out. Now she just wanted it to be over. *Let me be unconscious before he mauls and shreds my body with his teeth and claws to stop my body healing itself. I'm too far gone now.*

His raised paw dived down on her face and… tidied her long, bloodied hair. If possible, her eyes would have shown surprise. As it is, she didn't have much muscle control or stamina and instead stared back with a blank expression.

Human voices from the dairy farm in the distance stilled his movements for a moment. He stared down at her before he shifted his gaze and her own eyes popped open wide. Her once limp body spasmed violently as he tore at the knife embedded in her side using his teeth. His teeth grazed her skin but the pulling out of the knife caused every cell of her body to scream. No one heard her. He had already smothered her mouth in a steel grip. Hot tears arrived from the depth of anguish as his movements dug the knife deeper instead of releasing it. He stopped and waited. When the ripples of her silent scream quietened, he relaxed his paws. She lifted her head clear of the fur that was trapping her mouth for a moment. Her eyes tried to search his dark ones. He dodged hers. Instead of meeting her eyes he gently closed her eyelids and raised her clear off the boulder, pulled her into his hairy chest and carried her with her feet dangling several feet off the ground on his hind legs.

***

Minutes earlier

Avi's heart and brain stilled. In the distance lay Una – naked and from what he could see, dead. The nausea, similar to the violent bouts he suffered, brought on by grief and guilt when he couldn't find her or her body in the long night, threatened. His last-minute adjustment didn't vindicate him. After all, he had deliberately set off to kill her. A split second before he threw the knife, he had a change of heart and changed its course to no avail it seemed. When he looked for her, he thought a swift removal of the knife would allow her to heal. He hadn't accounted for the force of the knife to propel her body backwards. If she had fallen differently in Forced Blessed territory Kulkil would have saved her.

"Be alive. Against all odds please be alive," he pleaded as he bound towards her.

Halfway to her, he still couldn't tell if she was alive. Ravaged in grief and urgency, his feral self, bolted forward. Dead or alive, he had to be quick and remove her before the OTHERS or the tribesmen recognised her. To think they would quarter her and distribute her to the four winds was too gruesome to imagine. Yet an even more torturous possibility rose in his mind as he closed in on her. *If she is alive but suffering, do I put her out of her misery?* His stomach knotted in pain.

As Avi approached the rock he went from all fours to two. Large emeralds stared back at him and stopped him in his tracks. Between matted spikes of hair framing her forehead and her slashed cheeks, her face rested motionless over her torn fingers. Unnaturally her eyes did not flicker. Could she be dead? He hurriedly looked for signs of breathing and discovered the gentle rise and fall of her hair draped around her chest.

He took a short intake of breath. Even in this near-death state her body pulled on his human hormones. He could feel his body threaten to transform. Quickly he pawed her hair over her body covering her shape as much as he could. Salt invaded the innards of his mouth and giddiness made him lose his footing slightly over the riverbed pebbles. Inconveniently the internals of his own body began to rearrange itself to his human form. Tilting his shaggy bear head up to the sky he cast his eyes upwards and witnessed circling black specks. He had delayed too long – Avi picked up nearing human activity in the cowshed. He couldn't carry her with a knife in her body. He had to risk opening her wound. Desperately he grabbed his knife's handle in his teeth and pulled hard. All the time his paw blocked the screams he knew would come. A rusty iron smell hit his nostrils as he thrashed his head sideways. The knife refused to budge. It just cut through deeper.

He drew himself to his full height of six foot and moved onto his hinds and carefully lifted her off the boulder to his chest, averting his eyes from her body. It was torturous. Her skin was burning like an inferno and he flinched. She seemed to try and say something. He moved his chest slightly backwards, removing his fur from her mouth and then used his snout to push her jaw up slightly so that her mouth would shut. Relieved, she moved a millimetre closer and his chest muscles relaxed, removing all space between them. Unnerved by her body relaxing he felt the air in his lungs whoosh through his gritted teeth leaving him gulping. Slowly he lifted her from under her knees and began to carry her to the temple overhanging the north of the river. He felt his own body fast beginning to melt into hers, every moment he held her. He was at risk of losing himself.

The cackle of a crow and the clip of his ears by the departing wing brought him back to reality. But not before he faltered on the saucer green pools staring up at him. He used the soft padding of his paw to close her eyes. Her lips cracked open and against his fur he felt her breath spell out Avi.

A gun went off in the distance. He was not getting anywhere on his hind legs so he slipped her over his back and just as a cub would she held on to his shaggy ears. The difference was she was much bigger than a cub and he could no longer hold back the human in him. He had to get to the temple before he began to alter too much.

Just as he arrived at the steps of the temple, he felt her arms around his neck disappear and then her body slide down his human back. Now that he had fingers instead of claws, he caught her dangling legs and wrapped them around his naked waist and took two or three steps at a time to reach the top of the one hundred and eight steps. Her breath tickled the ends of his hair at his nape. He chanted for the wind and monkey form of Hanuman *Jai Bajrang Bali* more than one hundred and eight times using the steps instead of chanting beads, to give him strength. The temple was a Hanuman shrine.

At the top he was loathed to put her down, but he had to take care of his nakedness first. He cautiously propped her against the peeling, sculptured pillar and picked a loose kurta pyjama off the wash line at the back of the temple.

He felt awkward dressing in her presence. He knew he was more angular and muscular than in his teens but besides reflections in water he had not yet glimpsed himself properly and felt too conspicuous.

If he felt like this then he could only think how she would have felt if she were not at death's door, even though she needn't had. He quickly dragged a cream kurta over his head, ready to find something for her.

A red and gold length of cloth, the dupatta usually on Hanuman's statue flew past his vision and over Una, covering her effectively. They weren't alone. The Sharman was somewhere in the room.

"How fast will she heal?" asked Avi.

"Not fast enough," answered the Sharman.

"Give her something to grip on to, in her mouth."

Avi turned to one of the buckets of ice-cold water from the spring trickling from the hill rock which formed the back wall of the temple and tore a strip off his kurta. Before he could dunk it, it was snatched from his hands.

"Ice water? Hoping to finish her off, are you? Go fetch the bucket that's been in the early morning sun."

The Sharman, unlike the youngsters, was able to shift shapes instantly and when Avi returned he roughly pushed Avi down to where Una sat. "Hold her tight so I can close the wound quickly." Avi moved behind Una and held her tight as he leant her body down on him. The Sharman dampened the strip of Avi's kurta, prised her mouth open and pushed the strip in her mouth. Una's eyes opened in alarm.

"I'm on your side. I've always been on your side." Una blinked on hearing the Sharman's words. "Una, bite hard on the cloth and on the count of three I'll…"

Clunk! Avi's bloodied knife fell on the floor.

Una's body spasmed and she passed out.

Avi tore another portion of his kurta to clean her wounds.

"Leave the water alone, Avi. Lick her wound to help it heal quickly," said the Sharman as he walked out of the temple with the bucket of water in one hand and the knife in another.

Dumbstruck, Avi stared at the Sharman's disappearing body. *"Are you really trusting me, her murderer, to give her the kiss of life?"*

"Murderer? You missed your target deliberately."

Because killing her was just the same as killing himself. She was still his nemesis, but he wasn't ready to let go of her yet. Avi bent his head over her shoulder and licked her wound gently despite his fierce emotions. Her skin awoke under his tongue. Greedily it drank his saliva and rushed to mesh her skin at breaking speed on its own accord. It was mesmerising. It was dangerous for his heart. He pulled his mouth away and just watched, staring at her helplessly.

The Sharman re-entered the room empty-handed.

"I didn't need to help her, did I?"

"I imagine not."

"So why did you ask me to?"

"To help you discover what she is."

"Help me…" Avi swung his attention to his nana. He smiled gently back at him. "How long have you known she is a born Blessed?"

"Since she was conceived."

"But how is that possible? Neither of her parents are tribesmen or Blessed? I have Blessed blood from the tribe's leader and you, the Sharman, yet I still don't heal as fast as she has."

"You will soon work it out."

Avi began to protest. The Sharman cut him short. "Sort her clothing out. As soon as you finish, let her sleep and when she wakes up tell her to leave."

"LEAVE? No, she needs to be here!" The Sharman shook his head. "Wait, you just said she was Blessed."

"Avi, listen to me carefully. If you want her to live, she needs to leave. When she wakes up you will show her the way out of here," said the Sharman in a quiet voice. Before he left the temple, he added, "Don't let anyone see you and don't let your mother know either. She must not know of Una's presence here and she must believe Una is dead for a little while more. I will keep everyone away from the temple for as long as I can."

Avi watched his nana transform in the blink of an eye back into a langur.

Healed she might be, but Una was still burning up. Avi pulled the cold-water bucket nearer, used the cloth she had in her mouth and dampened her forehead. He repeated the action several times. Next, he washed her face. His thumb pressed water to her cracked lips. She squirmed.

Her shivering, barely wrapped body brought him back from his wayward thoughts. He shrugged off his tunic and dipped it into the water. He ruffled it so it would be easy to slip over her and then gently brought her head forward and put it through the neck hole of the tunic, gently pulling the sheer dupatta down over her.

Despite his best intentions he looked. Luckily, her hair still covered most of her under the sheer material. Before he leaned her back against the pillar, he gently tugged the tresses of hair from her neckline and left the dupatta under it.

Once she was clad, he held her snuggly to him. *As soon as your temperature lets up, I promise I will find you something better to wear.* He propped his head back on the same pillar Una had leaned against earlier when she took her first peek of Avi pulling on his baggy trousers. Whilst stroking her hair absent-mindedly, he fell asleep.

Chapter 43

Red Alert

The evening before

Wolf did have his doubts about Kulkil, but not anymore. Whilst transforming near the Modern Ruin he easily picked up on the interaction between Kulkil and Avi some distance away from him and sprinted in their direction. Although he could not see them, he heard Kulkil desperately trying to push through the bushes but couldn't. Avi's words about his old friend being ostracised because he was now a Forced Blessed meant Kulkil was telling the truth and was truly barred from the Blessed territory without a second chance.

Wolf was surprised. Before now the Sharman hadn't stopped him or his Forced Blessed cohort from entering the Blessed territory by using chants like he had. Disgruntled by Avi's illegal presence Wolf made a note to set the others to find the obvious chink in the Forced Blesseds' armour. He couldn't have the Blesseds finding Una so easily.

Until a few days ago, Wolf was sure the Blessed had just patrolled the boundary. It had to be a very new development. *I'm sure it wasn't that long ago when I dipped my toe in their territory to show Una and all the other initiates where the boundary was.*

The Sharman hadn't believed in using an enchantment on the boundary for the simple reason that he did not recognise Wolf's distinction of being a Forced Blessed and right up until Una arrived in Khamosh Valley he'd believed Wolf would come back to the Blessed way of thinking. In fact, until then he had not protected the Blessed boundaries from them in any way at all. Wolf remembered listening in astonishment to the Sharman's optimism when he had first met Wolf, after he returned to his parents. In reply to Wolf's question about why the Sharman was not wary of the new Forced Blessed cohort, the Sharman's exact words were, "Beta, son, ALL Blesseds are protectors to all in the jungle and can never be a threat to each other. I believe that not even you, Wolf, would go against that."

Wolf was glad of Avi. Because until Avi became Blessed no one on the other side thought to challenge the Forced Blesseds. They had been treated as juveniles rutting. According to Kulkil, Avi had made the Blesseds take the Forced Blesseds' threat seriously and was training them in modern combat techniques.

When Kulkil was in sight, Wolf stopped his sprint and changed his pace to a casual stroll. Avi was nowhere to be seen.

"What are you doing here at the border?"

Kulkil turned to face Wolf who had suddenly emerged from nowhere. He winced. "I'm hunting for Una; she fell on the other side."

The sight of Kulkil's face and his words hit Wolf with the abruptness of a collision.

What? "How?" gasped Wolf.

"She fell after she was ambushed. A Blessed threw a lethal tribal knife accurately into her side. It lodged in her and the momentum threw her backwards into the boundary growth."

"What?" exclaimed Wolf incredulously. *How was that possible? She had always managed to duck his knives during training and actually even before she was trained.* "Did you see who threw the knife."

"Yes…" Kulkil struggled to say the rest, "…it was Avi."

Perhaps he had misheard.

"Who?" He didn't really need to ask again; the disbelief and anguish was written all over Kulkil's face.

"It was Avi?" Wolf couldn't comprehend anything he was hearing.

"Did he kill her? Kulkil, think carefully, did you see her die?"

"I don't know..." Kulkil's voice faltered and then to himself he said, "...I thought Avi loved her."

Wolf's shock changed to suspicion. "Did you come to this side to kill her?" Kulkil shook his head. "Because of Gopan?"

"No! If I wished to do that, I could have done it earlier with much ease. Plus, what motive would I have to kill her? Gopan isn't a relative of mine." Wolf conceded that he indeed could have killed her earlier, but had he herded her here instead?

Kulkil nipped Wolf's train of thought in the bud. "If I was sent by the Blesseds, they would have allowed me back into the jungle. I changed sides and like some of the returned defected Blesseds, I have been ostracised." Kulkil's voice wobbled slightly as he contained his tears.

"Are you sure about the Blesseds who returned?" Wolf himself had wondered about the fate of the returned Blesseds as they were noticeably absent during the Forced Blesseds' initiation spectacle.

Kulkil's voice was shrill with hurt. "If not, then can you explain why they have disappeared from the tribal community entirely, along with their families, without a single trace. This is crazy. If you don't believe me then explain what I have done this all for? I've lost my best friend who only feels contempt for me even though he wronged me first."

"I believe you, but does it make sense to you that Avi wanted to kill Una?"

"Not at first but then he raged on about his contempt for her being greater than anything else. He said he had to finish her because she'd betrayed him repeatedly. He still couldn't fathom why she chose to hook up with the Forced Blesseds, his mother's murderers and the ones responsible for him not transforming to a snow leopard. You made him so wretched that she... chose you over him. He couldn't forgive her choosing you instead of him."

Wolf couldn't comprehend what Kulkil was telling him and mulled over it in silence. Was it possible that Avi and Una had met since her initiation and she told him that she had chosen to be a Forced Blessed? Did she really have feelings for Wolf as he did for her? Wolf went over his memories. There were many times they had been at ease with each other, even in the earlier days when she was first initiated and then when she helped him train the new recruits.

"What are you going to do about Una?" asked Kulkil, overwhelmed with worry.

"If she dies on the other side, we will know. As you know a Forced Blessed or Blessed death can't be hidden."

"Then what…"

"Then, Kulkil, we go to battle earlier than we thought. Unlike Avi we will make sure that Avi knows who his murderer is."

Kulkil didn't utter a word. But Wolf knew Kulkil understood. His eyes were hollow and listless as they wandered over the vast darkness. Was he torturing himself for not saving Una or was he devastated by the contempt Avi, his friend, felt for him? Wolf did not miss how he fisted his hands on either side of him. It was obvious that Avi's knife had dug deep into Kulkil too.

Had Kulkil expected Avi to forgive him for defecting or even understand why? Did it scare him and stun him that Avi, who protected and loved Una enough to try and send her back to England, would be the one to kill her? Did he think that if his relationship with Una meant nothing, then it made him question theirs? Or did it scare him that he really didn't know Avi? Wolf wondered how the Sharman and Avi failed to see the building frustration in Kulkil and in doing so enabled his deliverance to the Forced Blesseds. Had Kulkil truly realised all his ties would be cut permanently? Heck, even Wolf had been given a chance over a long period of time to go back to the Blesseds. Somewhere, Kulkil's mother would be worrying about him like his parents had too. Sad as it all was, Wolf knew he had to bring Kulkil out of the doldrums.

He changed tact. "Una is very resourceful, you know. She nearly outwitted me on her first day here."

Wolf hoped she had this time too. He thought talked to the pack of wolves, telling them to look for Una before the Blesseds found her. They reported back that she wasn't on their terrain and it looked like Kulkil was telling the truth as no one could penetrate the Blessed territory.

Wolf was struck by this conundrum. If no one on the Forced Blessed side could pass the bewitched boundary then how did Una fall backwards into their territory. There could only be one explanation: that the Sharman was involved and had opened a gap for her.

Chapter 44

Return to Status Quo?

"Nana, did you save her to avoid me being cursed by the snow leopard curse?"

"Being a Sharman does not mean I blindly follow faith."

"Doesn't it?" Avi asked disbelievingly.

"Believe what you like, but no, this blind faith is more dangerous than not having any."

"So, you don't believe the curse, yet you wanted to save her?" Avi was not buying it. There had to be more.

"She is Blessed and that's enough of a reason to save her life. I would save Wolf if he lost his cunning ways and was found in this predicament."

A brief, incredulous silence followed the Sharman's statement.

"She killed your grandnephew!" whispered Avi.

"Yet that's not even your reason for attempting to murder her… Don't balk at the word murder. How could you even contemplate it, when I explicitly told you to ignore your mother and the Blessed assembly's folly of agreeing with her and to leave Una well alone?"

Avi's gaze roamed over the sleeping Una.

The Sharman watched his grandson.

"Are you still in two minds about finishing her off because if you really wanted to save her you could have taken her back to the Forced Blesseds instead of bringing her here?"

"I don't know," he lied. How did he explain to his nana that she incited rage within him when he pictured her Blessed form, in direct contrast to the heightened emotion her sleeping pose evoked? He wanted to both kill and save her in the same instance.

"Don't forget I can read your thoughts." The Sharman shifted around uneasily. "You have to send her back before the Forced Blesseds notice."

"They've noticed." Avi looked up from Una's sleeping body. "Kulkil will have informed Wolf by now."

"Wolf knows?" exclaimed the Sharman. Avi shushed him. The Sharman looked over at Una. "He'll panic if he knows Una is missing… This puts us all in danger." The Sharman moved to wake her but Avi stood in his way. The Sharman spoke over his arm. "Fool! Wake her up and smuggle her out of here. Now!"

"I can't."

"It's not up to you, Avi." Both the Sharman's and Avi's attention swung to Una as she tried to stand on her feet but tripped on the dupatta ends.

Una gazed up at Avi and the Sharman. She had never seen him close up in his langur state.

The Sharman was nonplussed, in striking contrast to the heated state he had got into before she awoke. He leapt high onto a shelf and then returned with something wrapped in his tail. Una was surprised to find the langur's tail uncurling and revealing her personalised combat uniform.

"How…" Una uttered as she caught her uniform before it fell.

"You're not the only one who can use a window," the Sharman replied and then signalled Avi to give her space to change.

Avi nodded and made to follow his nana out the temple.

"No, Avi… stay. You have to explain yourself."

Avi hesitated at the door.

"You've seen everything anyway," Una uttered shyly.

"I can't."

Una's coyness dissipated into anger. "Unless the Sharman wrapped me in this red cloth thingy. I would say you've seen everything."

Her words had the undesired effect of him stepping out of the door.

"Avi, I'm not a shrinking violet… even if I was, it's too late… you carried me butt naked for heaven's sake."

For heaven's sake! Avi marched back to where she was and sat down.

The Sharman shrugged his furry shoulders and made his way to the door instead. Through the slightly ajar door he stared up at the sky.

"Avi, it's nearly dusk, make sure she is gone before she transforms back into a snow leopard." Then he leapt through the doorway and paused momentarily. "It seems you might already be too late."

Avi scuttled to the door, watched his nana disappear into a speck in the weakening brightness of the day. Avi pulled himself up against a column that formed part of the door and stood. He closed the double wooden doors and remained there, still facing the doors.

Una wasn't shy. She and her British male and female school mates often stripped to their underwear and jumped into the River Mersey at the back of their school in Manchester.

Una smirked and spoke under breath, "A pointless bit of chivalry after what you have seen and touched."

She unwound and removed the borrowed kurta and the dupatta from herself and chucked them at him. He turned in surprise just as she began to pull her T-shirt over her head and torso. Avi had never come across a woman dressing or undressing before. Una didn't seem embarrassed, but God, he was.

"He's right. You have to leave before any one of the other Blesseds find you or worse still, I come to my senses and…" Avi's voice rasped as his eyes connected with hers causing the air around them to fizz with their frustrations and unwelcome chemistry.

"And?" Una hooked an eyebrow.

"…And kill you."

"Because of Gopan?" Una's raised arm stilled. Relief set in

when Una straightened her T-shirt and then she caught him staring as she lifted her hair so none of it was stuck in her T-shirt.

"Yes." Avi turned around to hide his reddened face. "Lucky for you they think you are already dead."

"Would they not spare me if they knew that Gopan double-crossed them and gave me up to the Forced Blesseds?" Avi turned back to address her question only to find her nose almost touching his.

Avi leaned in. "It's your word over theirs. Besides, our leader isn't keen on you."

"Leader, but I can see the Sharman is on my side?" Una whispered, focusing on his mouth.

"He's not the leader, it's..." Avi stopped himself before he gave the cub or Rosetta away.

"It's Burfani, isn't it... so your mum is still alive?" asked Una.

"We don't have time for this now." To make the point Avi pulled her by her arms towards the back door. His strength raised both her eyebrows this time.

Una let him lead her out through the back entrance after scouting for onlookers first. She knew her way, but he wanted to make sure she left so this time she let him lead her without a fuss from one bush to another. It felt like old times when they explored the jungle in the then forbidden areas, but this time they could not make light of the gravity they faced if they were caught by either side. There was a desperation.

Una belatedly realised he was still with her when she crossed over to her boundary. Worse still, she could see Gagan hovering above them on a higher plane.

She ducked down in the bush, gave Avi a kiss on the lips and charged to the next bush. Seconds later the howl of a wolf boomed between the cliffs. Avi had to leave.

"Avi, go."

Avi stayed. Frustrated, Una moved forward to another bush. In the meantime, Gagan had come down to the lower bushes and stopped at the bush Avi and Una had been at earlier.

Had he picked up their scent?

Avi wanted to take him on, it would be easier now. Avi's body had begun its transformation. Before his forearms became forelimbs and fingers became claws, he quickly undressed himself.

His gaze hovered over to where Una was hiding. Witnessing a snow leopard emerge from a bush flicked a switch in him again. His shoulders tensed, ready to pounce, but he was stopped when a white furry langur arm covered his vision and his snout.

"They are guarding her Blessed identity from us and I want them to keep thinking we are still in the dark about it." Avi stepped back in subjection. Satisfied, the Sharman dropped his arms.

Avi gulped for air.

Back in Blessed territory Avi picked up Una's scent everywhere but it was strongest between the columned walls of the temple. It angered him. Try as much as he wanted to, he couldn't suppress his envy and fury just because the Sharman and his heart wished him to. Enraged, he tore her scattered dupatta to shreds.

"Have you finished with tearing the place apart?" The Sharman picked up his clothes and chucked them at Avi.

"She's stolen my birth right."

"No, she hasn't but if you want me to explain why, you have to take on your human form so you will do my temple the least amount of damage."

"Least amount of damage?" Avi noticed several objects had been thrown about from the prayer altar.

Satisfied that Avi was back in his human form even if all he could find to wear was a newly tattered T-shirt and jeans, the Sharman began:

"Your mother, Rosetta, was given the greatest honour when Burfani chose to be born to her. Your dead sister was meant to be the incarnation but instead…"

"But Dadi snuffed her out, I know…" Avi's frustration grew.

"Forget all that history. I can't see how someone born in England gets to be the snow leopard."

"Una was born in England, but she was not conceived there."

Avi couldn't see the significance at first, but then he realised the enormity of what his nana was saying.

If not there, then was she conceived here?

The Sharman nodded in agreeance.

Did that mean she was born here?

Open-mouthed, he gaped at his nana. Able to share his burden for the first time in seventeen years the Sharman released all he knew in a torrid of explanation.

"Una's mother, Alice, took a role as a researcher in the Forestry Commission after she met and married Vivek while they were at university in England. She was treated unfairly by her in-laws when she couldn't conceive due to biological issues. Desperate, Alice came to me for alternative medicine which coincidentally happened to be on the day your sister died.

"Burfani's spirit had first-hand understanding of the Major's brutality towards his own so she knew what he would do to creatures that were not his equal. Her urgency to be born again was helped by Alice who agreed to Burfani's conditions of returning her to the Blesseds when she was eighteen. When Alice found herself pregnant, your Nani, my late wife, somehow persuaded Alice to leave Khamosh Valley just in case Dev's wife meted the same fate on her baby as your sister's."

"Wait, it can't be..." Avi's face dissolved incredulously. His voice turned in to a stammer. "Are you saying... that Una... that Una is Burfani and she doesn't know it?"

"It's obvious she still doesn't know."

"How can that be?"

"Because when Burfani cocooned herself in the womb, she came out helpless and became Una. She's still the daughter of Alice and Vivek, who wishes to be back with her father in England. She's not awakened from her stupor completely but it's not long before she will."

"Wolf doesn't know about her, does he?"

"If he did it would all be over."

"How ironic Wolf has the real Burfani but can't recognise her and is stupidly making her learn about folklores and about Burfani… herself."

"Hence your meetings in the library."

Neither spoke further. Avi lit the evening diya and sat in the flickering light, thinking. She was Burfani and he was…?

The Sharman made his way to the door.

"Don't predict outcomes, Avi, it never works out as you think."

"I suppose." Avi hesitated but knew the answer.

"Even without the magnolia flowers you always knew she was Burfani so why didn't you try to take her?"

"Because she belonged here, and I assumed she would return. She almost worked it out on her first evening, but she was captured and then she unwittingly killed a Blessed. She's still locked in as Una until her father is released."

"Do you think Gopan's family knows who she is?"

"No, but they now know she is a snow leopard and they know Wolf has her father, who they wish to take their revenge on."

"We should at least tell my mother."

"She knows." His nana spoke in a resigned and sad voice.

Avi gasped and watched the agony of her sins to claim what was not hers portrayed on her father's face.

Avi didn't feel much for the wretched creature his mother was. How could she? It was difficult to witness the cub's stunted growth and sad state without realising that she wanted Una dead so she could be the snow leopard.

"I know what you are thinking, Avi. Leave well alone. Burfani will bring justice and put an end to your mother's pretence. Whatever you do you must not allow her to think you know the truth."

Avi agreed and after much discussion with the Sharman he transformed back into a bear. It was time to spread rumours that Una was dead. He hoped Una would stay low for a few days. Not just for her sake but his. He wanted to keep her as Una, for himself, for as long as he could.

***

He needn't have worried; Una had thought the same. She let Wolf know that she had been knifed and that Kulkil had saved her from Avi by deflecting him. She wasn't sure if Kulkil was on her side, but she had to take the chance that he wouldn't harm her. He had had more than enough opportunity to do so.

"I sent him to protect you from Wolf, Gopan and now it seems Avi." The Sharman blocked her out before she could respond.

Wolf heard from his sources that the Blesseds were rejoicing in Una's death. Wolf was pleased. The next day he organised a public pier funeral and lit a fire. He was sure the Blessed spies would have taken note of her absence and of the photo of her stuck on the sheet over the covered body. The body disturbed Una. She found it hard to believe Wolf when he said he got the body from the morgue and the person was not claimed and remained unnamed.

Chapter 45

Found Out

Clang!

Una looked up from pouring out the cocoa to see Kulkil with his hand extended, ready with his tumbler and eyes out on stalks. Una suppressed the smile forming at the ends of her mouth and innocently asked, "Is the new recruit finding the early mornings difficult?" In a lower voice she asked, "Or have you seen a ghost?"

"How are you still alive? Avi is our best tracker… he would have found you."

"Move on, KK! You look like you've seen a ghost. You normally want to kill her but here it looks like the tide is changing and you've got the hots for the headmaster's daughter," someone yelled out. The whole dormitory burst out laughing. Kulkil jostled with the boys and then things got out of hand and somebody bumped Una, forcing her to spill the whole of the jug's steaming hot contents onto Kulkil's hand.

Kulkil yelped.

Una quickly passed the jug to one of the new recruits and took Kulkil to the medical room. Once in the room she let go of his arm and ran the water in the sink, making sure it was ice cold.

Kulkil jumped away from her.

"Why the fuss, Kulkil? There's no rule that I can't hold a younger boy's hand in your Indian tribe rules, is there?"

"How did you do that?"

"Do what?" Una was flustered by his reaction.

Kulkil transferred his gaze from her to the back of his burnt hand. Only it wasn't burnt. Staggering backwards, further away from her, he stammered, "It's not possible… that means you are a seasoned Blessed but how can that be?"

Una watched the different emotions cross his face.

She tried to thought talk, but he was not ready. Yet she had been at his stage. Why was that?

"Una?"

"Yes?"

"What kind of cat are you?"

Una clung on to the ends of the basin with her back to it.

"I'm Forced Blessed, and I've already told you that I'm a leopard."

Her words seem to frighten him further.

"What kind of leopard? No, wait… you don't have to answer that, the Blesseds already have a leader." His own words failed to soothe him. He continued to back away.

"This is ridiculous. How can you be more scared of me if you think I am Blessed?" Then something occurred to Una.

This time she stumbled and felt the basin dig into her small of her back.

"If I am what you can't bring yourself to think I am then the Sharman would have told me to stay."

Kulkil rushed forward. "Wait, the Sharman let you come back?" Emboldened he gently shook Una. "Are you telling the truth?"

"Why would I lie?"

Kulkil sat on the respite bed, as confused as her.

"Who is this leader? Avi said there was a leader, but Rosetta is dead," Una asked, sitting beside him, just as confused.

"Yes, but Burfani is alive."

Una didn't quite understand the connection.

"She has merged with the cub snow leopard," Kulkil explained.

"So that's what I heard and felt. It really doesn't explain why Burfani asked for me to be killed but the Sharman let me go."

Kulkil kneeled down. "Unless he's not sure…" Wild-eyed he asked, "Una, where did you enter the jungle and become a Forced Blessed?"

"Enter? I was thrown over the bridge…"

Kulkil interrupted Una. "Was it on the last day of July?"

"Yes… but how do you know?" Una was stumped. She hadn't surfaced before Gagan's initiation in the autumn.

"Because that was the same day Avi found Burfani. He was so sure it was you who was in danger."

Kulkil sighed as he saw her face wear the same soft expression that Avi's used to when he heard her name. He continued:

"Instead of finding you he found Burfani. He didn't know he was Burfani. To both of us he just looked like an oversized cat with blue eyes and maybe… It's just that…"

She needed Kulkil out of her space.

"Kulkil, it's time to leave. The others will get suspicious – running your hand under a tap doesn't take that long. The boys might really believe I am seducing you."

That got a guffaw out of Kulkil. Una proceeded to push him towards the door.

"In any case I'm not Burfani, I'm just a leopard. Think carefully. The Sharman wouldn't want me harmed and wouldn't allow me to remain here if I was whoever you think I am." Kulkil shrugged his shoulders. She pushed them hard. "I think I would know who I am." Then desperately pleaded, "Kulkil, please don't do anything to put my father in jeopardy."

"Your father, that's it… If you didn't come back, he would have been killed." Kulkil raised his hands just as she got him to the door and gave a twinkling, cheeky smile. "Perhaps you are right. In that case you'd better wrap a bandage around my hand, so no one knows about your healing powers."

Although the Sharman had let her know why Kulkil was here, she still asked, "Aren't you going to tell Wolf?"

"About what?"

"About everything."

"No, it doesn't serve me to do that."

"You don't really hate the Blesseds, do you?"

"Shut up!" It was Kulkil's turned to look scared of being found out.

Una complied and busied herself with bandaging Kulkil's hand. He ruefully tried to manipulate his fingers but couldn't. "The annoying thing is that, in a year it would have been quite natural for them to believe my hand healed itself."

"There, all done." Una smiled and cut the bandage with a pair of scissors and tied the ends.

"Una, you do realise that when we leave this room, they must believe that I still hate you."

"I'll remember."

Kulkil moved to the door once again.

"Wait, Kulkil! The dead body earlier, it wasn't… my father?"

"No."

"Are you sure?"

Someone was banging on the door.

"Yes."

"Can't hear the springs moving but make sure you're decent, both of you, we are coming in!" Laughter and cackling followed as several boys walked into the room.

Chapter 46

The Waiting Game is at a Close

Una had worried that the dead body with her photograph was her father's. She hadn't dared to think otherwise. In happiness she leapt down from the high post she was on, without noticing the person walking below. Unfortunately, it was Gagan she brought down.

"What the fuck do you think you are doing?"

"You won't believe me because you're a prick, but I was just happy and didn't notice you."

"Repeat that again, you fucking bitch."

"Which bit? The bit that you were a prick or the fact that I didn't notice you?"

Gagan jumped on her and went to smash her jaw with his fist. She outmanoeuvred him by ducking. His hand hit a pole instead. His technique was better, but he hadn't managed to outsmart her since the first time she met him on Meeru's wedding day.

Under his breath he muttered, "I know how to get to you without even touching you. If only Wolf hadn't replaced me with the new boy, Kulkil, to guard your father."

***

Gagan had outgrown his purpose. Wolf never had any intention of hurting Vivek. As soon as he realised Gagan had taken out his frustrations with Una on her father, he had replaced him with Kulkil. She will have her father soon. *Soon she will understand and will forgive him for keeping her father hostage.*

Wolf climbed the Modern Ruin roof wall where, in the summer, Una had lay looking up, wistfully reading the clouds. The day he decided to take Vivek and bring her here as soon as he could.

It was finally time.

His cohort were ready. From what Kulkil had told him it sounded like the Blesseds were fighting amongst themselves. Further divisions were caused by the new Forced Blessed initiations. He never thought Avi would be the catalyst and that too by killing Una, his supposed love. It still niggled Wolf that Avi had targeted Una on Forced Blessed ground. He still hadn't found the chink in his security. Thankfully, Una came back but she looked like she had lost her nerve. He had to strike soon. *Tomorrow? No, it had to be this evening.*

The afternoon dragged with a strange air of normalcy for all but Wolf as he paced along the ledges of the roof walls.

Impatient, standing still on the wall, he tilted his Wolf head and howled the wolf call of curfew at 4pm instead of 6pm. His body shook with anticipation and thrill. He knew he had their attention, the jungle stilled and in the nakedness of daylight when the Blessed defence was weak, unable to come out in full offence in accordance with their treaty with the Forestry Commission and the Indian Army. The game was on!

Chapter 47

Smoke or Fire?

In the temple, there was a commotion. Once again.

Avi shook his head and sighed. Snow leopards were always at the root of it. So much for being an elusive species.

"What do you think Una's death means?" asked one of Kulkil's friends, who now held Kulkil's position as second-in-command of training.

"It means they have killed her themselves," Avi's great uncle butted in.

"Why would they do that?" Avi pointedly asked his relative.

A shadow passed over his great uncle's face. His eyes screwed up. "Perhaps they don't want a war."

Avi nodded. "Perhaps…" his uncle's facial muscles relaxed, "…perhaps they do." Avi smiled and moved to the front of the elders to position himself with his Blessed soldiers.

Both Avi and the Sharman pointedly stared at his great uncle in anticipation of a reaction to Avi's doubts. He uncomfortably shifted under their gaze and then hastily turned his back to them and addressed the rest of the Blesseds assembled on the steps of the temple. "It means we don't have to take revenge for Gopan now. They showed us her body, so we did not take revenge."

"So, no war?" someone shouted.

"I believe so." The great uncle's voice was buoyant.

"Really? Do you really believe that? Gopan's untimely death was part of the reason to wage war but not all of it. What about the abhorrent Forced Blessed initiations?" Kulkil's substitute asked.

"Quite right. The young understand that one death each does not mean the war is over," the Sharman replied.

"Besides, how do we really know if Una is dead? What if she is alive?" a Blessed in the crowd shouted.

I really hope Wolf didn't actually go and kill her, Avi thought, but dismissed his doubt. His body would've known if she was truly gone.

"Oh! She is dead! And they will definitely wage a war because it was a Blessed that killed her…" The Sharman looked directly into the dark depths of his brother's eyes. "By breaking their boundary security, and because they murdered her on Forced Blessed soil. Originally, I thought Burfani had been killed because I was sure a snow leopard's soul languished on our side." The Sharman's brother's countenance turned grey. "But then the patrol heard Kulkil shouting at Avi," finished the Sharman, watching the colour return to his brother's face.

"We heard them too…" The two who normally patrolled exchanged confused looks with each other and the great uncle. "We saw him do it."

A murmur of "Avi killed Una!" went up and down the temple steps.

The Sharman patted his brother's shoulder. "Avi, tell them how Kulkil reacted to you throwing the knife and killing Una on Forced Blessed soil."

Everyone turned, open-mouthed, towards the Sharman and then at Avi.

"I'm sad to say that Kulkil tried to warn Una but he was too late. He was beside himself with anger when he couldn't help Una. I hate to say it, but he wasted no time in informing Wolf of what I did. Although he was quick to leave, he did so after cursing me and the whole lot of us to damnation, and he left me with a warning. He said the way he felt trapped by the Blessed ways was how many others in his age group felt and it would be days if not hours before more of them joined him."

Avi stopped to breathe. There was a stunned silence. He

couldn't decide if they were shocked that Kulkil had betrayed them all or that Avi had killed Una.

The Sharman continued on from Avi. "Even if Wolf does not avenge us for Una's death which I think is unlikely as they have declared Una's death to us loud and clear, he is more than eager to convert more of our young, perhaps even today."

Avi straightened up. "That's why we need to be ready for his offensive. You have been called here because we believe Wolf will act in the next twenty-four hours. No, we actually think he will act in the next few hours…"

As if on cue a harrowing Wolf cry bellowed across the valley. The call was early… two hours early and in broad daylight too. The Sharman and Avi once again shared looks. They and his band of boys and girls and older men had prepared for this.

Avi had predicted Wolf's move only because they both had a tendency to go rogue. Neither were good at abiding by old traditions.

The Sharman pressed a conch to his lips and flew down the steps, changing into his Blessed self by the time he was past the bottom step. Avi and the shell-shocked Blessed elders followed suit in their Blessed form, but the others remained in human form. Avi gave a backward glance to his great uncle who remained where he had stood in complete shock. Avi smiled.

Chapter 48

Showdown

The river was transformed into a battlefield with an army stood on each of its banks. There was no water in the monsoon river, no water in sight yet there were alligators crawling along the riverbed.

The Blesseds and the tribesmen were garbed in their colourful tribal costume, army combats, with a handful as their Blessed animal selves in feathers or fur.

In striking contrast, on the other bank standing in a ribbon of combat sky blue and grey were the Forced Blesseds, all in human form. Wolf, even in his human guise, howled his wolf call as he marched ahead to the centre of the river carrying the Forced Blessed standard which had a coat of arms. Una ignored the icons in each quarter and just focused on the black streaks throughout the red flag, which revealed the camouflaged symbolic of Wolf's tattoo. Una wondered if she were the only one who could make it out.

In contrast the Blesseds' voluminous white flag, trimmed with sky blue ribbons, displayed a pouncing outline of a snow leopard encircling the tribe's standard bearer as he too approached the median of the riverbed. Once there he stumped the flag in the riverbed and retreated to the bank from which he came. Thirty seconds later, the flag material fluttered aside to reveal a familiar langur, a lesser known sloth bear and a shock of white fur with spots.

The sight of the cub with its snow leopard spots ruffled the featherless Forced Blesseds.

Una couldn't help herself and whispered up to the Blesseds.

"Keep staring ahead. No one react. A snow leopard cub means nothing," Wolf commanded through their shared thought talk.

Una chuckled. *Who was he fooling? He was clearly rattled.*

Wolf picked up on the word rattled and, to Una, said, *"Keep your nerves together. Don't give yourself away, not yet."*

Wolf then blocked Una out to talk to his cohort, so she blocked him out in retaliation. Alone in her head, Una was curious to see the cub close up. It looked a little like Cat, but it couldn't be because Cat would have grown larger by now.

Una zoomed in on the snow leopard cub and based on the patterning, was sure it was Cat. *How could it have remained almost the same size? Besides the size there's something else wrong. Una's focus was drawn to its limbs. The cub is struggling to walk steadily. I can't imagine why.*

"Really! But then could you imagine yourself doing what you are doing now?"

"Whatever do you mean?"

"Look down!"

Una dropped height in surprise. SHE DROPPED HEIGHT! She was in a bird's body. The flycatcher's body she was in cried independently of her. Black wings stretched out, she dived towards the Sharman's upturned langur face.

"I wondered when you would remember your expansiveness. However, for now, Una, save the poor flycatcher's life and let it fly."

Thump! She was back in her slumped body.

"*How did I do that?"*

"Your curiosity is enough to take you there. However, it's a bonus that you have an affiliation with flycatchers. They seem to be handy when your inquisitiveness is not sated by what you can naturally see."

"Sharman, what are you on about?"

"Remember Meeru's wedding day when Avi tried to warn you about the jungle through Kulkil's message?"

"Yes?"

"Then you have the answer."

Una rummaged through her memories of that day. She remembered how the Sharman had intercepted Avi's message to her by taking over Kulkil's voice box and after a little more effort she remembered her voice coming out of a flycatcher bird's beak. Una's body temperature rose.

"On that day you said you can only use a non-Blessed's body senses, but I have used Wolf and Avi in their Blessed forms when I hadn't even converted."

"You did?" A pause, then the Sharman asked, *"When?"*

"When the monsoons began... Never mind that... did you just miss the important bit of what I said?"

"No, you said you were able to manipulate the Blesseds."

"I travelled in their bodies more than mess with them, but yes. So, did you lie to me that day?"

"No, Una, I can't manipulate a Blessed."

"But..." Una protested.

"But, Una, you can."

Una was dumbstruck.

"Work it out later, Una. Your leader, who doesn't really have a clue about you, is speaking."

"I don't have a clue either."

Una could hear thought laughter.

WONDERFUL! The Sharman was amused by her in the midst of the beginning of a battle.

Their conversation came to an end with Wolf's exclamation: "Show your human selves so we know who we're dealing with."

Una's gaze fell on the movement in the Blessed camp.

Without any obvious command, several tribesmen encircled the threesome. A gap was temporarily created to allow two more carrying material to enter the closed circle.

Una shifted her attention between the circle and the Forced Blesseds as they watched on with curiosity written all over their faces.

No one was shocked to see the Sharman in his white dhoti and red band of material at his waist. Then the snow leopard, led by Avi, emerged.

Louder gasps than before left the senior Forced Blesseds but notably, not from Wolf.

They clearly hadn't expected Avi to appear from the bear guise and couldn't take their eyes off him.

Nor could Una for different reasons.

Avi stood at his nana's side with an air of ancient nobility with his muscled bare chest wrapped in volumes of black tribal material.

Someone, Gagan in fact, sneered loudly and then coughed as he caught dust in his mouth. Everyone was drawn to the dust that whirled as Avi kicked his leg high and lifted his whole self into the air, then twisted his body backwards to land. When his feet touched the ground he deliberately and slowly tucked in the end of a wide strip of red material held out to him by one of the tribesmen and repeatedly pivoted so the material wrapped neatly around his waist. Then he expertly tied the ends securely together and whilst planting one foot firmly on the ground he crossed the other over it and twisted his arms around each other to form a two-headed snake pose.

In the meantime, another tribesman came forward with a coil of metal more flexible than a metal tape measure and wrapped it around Avi's waist, on top of the red sash, leaving the handle at his side like a conventional sword.

The spectacle spread unrest in Wolf's camp.

Una caught Wolf's unguarded fleeting thought. *"Damn! The boys were already rattled by the manic bear who without fear had tried to enter their domain and prevent the initiations and now he is wrapped in a urami, a double-edged metal sword, and taunting them. Perhaps I should have shared Avi's guise with the others before today."*

An urami… Una remembered reading about them in the library. An urami was a quivering double-edged flexible sword! She had been left at the back and even there she felt the ripple of agitation and cautious hesitation from her peers. A curious sensation of wariness and pride arose in her for Avi, which she checked.

Someone was knocking at the door of her thoughts. It was time to lie.

Una let her thought shield down: *"I'm shocked... I thought..."*

"You hoped that the cub was Avi? Looks like he fooled you like the others."

Wolf's smugness made Una flinch.

"I thought he hadn't transformed yet or was a snow leopard..." Una lied.

"Guess I was the only one who knew. I'm surprised that you never connected the cowardly ex-boyfriend of yours with the bear though." The Wolf was enjoying this too much.

"You could have used his lowly form as ammunition against..."

"Against you?"

She meant to say against the Sharman, but Wolf greedily held on to the conversation.

"Really? Would you have given up on him and taken up with me if you knew he was a bear?"

Una couldn't pretend that and changed tactic.

"Wolf, it's more like it suited you that they thought Avi was too weak to be Blessed. If he just stayed as a sloth bear, I bet you would have told them, but he showed up as a threat during your initiations. It was him, wasn't it?"

Silence.

Una chuckled. *"Instead your silence now allows him to take advantage of their shock and show his metal, metaphorically speaking of course."*

"If he had so much metal, then how did he allow himself to be initiated by a lowly sloth bear?"

Guilt rose in Una. Una hurriedly suppressed the distant faint memory of an elderly bear and Avi throwing himself at the bear in her stead while pushing her away. Although useless information to Wolf now, it would reveal the feelings she still had for Avi.

"*Wolf why are we having this conversation. Forget about Avi. What about the fact that there is another snow leopard?"*

"Ah yes, the snow leopard cub. He is a curious thing."

"Curious?"

As if forgetting she was still connected to him, he sinisterly added, *"Curious, yes... Kulkil forgot to mention it."*

The connection between Wolf and her was lost.

Una shuddered for Kulkil. The fact he was missing from the line-up meant he had to be with her father. At least he was safe until Wolf got back.

Between heads Una caught sight of Wolf, Raul and Gagan moving in unison to where Avi, the Sharman and the snow leopard cub stood. Behind them the Forced Blessed bow men stood poised with their metal strong bows ready.

The tension in their bows was apace with the tension and nervous anticipation of what was to come.

Una was too far to hear, and she was desperate to know what was going on. *What did the Sharman say? She was expansive and just needed curiosity?*

"Hi, Gagan!" It was easier to hold on to Gagan than a bird in flight.

Gagan tried to get rid of her but instead, to the others, it looked like his body had gone into spasms as she jerked his body about to make herself comfortable.

Gagan screamed. "How is it even possible?"

Avi laughed. "What, brother, you thought I would be dead?"

"No… I… I wasn't talking to you; I was talking to… Get out of me!!"

Avi stood agog. The Sharman impatiently cleared his throat in response. Avi averted his eyes back to Wolf.

Una used Gagan's eyes to gaze at Avi. His stern face finally broke into the smallest of a smile when he caught Gagan's hand move to shift non-existent hair behind his ear; her tell.

Unaware of Una's presence, Wolf's attention was solely on the cub. When he had studied it enough, he bellowed, "Reveal your human form, snow cub."

Una wondered what Burfani would look like in human form. The cub was male, so was the human form male too?

"How dare you speak to me – the leader – like that?" the cub spoke, surprisingly, in a familiar adult female voice.

"Rosetta?" Wolf exclaimed.

Of course, thought Una. She remembered how Cat had sometimes been more energetic and had led her own parkour practice on the roof. She had known it wasn't Cat but had assumed it was a "normal" ghost that helped her until the Sharman had put her right on Meeru's wedding day.

Wolf recovered his stance. He drove his shoulders back and stood tall, pushing out his chest. "Leader! You aren't Burfani! You're a cub, a sickly one at that." Wolf was openly laughing.

Avi stepped forward but the Sharman pushed him back.

"Surely you can see that this is an imposter?" Wolf snidely remarked to the Sharman. When the Sharman didn't react, he added, "Or is this your way of staying as leader in the absence of your deceased daughter?"

Avi moved forward again. The Sharman placed himself between Avi and Wolf.

Wolf didn't really care about the Sharman's lack of response and he didn't even acknowledge Avi. Instead he sidestepped both of them and stood in front of the cub.

"If you are what you say you are then it is easy for you to transform into your human self. Burfani is meant to be able do it instantly according to legends."

"Didn't realise you were a keen researcher, Wolf."

Wolf didn't care for Avi's raised eyebrow and amusement. Wolf held his temper for a little longer. He was sure that he only had to bring Una forward to wind up Avi.

"You're not the only keen researcher. Una was very thorough; in all things she worked on."

Avi visibly recoiled when he heard her name. Wolf smiled.

Una hoped Avi was only acting.

Evidently enjoying himself Wolf taunted Avi some more. "Do correct me if I am wrong, Avi, but Burfani is meant to be female and fully grown to be the leader. In all the myths Burfani never appears as a cub because to be 'officially Blessed' you have to be at least eighteen years of age."

Una fielded a thought to Rosetta.

"He's right, Rosetta, you can't be Burfani because I don't believe Burfani would strangle and possess the cub's body. She just wouldn't allow it!"

"It's true that I'm not Burfani but if what you say of Burfani is true then why is she in Gagan's body."

"I'm in Gagan's body... not..."

As the penny dropped the jungle behind the tribesmen shook as if it were ravaged by a demonic storm.

Wolf took a step back and mistook the situation. A plethora of thoughts chased through his mind.

He had to be wrong... Only a leader can manage a response like that.

Wolf couldn't reconcile what he just saw and heard.

How is it possible that Burfani is the cub? The Sharman told him that a dead snow leopard was removed from Dev's roof and Una only received the cub six months later... None of it makes any sense. But if they were bluffing, how is it possible for the jungle to react? Rosetta had to be dead otherwise Avi would be a snow leopard today.

Wolf was worried that if he thought all of this, then his cohort would be doing the same. The disturbances from the jungle didn't help either. He had to pull himself together. Turning his back to the Blessed three he addressed his cohort.

"I see no Burfani in front of me, Forced Blesseds. Close up the cub looks sickly and close to death."

Then before Avi or the Sharman could stop him, he picked the cub up by the scruff of its neck for all to see.

The Forced Blesseds roared behind him in jest.

Something in Una burst and using Gagan's body she pushed him into the Wolf's body. The cub leapt out of Wolf's hands and sprung onto a boulder facing the jungle behind the Blesseds.

The jungle foliage behind the cub twitched with movement but from where Una had fallen with Gagan, after he was knocked down by Wolf, she was unable to tell what was happening.

Una had been reluctant to join the war, but a strange sensation overtook her. She became sure she was standing on the wrong side of the battle. *Yet how was that possible? They already had a snow leopard who seemed to command them easily.*

The jungle seemingly lost patience with her thoughts and began pulling Una's soul out of Gagan's. It wasn't just the jungle pulling on her, it was also the countless thoughts, all shouting… from both sides.

"Save yourself, Una, and release Gagan!"

Una obeyed the Sharman and returned to her body hidden in the back a little away from her fellow soldiers. Gagan had left the front. Just Wolf, Raul, the Sharman and Avi remained.

Chapter 49

Let the Battle Commence

Wolf stood on an invisible line. He sensed the growing urgency in his men to fight. They had trained for this and were desperate to begin the war. That was not going to happen.

Motionless, he waited for the Sharman to make his move.

His patience was rewarded. The signal came, but not from the Sharman as expected, but from the snow leopard cub, from Rosetta. The cub's fluffy head deliberately swayed from right to left. It was a definite signal. Wolf watched in horror. A signal of war. Since when did the Blesseds start wars? Something was wrong.

Una could hear Raul's thoughts. It was louder than most. *"Surely the Blesseds aren't planning to fight? You said they wouldn't. Wolf, how do we respond? It looks like they want to fight, and right now!"*

Una was shocked. *Had Wolf not intended to fight at all? Had all of this been just for show... Why?*

Wolf barked back in thought. *"Raul this war just can't happen."* Then, more to himself than Raul or to the eavesdropping Una, he thought talked: "The weapons we bought were meant to deter them from any actions. I had not intended on fighting them. I require theirs and our numbers to fight the property developers. I've got to stop them."

"How?" Sid asked. *"Should we retreat."*

"We can't retreat."

"Then?"

"It's time you came forward, Una."

She had already done that. The jungle's will had been too strong to disobey.

"Come forward, Una!" Wolf bellowed as he looked back. Surprised that he hadn't noticed her standing next to him, she went to tap his arm. Only she didn't tap it as much as put her fingers through him. Una froze and slowly turned to where Wolf was staring. He was staring right at… her.

At her unmoving physical body in the last row of Forced Blesseds. The jungle's unnatural rustle had pulled her ethereal soul out and was still trying to pull her to the Blessed side. Una looked forward. Avi didn't see her but the Sharman was staring at her almost in adoration. The cub was snarling. The tribe took this as another signal as they picked up their spears and held them overhead.

Una missed Wolf's verbal commands. She watched his lips move but neither heard his words or the clamour of spears and stamping feet to the tribal drumbeat.

She did hear something else though. Una moved her gaze to the Sharman who was blowing a cow horn. Everyone stayed still and then she noticed a movement, it was Avi. She called out to him, but he didn't hear her. He was in a zone of his own.

Avi moved oddly in a combination of quick low and high movements, stopping momentarily only to make deliberate poses. One hand was poised above his shoulder with his fingertips pointed upwards almost touching his ear and the other extended in front of him, his palm in a stop sign, and then he pushed his body forward while undulating. The first movement resembled a charging elephant with its trunk swaying forward. Slowly it dawned on Una that Avi was performing martial arts of a different kind, a more animalistic kind. All the time backing Wolf to his starting line.

The cub on its alleviated pedestal was no longer visible as at least twelve tribesmen with shields surrounded it. The rest of the tribesmen had moved forward with Avi. When they stopped moving the Sharman took his place in front of the Blessed line.

Wolf gawked at their formation. They had replicated his cohorts. Never had the tribesmen organised themselves in this way. There was also a lack of animals. The Blesseds usually had the animals in between. Come to think of it, Wolf looked across at the tribesmen, none of them looked familiar. None of the Blesseds were there except for the cub and the Sharman. Worse, the tribesmen in the tight rectangular formation were stamping their feet and raising dust from the ground, covering their exact position which was moving towards the Forced Blesseds. They were prepared for war!

Wolf had no choice.

He howled over the tribe's din.

Una returned to her body and slumped down from fatigue. Her cohort had left her behind without a backward glance. Even at a distance she could feel the release of the collective tension in Wolf's camp. Confused but eager to show their metal, his crossbar soldiers moved forward and readied themselves to fire their crossbows. Mirroring them the tribesmen archers came up the ranks and took the place of the tribesmen with their spears.

Una could not help but smile, the tribesmen were better prepared. They lifted their traditional bows already fitted with long arrows.

Before the Forced Blesseds could react, Una watched in dismay as the archers' arrows tore through the Forced Blessed ranks behind like thunderbolts. Una's breath hitched. It hit her; the war was real. People she had spent time in the dormitory and in the gym training with were going to die or be wounded. Una's allegiance for the moment lay with the Forced Blesseds despite Avi, or perhaps because her captive father was with the Forced Blesseds.

The Forced Blesseds' army stared above themselves in horror. Una squinted. As the arrows rained, they turned from their rigid shapes into snakes with bloodshot eyes, open mouths, and dangling fangs.

The Forced Blessed soldiers ducked and dived, breaking their tight formation. The snakes however found their targets and pockets in the formation were formed where the Forced Blesseds fell to the ground writhing. Most snakes slithered away but some were pinned and killed by the brave Forced Blesseds. The deaths maddened and spurred the remaining Forced Blesseds into action as they loaded the crossbars and reined their revenge.

Screams were heard as the tribesmen behind Avi and the Sharman fell. The undeterred tribesmen stepped over their own dead to advance towards the Forced Blesseds' line.

Neither side had gained the advantage.

The tribesmen archers ran out of snake ammunition and hastily moved back to allow their spearmen to release their spears. The spears found purchase and several Forced Blesseds were mortally wounded.

The opposing warring lines were upon each other. The Forced Blesseds wreaked havoc with their maces but then the tribesmen changed tactic and used unfamiliar fluid martial arts techniques to reduce the impact of the maces.

Finally, a cow horn pierced through the metal and war howls. Wolf shielded his eyes from the golden sun behind Avi shadowing him as he continued to blow the cow horn. Next, the sunlight was obscured by clouds of kicked up dust. When it finally settled silence fell over the bloodied ground.

Wolf and the Forced Blesseds looked around frantically. The tribesmen had fled!

Wolf turned to his army. Their metal guns and other weaponry shone with a special lustre, temporarily blinding him.

There was no time to analyse what had just happened.

"Forward charge, company!" he shouted with enthusiasm. He still had one trump card and he intended to use it.

Una held her head. Wolf was wrong again.

Through the golden light a silhouette of dark bodies made their way forward from the jungle.

Una shook her head.

Again, it seems you underestimate them.

The curtain of the jungle parted and from all heights and the width of the jungle, ferocious rhesus monkeys poured in.

Monkeys swung from the trees and fell flat in front of them, posturing in reverence. Others leapt about, landing their palms to a rhythm. A hypnotic drumbeat. The juvenile ones flung dust in the eyes of the Forced Blesseds whilst the larger and older ones paced horizontally to and fro, growling and posturing their agile bodies every which way.

"Where has this desperate courage come from?"

If only it was just courage. Una winced when a painful cacophony broke out.

And then… before her eyes the monkeys fell upon Wolf's cohort mercilessly; cracking and smashing ribs; severely wounding the boys on the frontline. Una could visibly see Wolf reel from the ferocity of the onslaught from his enemy.

The horrific dissonance and frenzied activity dispersed the Forced Blesseds out of their formation.

From his boulder Avi watched Wolf's disbelief turn to anger.

It was time for the second onslaught. Avi raised his head and growled his command. The monkey bodies stilled and without a single chatter or shriek they fell into formation, not an ordinary formation but a tall tsunami wave, and crashed into the remaining loose Forced Blessed human wall.

From Una's vantage point she spotted a sloth bear shimmying down a tree. The Forced Blesseds spotted him moments later, then charged and surrounded him as he dropped to the ground.

The ferocity of his own growl was joined by other growls and a deluge of sharpened wooden daggers. Avi caught Wolf staring at the sloth bears in the boughs of the trees as they aimed sharpened wooden daggers at the Forced Blesseds below.

Raul, in the mix of it nearby, shouted out loud to the Forced Blesseds, "Transform!" The whole army was transformed as the sunlight dipped out of the sky. Their ragged torn uniforms littered the ground. As did their weapons of warfare.

The Blessed monkeys grabbed the new Forced Blesseds by their hair and bit and scratched with their teeth, trying to injure the Forced Blesseds before they could transform. The newest recruits lay doomed as their transformations were time of day dependant. Wolf howled at the waste. His eyes looked for his prey and found Avi staring back with bloodshot eyes.

Una could no longer see the wolf and the bear. Rhesus monkeys had blurred her line of vision as they fell upon their enemies, both sides were reduced to butchering and pummelling the other to death. She could see the end for both sides as they would not surrender. For a minute she thought it suited her, she could escape but the urge to bring it to an end was greater.

From the corner of her vision, Una gasped as she watched the alligators everyone had forgotten about move in quickly for the available meat. The metal weapons had kept them at bay before now.

The long wails of pain from both sides stirred the Sharman. He tried to thought talk to Rosetta, but she had shut the cub's brain.

Despite the mangled mutilated flesh and bloodshed, the cub did not move to stop the two factions from fighting but instead had an expression of enjoyment.

He was appalled by his own flesh and blood, only she was no longer flesh and blood. The Sharman could not let it go on. Whilst surveying the numbers on the ground he decided to stop it but then realised he was no longer a leader. The Blessed now followed Rosetta and the cub.

"Why do you hesitate? Stop it," Avi asked him. Everyone was tiring.

"I do not have the power to do it, only Burfani can do that and it looks like she has finally recognised her power."

Avi swung his head around to find Rosetta and the snow cub, but they were nowhere to be seen. Instead an unnatural wind blew, and flags staked in the ground fluttered as did the torn rags. A hush fell on the river battlefield.

Wolf looked back from where he stood, over to Avi, and smiled. Silence seeped through the factions and all stilled except for Una.

Avi watched Una deliberately walk towards the battle – in her snow leopard guise, carefully negotiating her way between the fallen and slayed as they waited for their death.

Chapter 50

White Flag

In her snow leopard guise, death and mutilation hit Una's senses all the greater. Perhaps it was because her head was closer to the ground. Shredded arms and legs and bleeding sides of the fallen bodies lay on either side. In death, Blessed or Forced Blessed transformed back to their human forms.

No patience for her slow steps to the epicentre of the war, a gust of wind engulfed her and, finding little resistance, carried her away from the battlefield. To trees of magnolias. Her instinct pushed her to jump from branch to branch on the magnolia trees surrounding the temple until the purplish, pink wide petals feathered through the air to the battlefield and swept over the b.odies on the ground and those still standing.

Loud sighs rather than moans of pain were released from the different quarters where they fell.

Una didn't know how but she understood it was her awareness beyond the definition of her body that had caused the petals to fall. She was able to manipulate each petal just as if she were wiggling her fingers. Just to prove it she swirled her tail around. The petals momentarily paused and then like a shoal of fish weaved between all beings. The magnolia petals soaked up the blood and wrapped around limbs and the sides of bodies. A collective sigh filled the air.

Driven by something deep in her gut. She deliberately leapt onto the boulder from where the snow leopard cub had previously commanded the Blesseds. Blind to all eyes on her, she stretched on the boulder and let out air from between her open jaws as if she were yawning – loudly.

The bloodied petals rose and flew to the centre of the river and when every single petal was there, they combusted in the dark evening air.

Wolf made his way to the boulder where Una stood. Free of the weight on his chest, Avi caught sight of a furry ball launch itself into the sky.

Quick footed, Avi fielded and caught the snow cub as it leapt in the air to attack Una.

Avi held the pretender in his bear grip.

The shock of nearly being attacked began Una's transformation back into her human form.

"Look, she is transforming!" someone shouted.

The Sharman snatched the Blessed snow leopard standard from a Blessed bearer. He swiftly but carefully freed the flag from its stake and draped it over her. Several other langurs held their flags wide and faced out as they circled Una's body, creating a circular curtain all around her. Wolf grabbed the hand of the last langur bearing a banner. When he dropped his banner, Wolf let him go.

"Don't react, Avi," the Sharman warned.

Avi growled.

Undeterred, Wolf crossed over to his standard bearer. He struggled to get the flag off its pole with the help of Raul, who had already transformed into his human form. Between his canine teeth, Wolf carried the standard to the curtained circle. He gave the Sharman a look. The Sharman nodded. Wolf dropped it on the ground. Female langurs pounced on the material that had dropped into the middle of the circle from above.

The Sharman proclaimed, "This is the real Burfani!"

A rumble grew in the Blessed quarters.

"But who is he then?" An angry Blessed pointed to the little cub in Avi's arms. "You told us he was Burfani."

"Remember carefully. It was not I but in fact you, amongst others, that proclaimed him to be Burfani all because of the magnolia petals."

"You never denied that he wasn't, so you are still guilty," another Blessed shouted.

"Perhaps but hope gave you unity."

Avi didn't care about the cries. At this moment in time all he cared about was Una and she was safe. Avi glanced over at the curtained circle and watched the indentations of elbows and shadows. Flashes of the langur's limbs and corners of the different standard appeared as they dressed Una. When all activity ended, the Sharman and several other langurs broke away from their positions thus parting the standard curtain.

Avi's eyes like everyone else's were peeled on Una as she emerged. She was breathtaking in her warrior outfit. The awakening, he didn't know if that was what it was, had changed her body somehow and made her godlike. The Forced Blessed flag that had covered her formed a bodice while the longer Blessed standard was wrapped around her legs like a dhoti that men wore.

Avi could barely breathe. Her awareness tugged at his organs to change back to human form. Feeling his distraction, Rosetta cum cub were quick to take their chance and chose that moment to leap from his arms to attack her. Avi awoke in time from his stupor, stalled his transformation and grabbed the thing in his claws brutally, almost strangling the cub. The cub, aka Rosetta, mewed in terror.

Just as the Sharman stepped forward to speak, Wolf hijacked him and addressed the Blesseds first.

"I am the one who has brought Burfani to you. Your Sharman has shamefully lied to you all these years. He has abused his position for his own ambitions and made you believe that first Rosetta and then this cub was Burfani. Who are you going to trust?"

All ears and eyes were on Wolf. "The Blessed laws do not allow more than one snow leopard to be Blessed. And the same cat could not have made both Una and the cub Blessed so that surely means you are already Blessed because you were not actually changed by the cub because he still lives."

One of the Blesseds shouted out, "We should have understood that. He told us that by her marrying the property developer's son, it would have safeguarded the jungle but look where that has got us."

"That's not true. Burfani was meant to be born to Rosetta, she was, and she lived for a short while. Even Burfani didn't know that the Major's wife would murder her own grandchild because she was a baby girl."

"Burfani chose to be born again from Alice's womb," the Sharman protested.

"Quite right. Is that why your wife encouraged Alice to leave so that you could pretend that the remnants left from carrying Burfani made Rosetta Burfani?" the great uncle asked.

"No, you all knew my wife. She was innocent. She told Alice to never return to India in case her baby girl was killed. Alice, being a researcher, soon found many accounts about how the Major's and Dev's culture batted a blind eye to female infant and baby deaths."

Avi could tell that some of the Blesseds were swayed by the Sharman's explanation.

"*Bakwaz hai! Sabh bakwaz hai!* It's all bullshit. Don't be conned again by this man!"

Wolf held the Sharman's langur jaw up by his nozzle. "The only person who has brought Burfani here is me. A Forced Blessed. A Forced Blessed who by just forcing her over has shown that I care for your way and manner of order more than your Sharman. He knew who the real Burfani was and was happy to keep her away. Rosetta was party to that and now perhaps her son, Avi, too. That's possibly why Avi attacked Una. They are all traitors."

Una had stopped listening. Her mind slipped back to the night when she first met Rosetta in the dark when she was looking for her father in the field between Major's house and her own grandfather's property, on her very first night in Khamosh Valley.

Rosetta was terrified when Una had shone the lantern light on her. At the time Una had mistaken her shouting Burfani to mean it was Rosetta's name instead of her own. Wolf was right, Rosetta had recognised her to be the real Burfani straight away.

Though at that time and the time up to her death Una was sure Rosetta had not meant to deceive her. She remembered a later incident in which Rosetta asked her why Alice hadn't taught her, her daughter, her Indian native tongue. Una clearly remembered Rosetta saying that she would learn languages besides Hindi very quickly and... she was right, she'd learned everything including languages very quickly. Even the language of other species... Yes, other species!

Finally, the penny dropped, and she thought, *it wasn't that I was learning things quickly it was more that I was remembering skills I already had!*

Whilst Una pondered over her new discovery of herself, many of the Blesseds sat in disarray where they had stood earlier. The dawning of Wolf's words had some tribesmen posing with their spears aimed at the Sharman and yet others were walking away. Others, still, the younger ones, were dropping their weapons and walking to the other side of the bank to join the Forced Blesseds.

This was Wolf's chance to finish the Sharman and Rosetta off completely. He remembered his own obsession for looking for the cub when Una had fallen to check it had moved on. If only he had found it alive, he could have avoided the war.

"And use Una better?" the Sharman added.

"Why didn't you?" Wolf asked. "Why did you wait and not claim her? You could have stopped this war. You really are the one your people should fear."

"Perhaps, but your good intentions have brought what?"

One tribesman with his spear screamed, "Kill Rosetta, Avi and the Sharman – they have tricked us."

Pandemonium broke out.

"Wait!"

Everyone turned to Una with degrees of embarrassment

written across their faces, most had forgotten about their Burfani, their true leader, the whole reason for their contention with the Sharman and Rosetta.

"Put your spears down! No one is going to kill the cub, the Sharman or Avi. Leave the cub alone."

Una's voice shook, it was the first time most of the Blesseds would have seen her, let alone hear her voice.

She then addressed the cub. "Rosetta, you knew who I was and even tried to help jog my memory."

Whispers of confusion around Rosetta's possible innocence travelled through the battlefield.

Una paused long enough to shed doubt on Wolf's words and then carried on, "I even sensed you on the roof when you taught me how to be more agile through Cat."

She paused again and then finally asked what everyone wanted to know, "Yet, if you were helping me all that time why are you here, possessing Cat?"

The spectators nodded in agreeance.

The cub violently hissed in reply.

Una's benefit of the doubt hadn't worked.

Instead of answering her, Rosetta seem to be thrashing the cub's body about. Una was sure she could hear faint whimpers amongst the louder hisses.

The cub's pain and discomfiture became too much for Una to bear. From a place she didn't think existed, she raged in a booming unfamiliar voice, "Rosetta, release your soul from him. RIGHT NOW!"

The cub stilled and sat down with its forearms forwards and very deliberately swished its long tail about. As if flicking flies from its body and face.

"Una, may I still call you that?"

Una nodded. "Even if I'm inclined to do such a thing, which body do you wish me to invade instead because I have no plans to wander as a ghost amongst you."

The colour drained from many a face including the Sharman's.

"Enough, Rosetta! If you don't leave Cat, then I'll have to… I'll have to do it by force for you," Una thundered in absolute rage. A second too late she realised how foolish she was. *Even if I want to, I don't know how to.*

Rosetta chuckled. "Do you know how?" Una's silence told her she didn't. "Never mind, let me tell you this. For you to forcibly extract me from your precious cub, you will have to kill it first?"

"Are you crazy, it's an innocent!" shrieked Una and Avi, Una learning for the first time how much she cared for Cat after all.

"There must be another way," she asked, nervously glancing at the Sharman.

The Sharman, weary of the young one's obsession over Cat shrugged his shoulders in agreement.

"I can recite and repeat the incantation, but it is only you who can separate the two and keep the cub alive."

Una agreed.

The Sharman snatched the cub up and placed the squirming cub in Una's open arms and began his chanting. Affected, Rosetta, using the cub's incisors, tried to bite her. Una didn't even flinch. Instead she placed her thumb on its fur just above his snout and pressed gently. Straight away his body went limp. Then he closed his eyes and snuggled deep into the safety of her arms. Before he dozed, Cat purred the deepest sigh. He was finally home, where he wanted to be all those months ago when he first imprinted Una as his mother. Understanding flooded Una and she knew his strong imprint had brought on her maternal instincts.

"Una, stay focused." Avi's words brought her back.

He inclined his head at her and directed her attention to the Sharman who, while still chanting, was beckoning for her to follow him as he walked ahead of her. Una followed and then stopped. She swung her head back to find the lesser wounded Blesseds and Forced Blesseds lined behind her. She had been too wrapped up in the chant and was oblivious to their pounding feet, but their whispers of their new understanding of the new magnolia buds magically appearing and then unfurling instantly in the trees to replace the ones that had been blown away to nurse the wounded, gave them away.

Their adoration and expectation overwhelmed Una and made her nervous, and she faltered on the very first step of the temple.

Avi's hands caught her just in time. He must have gone ahead of her and changed into his usual black combats and T-shirt in his human form. Before she could protest, he swished her off her feet and raced up the steps. At the top step he put her down with an odd expression of concern for her on his face.

"Shouldn't you be concerned about yourself, the Sharman and about your mum?"

Avi shrugged his shoulders in response.

A sharp cough interrupted their interlude. The Sharman was waiting and ready in his tribal Sharman gear. His chanting had not ceased beyond the cough. Una paid full attention and when motioned to, placed the sleeping cub on the temple's altar in front of Hanuman's idol.

The Sharman signalled to Avi to open the cub's mouth carefully.

Whilst still chanting the Sharman took Una's limp hand from her side, fixed her fingers into a claw shape, and forced it into the cub's wide mouth. Una's digits tugged at something that was no more than energy. But the energy snapped at her. The Sharman held her hand in place, until she found her momentum.

Horrendous shrieks filled the temple. Most of the audience held their ears and cowered down. Then something like wind blew between the pillars of the temple. The Sharman, Una, Avi and Wolf were the first to gaze up. The others followed and together they witnessed Rosetta in her snow leopard form rise and envelope the small temple.

"NOW, UNA, before she leaves the temple."

Surprisingly, Una knew what she had to do. She opened her mouth and swallowed Rosetta's essence in one gulp.

Light exploded in Una's body and then she collapsed into Avi's arms.

"Burfani is now truly complete." The Sharman sighed loudly

and flopped to the ground himself.

What felt like an eternity to her but to others just seconds, she lifted Avi's stroking hand on her hair and then stopped. The Sharman had tears in his eyes, happy tears she thought, and the others were whispering while they pointed to her hair. She dragged a handful of her locks up close to her eyes and exclaimed in surprise. They had changed colour to platinum white in the main whilst the ends remained black. Una pulled at a wisp of hair. It was stronger and left her scalp sore. Ouch!

Una recovered her composure and stood up, and when she did the Sharman spread his arms forward, held his hands in a namaste and lay down on his tummy in reverence. All the Blessed tribesmen followed suit.

Wolf and the depleted Forced Blessed cohort remained standing. As did Avi.

Chapter 51

Flood of Memories

Una was more than complete. She was much more than Una. Thrilled, Una looked around her and noticed the Sharman's shaking body. It wasn't his fault. Though she instinctively knew that before she remembered it now. It was time to end the suspicions initiated by Wolf.

"You can't blame me for thinking them."

"I don't."

She helped him rise and made her way out. Determined that all fallen Blesseds and Forced Blesseds saw what she was going to demonstrate first-hand.

She chose the cliff closest to the river and projected a moment that she didn't even know existed before this.

The Sharman wasn't to blame, yet any words from him would not absolve him. But Burfani's words of yesteryear would.

"You summoned me from the Valley of Flowers. First, I was to bless your daughter on her eighteenth birthday, but you said she had been snatched and married off? Then you called me to merge with the foetus in your daughter's womb. Do you understand that my essence will remain in her too until the baby is ready to feed itself? She must safeguard me when I'm born. I will not remember who I am until I am independent."

Una jerked from her own vision casting. Avi put his hand on her shoulder.

"Stop, Una, that was enough."

"No, Avi, there is more they need to see."

"Then you will understand that I'm going to hold you steady from behind."

Una nodded.

Some time had passed in the vision. A young Rosetta wrapped in a white saree was crying on the floor, next to a small body wrapped in a white shawl. A baby cried in the hands of the Sharman.

Burfani was talking to the Sharman, as a lesser snow leopard stood over the dead baby. "I'm sorry, while I am whole again, your daughter still has my essence. For me to release it from her, she will die. I warned her to safeguard the baby. If you don't want her to die, she will have to take on my Blessed form at night."

"No, I can't, please just kill me!" Rosetta cried out.

The Sharman pushed the baby into her hands. "And if you do that then kill him too."

This time Avi's body, which was supporting her, jolted, causing her projection to tilt. She wrapped his hands around her midriff and corrected the tilt.

"Why do you cry for the body that you were born to? It is only flesh and blood not that different from the animal one."

"I know what Blessed is, but I can't now be an animal whist married to an OTHER."

"Not just animal but you remain part human too. When a human soul weaves with an animal's one our lives become greater, we become Blessed."

"But I am married to a non-believer. His family murdered their own. How do you think they will allow a monster like me to live?"

"Live it, remember you are not above the valley. Your father will give up his leadership to you. From now you are the leader, protector of the valley."

Rosetta was shocked. Her father had given away his leadership in the ultimate sacrifice just like that.

"Rosetta, I have already begun the change in you, you have a little of me, which can only be released when your body dies and your soul is ready to leave and become part of my consciousness, me. If another woman were pregnant and stayed in the valley then the snow leopard would not manifest in, you."

"Will I do?" Alice, Una's mother arrived. Una's heart clenched.

"You can't be here!" exclaimed the Sharman.

"No, Sharman let her speak."

"Are you pregnant?"

"I'm not sure, I've missed my period which probably means I'm pregnant."

"How many children do you have?"

"None."

"Then how…"

"I fall pregnant easily enough, but I don't seem to be able to carry them beyond the second trimester."

Burfani touched Alice's stomach.

"Yes, you have the beginnings of a foetus. Wait, will the baby be from a firstborn in this tribe?"

"Not of the tribe but he is living on this land."

"Then perhaps…"

The Sharman interrupted, "No, she's not acceptable. She is married to the son of the property developer who we are trying to curb."

Alice piped up, "So, I make a better candidate. Do you understand the pain of marrying a family's only child and then not being able to provide one? You know me well, Sharman. I have been working with you for months and by profession and my own research I understand the needs of the environment perhaps better than you."

Una's eyes welled up. She had forgotten how feisty her mother could be. In the end she had resigned to cancer and had quietly accepted her end.

"Perhaps you are perfect. Do you understand you will have to stay here? Away from the Himalayas? I am ineffective. I am the essence of the jungle and cannot leave."

"I will promise this: I will protect my child against everything, even the jungle if I have to and, Burfani, when you are eighteen you will be here in this jungle."

"Then I am to be born to you."

It was as if Una could remember herself saying that. In reality she had never been Una and was always Burfani, but her mother's body had given her flesh and blood so her consciousness could flow.

Now it made sense why her mother wanted her to come here.

Una faded and collapsed backwards onto Avi, not from exhaustion this time but from emotion. She hadn't expected any of this. Hearing and seeing her mother made her raw.

The Sharman faltered. Una had calmed the Blesseds and before Wolf exposed him, he had to expose his weakness, his loving, deceased, wife.

"But my wife advised Una's mother to leave and she took our Burfani away."

"We don't believe you, Sharman. You put your wife up to it. That way the essence of Burfani lived on in your daughter and she was forced to take her Blessed self," the Sharman's own brother shouted out.

"Burfani will be able to..." The Sharman turned to Una. In the spot Avi and Una had been, Kulkil now sat, tied up with a rifle aimed at his head. They were surrounded by the Indian army, Una's father and Gagan. Vivek shouted out, "Come out, you coward. Wolf! We've got your parents and sister."

There was no answer. Una was missing, as was Avi, Wolf and his cohort.

Chapter 52

Earlier before the Army arrived

Over Una's head resting on his chest, Avi saw Wolf and his remaining cohort disappear.

"Wolf is up to something."

"MY DAD!"

"Your father!"

Avi's eyes darted over to his Nana. The Sharman was floundering and needed his help but so did Una. Una won. Supposedly, Una was stronger than all of them put together but right now she was exhausted from her projection. Selfishly, Avi chose to believe that she wanted his protection. After such a long time apart, he was not ready to let her out of his sight. She needed him… he hoped. His Nana's life was not at risk with the army there. Yet Wolf was dangerous and could not be trusted.

"Avi I've got to get to Dad before Wolf does," pleaded Una.

"I agree. Lean into me so I can walk you backwards without attracting attention."

Una complied.

Together they slowly backed into the foliage whilst the Blessed were distracted by the Sharman's brother's discourse. Avi's tormented eyes never left his Nana.

When he backed into a tree trunk, Avi extracted himself from Una so she directly leant on the trunk.

Kneeling in front of her with his back to her he thought spoke gently.

"Until you get your strength its quicker if I carry you on my back and run".

Una was just about to protest but Avi shared his vision of carrying Una once before. Una blushed and climbed Avi's back before he shared anymore. Avi took a quick inward breath. The path would have been the most direct route to the Modern Ruins but her tribal flag garb in broad daylight would make her conspicuous. Instead he pegged it to the gap he used to enter the Forced Blessed territory. Soon they were scaling up the Modern Ruins' steps to Grace's bedroom.

They were late. Too late.

The door was smashed to smithereens. Behind it chairs and the dressing table were overturned. There was no sign of Kulkil or her father. Avi placed Una down and held her.

"Looks like Wolf beat us to it."

"No…it can't be!" Una wailed loudly. "I waited and was so careful. I did everything he asked. Wolf even gave me this as a truce…" Una fingered the trim of the Forced Blessed flag she was wearing draped over her body.

Frustrated she lashed out at Avi pushing him away. "None of you can be trusted." Without Avi's physical support she collapsed to the floor like a sack of potatoes.

Avi's chest tightened. He knew it was futile, but he still ran down and checked all the rooms and then ran up to the roof.

He returned alone.

"Una we've got to go, if we don't Wolf will be too difficult to track."

Una just stared at him through her angry tears.

A big sigh left Avi's body. He picked her up over his shoulder and climbed the steps to the roof.

"What if he comes back…"

"He's not coming back anytime soon. There are police goons making their way to the house. Two are already posted outside the gate. They must have been here earlier because the place is completely turned over."

"Wait…what about Kulkil?"

Avi stiffened. "He's gone too." Slowly he placed and stood Una on the roof wall, never letting go of her hand as he climbed up beside her. Una tried to pull away.

"We've got to go now" whispered Avi.

With the back of her free hand Una wiped her tears dry. She had recovered enough to claw her captured hand's nails into the back of Avi's hand. Satisfied with the sight of blood on the tips of her nails she relaxed her fingers.

Avi wasn't sure if she meant to hurt him or Wolf or both.

Grimacing inwardly, he held her hand tightly in his now stinging one and raised his foot off the ledge. Una mirrored his movement. In unison both stepped off the roof. They were swallowed by the canopy of the jungle below after displacing a flock of mynas. The unsuspecting police at the gates ran for cover to the Modern Ruins veranda from the pecking of the menacing birds.

Appendix A

Main Characters

Character Name	Description
Avi	Major's and Sharman's grandson. Short for Avatar. Full name Avatar Singh Rana
Una	Dev's grandaughter. Also Known as Ms Rao to the Forced Blessed.
Wolf	Wolfgang or Mr Hamilton
Sharman	Spiritual leader of the Blessed. Avi's Nana (Grandfather)
Nani	Avi's Grandmother.
Dev	Una's Grandfather.
Mrs Dev	Una's Grandmother.
Burfani	Leader of the Blessed.
Gopan	Una's grandparents' servant. Sharman's brother's grandson. Also known as Johnny Walker in first book.
Rosetta	Avi's Mother
Gagan	Avi's brother. Gag for short.
Vivek	Una's Dad.

Character Name	Description
Alice	Una's Mother.
Dada	Avi's grandfather. Also known as Major.
Dadi	Avi's Grandmother. Major's wife.
Meeru	Avi's Aunt.
Riki	Avi's Uncle.
Niki	Avi's Uncle.
Chaz	Avi's Uncle.
Sid	Wolf's father. Headmaster of Forced Blessed dormitory in St Anthony's school.
Grace	Sid's daughter and one of the Forced Blessed
Agnes	Sid's daughter. Grace's sister
Kulkil	Friend of Avi and local villager.
Raul	Seond in command to Wolf in the Forced Blessed
Christopher	One of the Forced Blessed
Vibu	One of the Forced Blessed.
Dr Verma	Doctor to Avi's family.

ACKNOWLEDGEMENTS

This book has been three years in the making and many people have helped me along the way. I would like in particular to thank Amanda Carroll at Studio Beam who produced an eye-catching front cover design that truly compelled me to stay focused and finish writing the second book; Shirley Khan who waited with admirable patience for the completion of the book and for her astute copyediting and shaping of the manuscript so it was a fast pace read. Thank you, Jyotsna Sindhi, for following my River Rule Series Facebook page loyally and being the first to read Broken Rule's manuscript before it went to professional editing. Her advice was invaluable but her love and excitement for the book and the paintings that you painted based on the emotions it stirred in you are priceless.

A host of readers through their reviews and critiques on GoodReads and Amazon of the first book River Rule positively impacted the writing and story of Broken Rule.

A really huge thank you to all my friends and supporters who made the printing and marketing of this book happen: Anu Bajaj, Rekha Balwada, Chris Bailey, Melisa Bassett, Anupama Bhalla, Deepa Bhartia, Alpana Bhartia, Hamish Blackwood, Michele Blackwood, Papia Chatterjee, Sumitra Choudhry, Ashley Davis, Chris Davis, Natasha Davis, Russell Davis, Val Davis, Kim East, Jason Goldberg, Maureen MK Hahn, Sangita Jaiswal, Christopher Jones, Jill Jones, Kimberley, Urvashi Khemka, Gwenda Lambert, Rosie Mann, Dr Brijender Singh Rana, Claire Randall, Sonali Sangwan, Anurima Sandhu, Parul Saxena, Jyotsna Sindhi, Pamela Srivastrava, Esther Uhlmann, Flavia Vincenzi and Laura Vincenzi

Thank you to Flavia Vincenzi and Gwenda Lambert for bringing the Forced Blessed and Blessed Monica Narula, tattoos and animal personality test alive to boost my KickStarter tiers.

And finally, my heartfelt thanks go to my husband Miles, who has done the final edit before I sent it to Shirley Khan. He has help engineer the book and did most of the emailing communication and ran the kickstarter. He had to live in the world of Khamosh Valley as much as me. The book just wouldn't exist if it weren't for his patience, effort and putting up with me disappearing for long hours and disappearance to India and my old school town and haunts. Thank you to Natasha for creating graphics of Una and Wolf for me to enhance my River Rule posts and for Ashley who researched on YouTube for GoodReads Viewers and heavily encouraged me to run a Kickstarter. Thank you, Mum, for your prayers and good wishes and Dad's blessings. Without my family's support none of this would have been possible.

CPSIA information can be obtained
at www.ICGtesting.com
Printed in the USA
LVHW110738141120
671534LV00015B/280

9 781999 892845